THE
WISH

THE WISH

Gonoa

Podium

Published in 2025 by Podium Publishing
www.podiumentertainment.com

Podium

THE
WISH

Prologue

"Today is the day the world has been waiting for for the past two weeks!" said the journalist in a way too excited voice. She, apparently, wanted to make it more believable.

"World-renowned scientist Dr. Becker did what no one could have imagined. He proved everyone wrong just two weeks ago. His prediction of the so-called 'unidentified energy source' is actually real."

The scientist in the background looked at the journalist angrily. He was standing in front of the camera, waiting to be interviewed. His face had flushed red, and he seemed like he wanted to say something. But he shook his head and stared at the crowd of people who had come to see what was happening for themselves.

"Dr. Becker!" the journalist said, now turning to the annoyed scientist. "For three years, everyone called you crazy! And you even got several prizes and titles revoked. How does it feel to be right in the end?"

Dr. Becker sighed and looked helplessly up to the sky for a moment, clearly trying his hardest to stay calm. Then he started speaking into the microphone. "I wasn't right 'in the end,' I was right from the beginning," he clarified. "But I couldn't care less about this at the moment. In approximately fifteen minutes, the unidentified energy source may impact this location. And no," he shouted when he saw the excited glint in the eyes of the journalist, "there won't be an explosion. This isn't a Michael Bay movie. And yes, even though the energy source is unidentified, I can say for certain that the impact will not result in any kind of explosion or other destructive force."

Dr. Becker had tried to avoid this unpleasant topic, but the journalist had a good nose for a catchy story and didn't want to give up. "Are you sure that it will not explode? What if there are injuries to civilians and damages to infrastructure? Will you take responsibility?"

It was clear to Dr. Becker that the journalist still thought of him as crazy. She just wanted another headline, one that maybe read "Crazy Becker Is at It Again." At this moment, something snapped in Dr. Becker's head.

Completely losing his cool, Dr. Becker started to furiously scream at the shocked journalist. While everyone focused on the argument, one of the onlookers pushed himself through the crowd of curious people.

This is it, he thought. *This will be the moment when I will awaken the system in me, and I will go on a journey to save the world and become the strongest!*

It was quite clear from the faces of the people standing near him that he had spoken those last words out loud. As if his madness was contagious, the crowd made some space around him.

While pushing himself through the crowd, a frantic teenage boy looked behind him. He was afraid the doctors or nurses would find him. For what felt like months, he had begged them to let him come here. But they just didn't believe him. He was meant for more. He had a mission.

And in the end, he was able to flee. He was very sorry about the nice nurse Sophia, but he couldn't help himself. It wasn't his fault what had happened to her. He just had to be here.

Now, he stood right in front of the barrier separating the crowd from the scientific equipment. The boy inched closer.

Dr. Becker didn't seem to notice that the time of impact was coming close. He was still screaming at the journalist for all the horrible things that had been said about him in the last couple of years.

Even when his co-workers tried to pull him away, he just pushed them back and started an even bigger commotion.

This briefly distracted the security personnel, and the boy took his chance. He jumped over the barricade and ran straight to the center of the equipment.

One security guard tried to grab him through reflex, but he tripped over a cable and stumbled to the ground. This alerted the guards next to him, who immediately looked for the perpetrator in the crowd. They didn't realize what the actual cause was. This allowed the boy to run straight ahead, which was only noticed by the crowd. They started shouting either words of encouragement or warning. The security guards noticed a moment too late that someone had slipped past them and began running toward him.

More by chance than anything else, Dr. Becker's gaze fell onto the wristwatch the journalist was wearing. He noticed that the time of the impact had arrived.

Shocked, he immediately turned around, only to see a young teenage boy in a hospital gown standing right in the middle of his equipment. He was screaming madly out of joy and lifting his hands in the air.

Dr. Becker paused for a moment, not quite understanding the bizarre scene in front of his eyes. When he regained his bearings, he wanted to run toward the boy and tackle him out of the way.

But his brief hesitation was a moment too long. A white light shot out of the sky and directly at the boy.

All sound and light vanished, and only the immense pillar of light was visible. Like a waterfall, the light crashed into the boy, making him shine so brightly that his body became translucent.

Reality seemed to vanish. The pillar and the boy in the middle were the only things that remained in a seemingly empty world.

Dr. Becker watched on in horror, not quite sure if he was still alive. The pillar of light started to spread, the light inching closer to him. He screamed soundlessly and stumbled backward, trying to get as much distance between him and the light as possible.

But before he could do anything else, everything went black.

CHAPTER ONE

Initialization

<System initializing. Please wait.>
<System initialized. Integrating life forms.>
<Life forms integrated. 23.67% successful. Certain errors could not be fixed. Resetting world.>
<World reset. 79.09% successful. Certain errors could not be fixed. Starting new world.>
<Welcome to the system. Welcome to the new world.>

A young woman screamed, lying buck naked in the dirt. She panted heavily and held her shaking hands in front of her face. She was still screaming, but she didn't really seem to notice.

After mindlessly flailing around for a while, she seemed to calm down.

"What the fuck?" Sarah asked herself breathlessly, after she regained her bearings. "Melissa?" she shouted and looked around her. But to her shock, she was alone in the woods. Or maybe a swamp?

The next moment, she noticed that she was totally naked. "Shit!" She said it loudly. "Did someone put something in my drink and drag me out here to . . ." She couldn't end the sentence. She couldn't even think it through until the end. Too disgusting were the images that waited behind the unspoken words.

"Melissa?" she tried again, but there was no answer. "What the hell is happening right now?"

For a while, she just lay in the dirt, trying to calm her turbulent mind. She wanted to remember what exactly could have happened for her to be god knows where. And completely naked on top of that.

"What was this weird dream I had?" she wondered. "Was it even a dream?" It seemed more like a movie to her. Or a bad trip from a drug she would definitely never want to take again.

Her memory was still fuzzy, and she felt like she had woken up from an eternity of sleep and was still drunk.

"I need to get out of here," she said groggily, trying to stand up. Just to be sure, she checked between her naked legs, but she didn't notice anything different or painful. With a shaky breath, she tried to orient herself.

She couldn't be too far away from the city. She often took hikes in nature. If her mind could only manage to be a little clearer, she was sure she could remember where she was.

At least she hoped that was the case. With her bare feet, she gingerly started to walk, stepping on soft-looking patches of dirt, and began shouting for help.

Her voice was way too loud for her fuzzy brain, but the combination of walking and screaming at the top of her lungs seemed to help a little.

"There was a light!" She remembered something. She was standing next to Melissa in the Caesar Club, talking with one of her co-workers, and suddenly, a bright light started shining out of nowhere. She even tried to close her eyes, but the light was so bright, it didn't help at all.

"And then . . ." Crouching down and holding her head, she tried to remember. She heard certain . . . things. Or did she see them? Both? She wasn't sure anymore. Weird stuff about some strange initialization of a . . . "System?"

Suddenly, she saw, and kind of heard, something.

<Welcome, Sarah Anna Fischer.>

"What the . . ." With a gaping mouth and her hands still clasped around her face, she stared at the white holographic words hovering in front of her.

It kind of hurt her eyes to look at it. It seemed neither close nor far away. It was more like it was imprinted into her brain. Even closing her eyes didn't work. The same was true for "hearing" it. It was more like she knew the words—like remembering someone saying something. It was very unsettling.

The system had more to say.

<Congratulations on adapting so well to the new world. You are now one of the chosen ones. Everything you could possibly imagine awaits you. And the system is here to guide you. Please enjoy your journey.>

"Please enjoy my what? Is this a joke? Hey, what the hell is going on? Who is doing this?" she screamed into the woods, but there was no response.

<For more information about yourself in the new world, please say or think of the word "Status." As a bonus, due to the low probability of survival, you will be informed about your circumstances. Your location was changed due to a spatial error that occurred during the world reset. You are currently inside the spatial error, and you will need to find your way out. Good luck.>

"Oh, well thank you so much for wishing me luck for having a LOW CHANCE OF SURVIVAL!" she screamed at the now gone words. But there was no answer.

"Are you kidding me? What is going on?" she asked herself. Part of her knew what she had heard was the truth.

It felt like there was new knowledge inside her head that just shouldn't be there. Like someone had just stuffed something inside of her.

As bizarre as it seemed, a system seemed to exist inside her mind, and possibly inside the minds of other people. This weird entity had placed her completely naked inside of something it called a spatial error. Whatever that meant.

The more she thought about it, the more the existence of the system seemed normal. Like it had always been there, just like her arms and legs. Her whole body began shuddering while her mind altered in real time. It was, by far, the most unsettling experience of her life. She literally saw memories just vanishing. Afterward, she was left with only a memory that she had forgotten something. And after a while, even this memory faded away, leaving her feeling completely empty.

The system took quite some time, rummaging through her brain and erasing everything. But at some point, the feeling subsided, and she sighed a breath of relief.

Sarah knew that only moments before, the mere concept of there being a system was bizarre to her. Now, it was completely normal. The disparity between what she thought she needed to feel and what she actually felt was enough to break most people's minds.

Still feeling disoriented, she heard a system prompt.

<Congratulations. You got the Achievement 'How the hell are you still sane?' for being the first sapient being in the world to experience the mind-altering function of the system while being awake, and not losing your mind and/or killing yourself.>

"Uhhhh." Sarah couldn't help looking at the prompt like a lunatic. She was trying to process all the things that had happened in the last few minutes. "What's up with this weird achievement name?" she asked the system, but there was no answer.

It was a deeply upsetting experience, but to the point of being the first person not to lose her mind or kill herself? That was a bit extreme.

Alright, she thought to herself, while trying to stay calm and rationalize the situation. *The system told me something about my current situation. Me being in a spatial error and all and having to find my way back. Soooo, what to do now?*

In a faraway corner of her mind, a voice told her that it was absurd for her to believe something like this. But the voice was continuously getting further away.

What did the system say again that I should say or think? Status?

Right as she thought about it, another semi-transparent holographic screen popped up in front of her. She gawked at it.

Details:
Level: 1
Name: Sarah Anna Fischer
Class: None
Race: Human
Status: Confused (50% higher MP consumption)
HP: 50/50 **SP:** 10/20 **MP:** 10/10

Achievements:
- How the hell are you still sane?

Affinities:
Mind (Mid) Body (Mid) Energy (Low)

Specializations:
- Mind (0/2)
- Body (0/2)
- Energy (0/1)

Basic Stats:
Strength: 4
Dexterity: 11
Endurance: 4
Resistance: 3
Intelligence: 20
Force: 1

Special Stats:
Magic Power: 1

Active Skills:
None

Passive Skills:
- Struggle (Conditional Passive)
- Slightly Crazy
- Mean Eye

She stared blankly at the information that served as her status. Especially the passive skills.

"What do you mean slightly crazy? Hey?!" she shouted into the air, but once again, the system didn't answer her. She was a bit grumpy about being labelled slightly crazy, but it didn't really surprise her. It was something a lot of people called her during her former life. She didn't care, but she was slightly sorry for all the people she had beaten up because of this.

"So sorry, Tom, for your genitals." She said a prayer for a guy who was once her boyfriend and had a restraining order against her. But she had a hunch that this wouldn't matter anymore. "Wait, what's a restraining order?" she asked herself, clutching her head due to a sudden headache. Some moments later, the whole incident was forgotten, and she looked at the status screen again.

She studied it for quite a while but didn't understand much. She only got more information about certain things when she thought about them. To be precise, the achievements and skills categories. The names of her one achievement and the skills were mostly silly, but they seemed to help her out.

Achievements:
- How the hell are you still sane? (Resistance to mind damage increased by 10%.)

Passive Skills:
- Struggle (Conditional Passive): Resistance is increased in dire situations.
- Slightly Crazy: Most things won't bother you that much. If certain conditions are met, however, there is a slight chance that you will go berserk.
- Mean Eye: There is a chance that other beings will momentarily freeze in fear when they look at you. Higher chance with sentient beings.

Somehow, she thought that she had seen things like this in the past, but she couldn't tell where or why. For now, what made most sense to her were her basic stats, which were mostly intuitive.

Strength, dexterity, endurance, and intelligence seemed pretty straightforward. But she didn't know what kind of resistance the system was showing her. Mental? Physical? And also, what exactly was force? If strength hadn't shown up on the screen, she would have thought that force would be muscular strength. But it probably wasn't.

For a short moment, she remembered a scene of two men in brown robes holding weird sticks made of light in their hands, and she chuckled lightly. In the next moment, she asked herself why she had laughed a moment before. Was "slightly crazy" really enough to describe her state of mind?

She didn't know if her stats were high or low. But she wasn't into any sports, so she probably wasn't as in shape as she could be.

With a deep sigh, she thought about closing the status window. It closed immediately, like it had never been there in the first place.

"What to do now?"

CHAPTER TWO

First Steps

Sarah had been walking for a while, and she was becoming more and more exhausted. She was looking for any sign of civilization or just another human, but she found nothing. And the further she got from the place where she woke up, the harder it was to walk.

Sometimes, she sank knee deep into wet, stinky mud and had to pull her legs out. From time to time, she also looked at her status screen to see if her activity had changed anything. And it really did. Her SP seemed to go down. It was now 5/20 and started to blink in a yellow color. It was most likely her stamina, which was low right now. It got harder and harder for her to move forward. And every time she had to fight her way through waist-deep mud, her exhaustion grew stronger.

HP on the other hand, seemed to indicate her health or something. At one point, she cut herself right above the knee on a twig that had been hidden in the shrubbery. Due to her wound, which had bled moderately, her HP had gone down by one point to 49/50. And even after it had stopped bleeding, her HP didn't recover.

Not wanting her SP or HP to drop any lower, she sat on some nearby thick roots and leaned her back against a tree. She recalled what she had found out about this place.

She seemed to be in some kind of swamp. A thick canopy of trees partly blocked out the sky, and thick undergrowth grew around the tree trunks.

Some parts of the ground were muddy, and she couldn't walk there. Different kinds of plants grew in these parts, and they looked really beautiful and exotic. If this were a normal hike, she would really be enjoying the landscape because it was so mysterious. But right now, it was rather cause for concern.

She didn't notice in the beginning, but when she woke up in the swamp, she didn't hear any wildlife. No birds, insects, or rustling in the bushes. But as she walked on, she started to hear more and more. Weird bird cries, the humming of insects, namely—and worst of all—mosquitoes.

She wasn't very knowledgeable about flora and fauna, but she was pretty sure it was a really bad idea to be naked in a swamp. All kinds of parasites, germs, and poisonous stuff were all around her.

While lying still on the ground, a cool breeze managed to slip through the canopy. It cooled down her overheated body, giving her some much-needed relief. The wind and the rustling of the leaves made her feel comfortable. This made her forget, for a moment, what was actually going on. *Maybe I can rest here for a while longer*, she thought to herself, her eyelids growing heavier by the second. Caressed by the breeze, and with the ground feeling uncharacteristically soft, Sarah drifted into a deep slumber. She was too physically and emotionally exhausted to stay awake any longer.

<Warning! You are poisoned.>

Sarah drowsily opened her eyes, not quite registering what she saw. She wanted to go back to sleep. It was so comfortable. But the message flashed again. This time in a bright red color.

<Warning! You are badly poisoned. Searching for options.>

When she finally realized what this meant, she was immediately awake. Only now had she noticed that her body was covered in a cold sweat and that her left arm felt really, really weird. She tried to move it, but nothing happened.

In shock, she looked down at her arm, which partly lay in some kind of spiderweb. Right in the middle of her forearm, there was a swollen spot with two very small bite marks. Weird white spots began appearing around the swollen spot on her skin. Something was very wrong.

She couldn't move her arm. And what was even worse was that she also couldn't feel it. The numb feeling almost reached her shoulder. She would have preferred it to be painful rather than numb.

In her panic, she still had the presence of mind to try to understand her situation better, so she opened her status, and one section was blinking bright red.

Status: Badly poisoned (HP reduced by 1 every 60 seconds). Left arm immobilized. Spreading at accelerating speed.)
HP: 23/50 **SP:** 2/20 **MP:** 10/10

Sarah was pretty shocked to see that her health was already halfway down. Was she dying right now? Should she try to suck the poison out of her wound? The arm was only immobilized according to the system, which meant it wasn't dead already. There was still a chance.

Just as she tried to lift her numb arm with her healthy one, another system prompt popped up.

<Solutions Found:
- Cut poisoned arm off (10% survival rate)
- Acquire specializations Adaption and Mutation (15% survival rate)
- Start praying (0% survival rate)
- Suck at the wound (Do you want to die even faster?)

Please decide fast.>

"What the hell are the last two options even for?" she shouted and then pulled herself together. "Dammit, I'll take option two. Make these specializations!" she shouted at the system again, as she felt the poison crawling into her shoulder, spreading the sickening numbness.

<Acquire specializations Adaption and Mutation?>

"Yes!" she screamed, hoping that the system would hurry.

<Initializing the acquisition of specializations Adaption and Mutation. Possibility of cell breakdown: 85%. Possibility of mental breakdown: 81%. Possibility of soul crippling: 43%. Starting in 10 seconds.>

"Wait, wait, wait," Sarah said, while reading the horrible possibilities that awaited her. But a countdown in the corner of her mind told her that the system wouldn't wait anymore.

"There has to be a different solution. Just wait a . . ." She drifted off when the countdown dropped to zero, and a foreign feeling hit her. It was like her body, mind—her very being—were melting down and reforming. Over and over again. She wanted to scream, but she couldn't. It was like her mind was trapped.

Strangely enough, it wasn't even painful physically, but the strain it put on her sanity was unimaginable. The feeling of something that shouldn't happen inside her body, and the inability to do anything about it except think about it made her nearly lose her mind.

After what felt like an eternity, the sensation subsided as suddenly as had begun. And with it came a new system prompt.

<Congratulations! You managed to survive the transformation with only a small scar on your soul. Please check your status window for more information.>

Sarah barely understood the system prompt. And when she realized that she was safe and that she had survived the procedure, she immediately fell unconscious.

CHAPTER THREE

Into the Wild

Andrew sat on a smooth stone, just big enough to be slightly comfortable. He groggily looked at the approximately fifty people around him. Everyone was sitting either on the grass, the ground, or standing around. Everyone tried, with varying success, to hide their naked forms.

Andrew was very happy that he only needed to hide one part of his body. He desperately tried not to stare at the women crouching down on one side of the group. They were trying to hide as much as possible from the men, who were awkwardly looking up at the sky.

No one said anything. They all woke up more or less at the same time and wordlessly stood near each other, and as far away as possible from the people who lay on the ground with wide open mouths and eyes.

When Andrew first saw them, he thought they were dead. But upon closer inspection, and while in shock, he noticed that they were breathing. They looked like they had experienced something so horrifying that their minds just stopped working.

"Is there a doctor here?" someone asked, while awkwardly pointing at the unmoving people a few meters away.

For some time, nobody moved or responded. Eventually, a young woman stood up and seemed very nervous while holding her arms in front of her body.

"I am," she said. The doctor took a deep breath, and walked toward the unmoving people. Some of the men took quick glances at the woman's backside, which caused many of the other women to stare angrily at them.

After a moment, silence fell over the group again. It was only disturbed by the wildlife in the woods around them.

Everybody knew what was going on. The system had told them. The world was different now, and they somehow needed to survive. Andrew thought it a small miracle that nobody was freaking out. Well, the people here were probably freaking out, but, like him, they could probably keep control over their turbulent minds.

After some time, the doctor came back and sat down with the group of women.

"I have no idea what's wrong with them. Their bodies seem fine, they have no injuries, no signs of trauma, or anything else. But they seem close to being brain-dead. Nothing reacts. Only the basic body functions seem to still work." She spoke with a hoarse and shaky voice, trying to stay calm and professional. Not everyone was able to do that.

One man suddenly jumped up from the ground and began running into the woods while screaming.

"Wait, stop!" shouted Andrew. He tried to follow him, but a sudden dizzy spell hit him, and he fell right on his face.

The other people stood rooted to the ground and looked at the man, who was getting further and further away.

Andrew stood back up and felt tension in the air. It wouldn't take long before the entire group would start freaking out. He tried to ignore the fact that he would also start to freak out.

He suppressed the overflowing panic inside his mind and thought about what to say next, and how to calm down the people around him.

<Specialization Equilibrium (Soul) is unlocked. Acquire?>

This prompt nearly pushed him over the edge, and he swallowed the scream that threatened to come up his throat. This prompt came right after he had tried to come up with a solution for calming himself and everyone else down. Did the system give him a solution? He could only guess and mentally affirm the acquisition.

<Initializing the acquisition of the specialization Equilibrium (Soul). Possibility of going into a vegetative state: 16%.>

He blankly stared at the second sentence and somewhat understood its meaning when a weird sensation washed over him. It felt like everything had calmed down. Nothing mattered anymore, and he was fine just sitting on this little rock. Deeper and deeper he drifted into this calmness, when a small part of his brain told him that this was dangerous.

Like a drowning man, his consciousness came back from the dead calm. He started sweating and breathing heavily.

<Congratulations. You acquired the specialization Equilibrium (Soul). Please check your status screen for more information.>

Still breathing heavily, he mentally summoned his status and saw one new active and passive skill each.

Active Skills:
- Emotion Manipulation: With moderate Magic Power consumption, you are able to influence another person's emotions to a varying degree.

Passive Skills:

- Equilibrium: You are unable to feel extreme emotions and are always in a state of balance. In a limited area around you, people will be slightly influenced by this skill.

This is exactly what we need right now, Andrew thought to himself calmly and stood up from his crouching position. He walked forward and stood tall before the nervous crowd.

"I know how you all feel. I also feel it. But we need to keep it together right now. We need to hold together. If we start panicking like the last guy who ran off, we will only be digging our graves." He calmly gazed into the crowd of people, who seemed oddly convinced of his words. Maybe they just desperately wanted someone to show them a way out of this fucked-up situation.

"The strongest of us will carry the unconscious people over there," Andrew said, pointing. "We will always walk in a group. And for now, we will look for fresh water and a place that will give us a little bit of shelter. Has anyone got some more suggestions?"

"I have one," said a scrawny young man, barely out of his teens. "I want to wear some fucking clothes."

A few people laughed and threw each other glances, again aware that everyone was naked.

"Yeah, that would be nice," Andrew said, "but sustenance comes first. Does anyone have experience walking through the wilderness?"

A gruff-looking man held up his hand and stepped forward. "I have experience," he said curtly and in a deep and raspy voice, while holding his other hand between his legs.

"Perfect," Andrew said and nodded to the man. "Let's go."

After some time, the oddly calm group started walking like a herd of sheep behind Andrew and the gruff-looking man. They started looking a little bit less hopeless.

CHAPTER FOUR

The First Mutation

A long time passed after Sarah woke up, during which she just lay around, staring at the softly moving leaves of the trees.

I almost died, she thought to herself. *I almost died, and I made it.* A normal person should probably feel dread and panic right now, but she couldn't help but feel excited. The thought of having survived alone and against all odds was exhilarating.

"Well," Sarah said, sitting up. "Sorry, system, for getting angry about the 'slightly crazy' thing. I guess you were kind of generous with your evaluation." As always, the system didn't answer her.

After relishing this great feeling, she finally opened up her status screen.

Details:
Level: 2
Name: Sarah Anna Fischer
Class: None
Race: Human
Status: Exhilarated (Potency of active skills increased by 10%)
HP: 55/55 **SP:** 10/25 **MP:** 0/20

Achievements:
- How the hell are you still sane?

Affinities:
Mind (Mid) Body (Mid) Energy (Low)

Specializations:
- Mind (0/2)
- Body (2/2)

- o   Adaptation
- o   Mutation
- Energy (0/1)

Basic Stats:
Strength: 4
Dexterity: 11
Endurance: 4
Resistance: 3
Intelligence: 20
Force: 1

Special Stats:
Magic Power: 2
Life Force: 1

Active Skills:
None

Passive Skills:
- Poison Body (Adaptation)
  - o   Poison Resistance
- Metamorphosis (Mutation)
- Struggle (Conditional Passive)
- Slightly Crazy
- Mean Eye

To Sarah's surprise, she seemed to have leveled up. Not much had changed besides having a bit more HP, SP, and MP. There was also a new special stat called Life Force, but for now, she didn't really know what it did.

The most interesting addition was the new specializations. Or rather, the new skills that seemed to come from them. She hastily signaled the system to give her more of an explanation about these skills.

Poison Body (Adaption): You are able to increase your resistance to hazardous substances and reinforce your body with their properties in combination with your "Mutation" specialization.
- o   Poison Resistance

Metamorphosis (Mutation): You are able to mutate your body. Drastic mutations and changes to your body's form and/or functions have a high chance of scarring your soul and destroying your mind (mostly immune to this side effect due to the passive skill "Slightly Crazy"). The number of mutations is dependent on your Life Force. Due to your "Adaption" specialization, there will be less Life Force needed, and you will have fewer limitations.

- o   Skin: None
- o   Bone Structure: None
- o   Muscles: None
- o   Brain, Nerve System, and Sensory Organs (not recommended): None
- o   Organs and Processes (not recommended): None
- o   Special Mutations (not recommended): None

"Uhhhh" was the only thing she could say. "Is this . . . good? It sounds kind of disgusting, honestly." The thought of a horrifyingly mutated body wasn't a very nice image. Especially if the system forced these changes on her, rather than her actively choosing them. She had only been in contact with the system for a short time, but it seemed kind of pushy and intrusive.

"Alright, just steel your mind," she said to herself, firming up her resolve to overcome this situation. She was alone and naked in a godforsaken swamp within something called spatial error. Looking at her lower legs and feet, she saw countless little wounds that were starting to look a little inflamed. Not to mention the freaking spider bite that had almost turned her nerves into mush. She had no idea how to make protective clothing with the materials around her. And she definitely didn't want to just wrap some plants around her without knowing whether they were poisonous or not.

"My best bet right now is to . . . well . . . mutate my skin. Gosh, that sounds disgusting."

Survival came first, superficial beauty later.

"Give me the details about mutating my skin," she said, trying to prompt the system; and to her surprise, something actually happened.

<Mutation: Skin. Listing available options.

Camouflage Skin (1 LF): Able to use Magic Power to lighten or darken the skin.

Dense Skin (1 LF): Dense and leathery skin. More force is needed to penetrate the skin, and shallow wounds close up faster.

Breathing Skin (1 LF): Able to passively absorb a miniscule amount of magic power from the surroundings.

Rough Skin (1 LF): Scaly and rough skin, which can injure by contact. Slightly more resilient than normal human skin.

Patterned Skin (1 LF): Skin with colorful patterns that can scare other beings by suggesting danger.

For more options, increase your level and/or heighten your Life Force.>

"Ugh, rough skin sounds disgusting. But luckily, some of these options don't seem to make a freak out of me." After a short pause and some mental preparation, she prompted the system again.

"I choose Dense Skin." And again, the system gave an answer.

<Initializing mutation "Dense Skin." Final affirmation needed.>

Before she could even say something, the system had already begun its damned countdown. Apparently, a mental affirmation was all it needed. She didn't need to speak her demands to the system out loud in the future. *Thank god, that would be embarrassing*, she thought to herself absentmindedly. The countdown was ticking down, and she tried not to think about the mental pain her last experience with the system had caused her.

Her fear only came partly true. This time it was her body that was in immense pain. When the timer hit zero, her skin started to literally melt in front of her eyes and started bubbling. The pain was excruciating. With gritted teeth, she endured the pain, while keeping her eyes firmly shut. The sight of her skin sloshing and bubbling was just too horrible.

After a short while, the pain ended as abruptly as it had begun. And with it, a system prompt.

<Mutation successful. Acquired the mutation "Dense Skin." In combination with "Poison Resistance," your skin, if intact, will ward off contact poison.>

With a low sigh, she just lay on the ground for a while. After some time, she dared to look at her skin. It actually wasn't that bad. She wasn't sure if there was even a visible change. The skin just seemed more . . . dense. Which made sense, according to the name.

To test her new resilience, she pressed one of her nails into the thin skin at her wrist. But she didn't even feel much pain. It felt like pressing her finger into thick, processed leather. The wounds on her feet and legs also seemed to have healed up.

The moment she stood up, Sarah felt that she had left something behind. Her hair! With shock, she touched her head. It was smooth. She didn't even have eyebrows or eyelashes.

"Shit, that wasn't in the description!" she shouted at the system with a raised fist, but soon she quelled her anger. She had gotten what she wanted. And, she definitely didn't need to look pretty right now.

"But still," she muttered, wildly pointing her middle finger in various directions.

Somewhat satisfied with venting her emotions, she reoriented herself. Or at least, she tried.

"Still in a fucking swamp," she said bitterly. For a moment, she thought about climbing a tree and trying to get a good look at her current location. But the sight of numerous spiderwebs decorating the thick foliage above her gave her the creeps. While she had thicker skin now, she didn't want to test it the hard way to see if it really protected her from these insidious spiders.

With no better option, she began to walk in a direction where the ground didn't seem to be too wet and muddy.

CHAPTER FIVE

Poison Gorger

While walking, Sarah realized several things. Firstly, she had no idea how she should sustain herself. She hadn't seen a single clean water source; nor had she seen anything edible. At least, nothing that she was familiar with. And she wasn't sure if she should try her luck with the various berries and weird-looking vegetable things.

Secondly, she wasn't sure if walking around would do her any good. The swamp didn't seem to end. The only things changing around her were the mushiness of the ground and the density of the foliage.

One time, she came upon a wide clearing and tried walking into the field, but after a few steps, her left foot sank so deep into the mud that she fell over. She felt as if she may have even ripped something in her leg. There was an unsettling snap when she fell over, with her leg stuck deeply in the mud.

Even worse, some kind of giant leech actually managed to penetrate her dense skin while her foot was stuck in the ground. She immediately ripped it off, but the wound bled for a long time.

Her SP was running low. She was insatiably hungry and thirsty, and the sun had started to go down. By now, the nocturnal animals were starting to come awake and filled the air with their cries. The swamp around her was full of the sounds of birds, insects, and other unidentifiable creatures. It was really spooky. At least the mosquitoes hadn't managed to penetrate her skin.

She sat down in the middle of a grassy clearing, which was surprisingly dry and stable underfoot. She was a few meters away from any trees or shrubbery. And the various spiders and other things they might contain were also far away, which calmed her down immediately.

While sitting there in the last light of day, she came to a difficult conclusion. She would have to trust in her poison resistance and drink the murky swamp water. Unless she wanted to die of dehydration. She had bled a lot and had some difficult experiences. She also started to feel pretty woozy. As far as she knew, humans couldn't survive very long without water. Her whole body shuddered while thinking about it.

"While I'm at it, I can also eat those berries that grow around here. It can't be worse than the spider poison," she told herself, trying to be optimistic.

With hesitant steps, she walked into a swampy area not far from the clearing and saw the slight shimmer of water. She took a deep breath and sank her hands into the murkiness. She scooped up some water and tried to see if there was anything in it, but in the disappearing light she couldn't see a thing.

Before she could change her mind, she swallowed as much as she could. A foul taste assaulted her mouth, and she felt some small chunks in the water. She immediately swallowed the water and started gagging because of the putrid taste. It felt like her stomach was also churning because of the disgusting stuff she drank.

She sat there for a few minutes, waiting to see if something happened. But her stomach seemed fine, more or less, and the system didn't mention any poisoning. So she went back to drinking again.

Holding back her reflex to vomit, she scooped up one handful of murky water after another until her stomach felt bloated and started to churn.

While sitting there and waiting for her sick feeling to go away, a system prompt surprised her.

<Poisonous substances resisted. Poison resistance became more effective.

The infection could not be resisted. You are now infected.

Parasites could not be resisted. You are now infected.>

"Uhhh," she said while looking at the screen. "Shit dammit!" she started to scream while holding her bald head. "Why didn't you warn me earlier when I took the first sip of this disgusting soup?!"

It was a really gross feeling. Her body was now infested with who knows what. While thinking about that, she wanted to vomit everything out. But, she knew that her body would need the water. So she kept it in. The infection and parasites wouldn't kill her, but dehydration would. Probably.

The problem was that the infection could lead to diarrhea. Which was a high possibility because the infection was in her stomach. In this case, she would die anyway because of dehydration. Great.

While agonizing over her hopeless situation, she came up with a crazy idea. Her poison resistance didn't seem to work against organisms like parasites that entered her body, but it was really effective against the poisonous substances in the water. What if she consumed so much poison that everything inside her died? A mad laugh escaped her lips.

"Let's see who dies first," she said maniacally while patting her stomach.

She stood up and looked around, trying to find the berries she had seen before, when she spotted some kind of flower growing next to a bush.

"Ah, might as well," said Sarah. She grabbed the flower and started chewing. It didn't even taste that bad. Very grassy and sweet.

From this point on, she started to eat everything that came into her sight. Berries, flowers, weird plants, some bean-looking plants, and many other things. She couldn't even properly see what she ate because it was so dark.

After her mad eating spree, her mouth, throat, and stomach were on fire.

While groaning, she fell to the ground, holding her stomach and shuddering. For a while now, her body had tried to vomit but she'd suppressed it, trying to keep everything in.

When the system prompt came, she fixed her gaze on it.

<Warning! You are badly poisoned by a multitude of substances. Poison resistance is only partially successful. Poison is spreading throughout your body.

Warning! You ate something acidic. It is corroding your insides.>

While waiting for other system prompts and feeling like her insides were melting, she avoided looking at her status screen. She didn't want to see how much her HP had dropped.

After some time squirming on the ground, she couldn't help herself and vomited. It smelled putrid, acidic, and bloody. That was not good.

Suddenly, her eyes began burning, and she grabbed her face while screaming. She felt a warm, sticky liquid coming out of her eyes, and she couldn't see anymore.

"Shit," she said in a coarse voice, regretting her stupid idea.

<Infection subsided. All bacteria have died due to the highly toxic environment.

Parasites have died due to the highly toxic and acidic environment.>

Even though she couldn't see anymore, she saw the system prompt. And she couldn't help but laugh while realizing what it meant.

"Go fuck yourself, you little shits," she said in a raspy voice, blood starting to pool in her mouth.

Sarah felt like she could black out any second, so she rolled over on her side. It would suck pretty bad if she drowned in her own vomit while unconscious.

Not long after she managed to roll over, her premonition came true.

CHAPTER SIX

Silver Lining

Sarah woke up and coughed for a few minutes. She coughed so hard that she nearly passed out again. While clinging to her consciousness, she tried to calm her breathing.

After some time, she managed to do it and was able to concentrate on her situation. To her horror, she realized that she still couldn't see, apart from the various system prompts. The rest of her body felt pretty sore, and her stomach still felt horrible. But apart from that, it could have been worse.

To avoid thinking about her lost eyesight, she concentrated on the system prompt. She was hoping for anything that could help her situation.

<Various poisons and acids could be integrated into your ability "Poison Body." A new sub-ability, "Walking Hazard," has been created.

The sub-ability "Poison Resistance" has been strengthened and upgraded to "Poison and Acid Resistance."

Achievement "Poison Gorger" has been obtained.

Due to overcoming a near-death situation, your Life Force has increased by 1.

Level up.>

"Shit," she muttered. There was nothing that could help her eyes. She continued looking at her status screen.

Details:
Level: 3
Name: Sarah Anna Fischer
Class: None
Race: Human
Status: Blind, injured (Strength reduced by 10%, dexterity reduced by 50%)
HP: 10/60 **SP:** 25/30 **MP:** 10/30

Achievements:
- How the hell are you still sane?
- Poison Gorger

Affinities:
Mind (Mid) Body (Mid) Energy (Low)

Specializations:
- Mind (0/2)
- Body (2/2)
  - Adaptation
  - Mutation
- Energy (0/1)

Basic Stats:
Strength: 4
Dexterity: 11
Endurance: 4
Resistance: 3
Intelligence: 20
Force: 1

Special Stats:
Magic Power: 3
Life Force: 3

Active Skills:
None

Passive Skills:
- Poison Body (Adaption)
- Poison and Acid Resistance
- Walking Hazard
- Metamorphosis (Mutation)
  - Skin:
    - Dense Skin
  - Bone Structure: None
  - Muscles: None
  - Brain, Nerve System, and Sensory Organs (not recommended): None
  - Organs and Processes (not recommended): None
  - Special Mutations (not recommended): None
- Struggle (Conditional Passive)
- Slightly Crazy
- Mean Eye

It was pretty shocking to see that she was really blind now. And it didn't seem like a temporary kind of thing. But she still had hope. She had leveled up, and her Life Force was now one point higher. That meant she could mutate again.

Show me the list of available eye mutations, Sarah mentally commanded the system.

<Mutations on the sensory organs are not recommended. Proceed?>

Without even having to formulate a *yes* in her mind, she was shown a list of possible eye mutations.

<Mutation: Sensory Organ "Eyes." Listing available options:
Farsighted Eyes (1 LF): You are able to see further and in more detail.
Predator Eyes (1 LF): Heightened sensitivity to movement. Higher chance of spotting camouflaged beings.
Nocturnal Eyes (1 LF): Better eyesight in the dark. Slightly worse eyesight in bright light.
Superior Eyes (2 LF): Enhanced eyesight and dynamic vision. Able to see in close to complete darkness.
Magic Vision (2 LF): While consuming Magic Power, magic vision is enabled.
Illusion Vision (2 LF): While consuming Magic Power, you are able to create illusions for yourself based on your memories.
For more options, increase your level and/or heighten your Life Force.>

Sarah was immensely happy that her blindness didn't affect her mutation choices. She was half worried that, with her being blind, it wouldn't be possible anymore.

She wondered what the difference was between the Vision and Eyes mutations. Would the vision mutations change her eyes, or her brain? She wasn't quite sure how it would work. In any case, it was quite possible that the Eyes mutations would change the basic structure of her eyes. Therefore, it could heal her blindness by restructuring her eyes and forming new ones. Just like with the wounds on her legs.

But seriously, what the hell was Illusion Vision for? Was this the system telling her that she could just lie around, living in a self-created illusion instead of facing reality? Was this some kind of sick joke?

Tired of thinking about the weird sense of humor the system sometimes seemed to have, she focused on what she should do.

Because she didn't want to spend both of her free Life Force points, she decided to choose Predator Eyes. They seemed the most useful, especially in an environment where many beings camouflage themselves. She hoped that with these eyes, she could spot poisonous animals and insects before coming near them.

As always, the system knew what she wanted. This time, it didn't even ask for affirmation. Maybe it was able to learn.

Luckily, the pain wasn't as bad this time. Maybe because her eyes were already destroyed by the poison.

When the transformation was complete, it was surprisingly unsettling to be able to see again. She gagged and tried to suppress the influx of information her newly mutated eyes gave her. It felt like her brain wasn't made to accommodate so much visual information. And it also seemed to be nighttime. She didn't want to know how it would be during the day.

When she closed her eyes, the nauseating feeling somewhat subsided. Now she could only see through a tiny slit, but it was better than the nausea. This seemed to need some getting used to.

"At least I can see again," Sarah mumbled to herself, as she made herself comfortable on the ground. By now, she was very dirty. She had passed out a lot in the mud. She didn't really care anymore about staying clean or whatever.

The change in her mindset happened surprisingly fast. In the end, one of the most outstanding abilities of humans seemed to be their adaptability.

With a sigh, she stood up. Being a bit disoriented with her new eyes, she stumbled around, looking for the spot where she had drunk water. She definitely needed some fluids right now. Her body was parched, as if she had been lying in the sun for a whole day without drinking anything.

She didn't find the same spot again, but at some point she toppled over, splashing in some muddy water. She quickly scrambled out onto more or less stable ground and checked her body over. She really didn't want some kind of leech sucking her blood again. But, to her surprise, there was nothing. She more or less expected by now that every mistake she made would cost her dearly.

With some reluctance, she kneeled down and started scooping up the disgusting water full of bacteria, parasites, and who knows what else.

It had a seriously horrible taste. Sarah was so thirsty that she thought about plunging her head into the water and drinking like an animal, but she had already seen one of the disgusting denizens of the swamp, so no thanks. She didn't want a leech stuck in her face or, even worse, her mouth.

She shoveled water into her mouth as fast as she could for a few minutes until she felt full again, spitting out the bits and pieces of dirt and other stuff from the water.

She sat down with a sigh and waited for the potential system prompt. But, nothing happened. It seemed that her resistance was so strong by now that it wasn't even worth mentioning what she had just consumed.

With a happy smile, she patted her stomach. It was now a toxic and acidic death trap for anything that wanted a piece of her. "Who is a good stomach?" she mumbled, while still patting her belly. While doing so, she summoned up her status window and was relieved to see that her status seemed to have improved.

Status: Injured (Strength reduced by 10%)
HP: 20/60 **SP:** 30/30 **MP:** 15/30

Her HP, SP, and MP seemed to restore themselves again, even though she didn't know why her MP was drained. Some abilities and mutations seemed to need MP, but until now she never used it. Well, she also had no idea how to use magic power anyway.

It was also nice to see that she leveled had up again. This seemed to add magic power, life force, and some improvement to her HP, SP, and MP. She was a bit disappointed to see that her basic stats hadn't increased at all. It would be really useful in this situation to be stronger or smarter.

She also noticed that her level seemed to increase every time she made some progress with her abilities.

"How nice," Sarah said in a dry voice. "I need to mutate and poison myself to level up, huh? Are you some kind of pervert, getting off watching me suffer?" she asked into the empty air, but as always, when she spouted nonsense like this, the system didn't answer.

Feeling a bit better after insulting the system, she thought about what to do next.

She had to survive and get stronger and more resistant. She didn't know whether she would have to swim through some parts of the swamp, and she didn't trust her dense skin enough to risk it. Even worse, she didn't know if there were insects or snakes in the swamp that could overcome her poison resistance.

For now, she would concentrate on consuming poisonous stuff and drinking the disgusting water. All of it was to improve her poison resistance. Maybe she could level up again and improve her mutations. Who knows, maybe she could just make herself some super muscles. Then she would swing around in the treetops like some weird, naked ape. Maybe, like this, she could find a way out of this cursed swamp.

With a firm resolution, she stood up and started gorging on some plants. Trying not to think too much about what she was doing, she repeatedly ate random plants and drank some water. She waited for some time afterward until she could feel that the poison she consumed had subsided.

At one point, she even ate something that temporarily paralyzed her. For a few horrible minutes, she lay on the ground, afraid she'd eaten the wrong plant. Luckily, she could also subdue the poison. She even got a system prompt that her resistance had been strengthened.

Most of the next day went by like this. When the light began to fade, she stumbled to the clearing and let herself slump down into the grass. She felt bloated and gross from eating so much stuff that humans really shouldn't eat.

As she lay on the ground, she watched the small part of the sky she could see get darker and darker, until the first stars could be seen. As the evening progressed and night set in, the sky was practically flooded with stars. It was breathtakingly beautiful.

"I must be really crazy," she mumbled to herself. "Here I am, in danger of dying, and having almost died a few times already, and I'm enjoying this shit?" Even though she thought she had to be kind of disturbed, for some reason she wasn't. She enjoyed progressing in level and getting stronger through mutation and her poison resistance.

"The taste is really horrible, though," she mumbled, "but I guess one cannot have everything."

With a relaxed smile, she watched the beautiful night sky and fell into a deep slumber.

CHAPTER SEVEN

Questions

Andrew watched the crowd of tired people. They were sprawled out in the wide clearing, completely spent from their last couple of days.

"That's a lot of progress for a few days, am I right?" said the young, scrawny man. His name was Dennis, and he sat on the ground next to Andrew.

He was wearing some sort of underpants, which had been made from spun tree bark and were somehow elastic. One of the craftier people came up with the idea a few days ago, and now he and a few more people were working on making clothes nonstop.

By now, everyone had at least some clothes to hide their sensitive parts, so everyone was much more at ease with each other.

Andrew smiled slightly and patted Dennis on the shoulder. "That is also your achievement, you know. I'm not quite sure how you do it, but you seem to know exactly when to make a joke to lighten the mood. You prevented a few people from freaking out the last few days."

Dennis smiled wryly and scratched his head. "I know you just want to make me feel important. And I also know that all of this is mostly because of you. I noticed that if people get too far away from you, they start to get more nervous. You got some of those powers right in the beginning, am I right?" he asked in a shy voice.

He was, of course, right. Andrew's passive skill, Equilibrium held the minds of these people here together. And when this wasn't enough, he could increase the calming effect with his active skill, Emotion Manipulation. He felt a bit guilty about it, but it was needed right now.

"Maybe," Andrew said with a somewhat somber smile. While exploring their surroundings, the group had undergone some changes.

More and more people had gained strange powers with the help of the system. They were mostly used to calm their nerves and emotions, like the power to suppress their minds' and bodies' reactions to fear.

A few got stronger, tougher, or more dexterous. Dennis acquired one of the most unique abilities. He was able to somehow identify if a plant was edible or poisonous. One of the other guys, Thomas, actually got some kind of beautifying skill, which he was really embarrassed about. Andrew didn't blame him for being embarrassed. He thought it was ridiculous too. When everyone else was trying their best to stay alive, and got corresponding skills, he got more attractive.

By now, they had found out that strong emotions or thoughts could lead to awakening powers, which made the beautifying skill all the more laughable. It more or less meant that it was more important for Thomas to look good than his very own survival.

Most people acquired their powers without much trouble, while some were in great pain, but nothing traumatizing.

Sadly, there was one case when someone became comatose in the process of gaining powers. It was the female doctor who had initially tried to help the other comatose people. The doctor and others had tried to feed the unconscious people, but it didn't work. One of them died when someone tried to shove berries in his mouth. Unfortunately, the rest of them were now slowly dying. Of the initial seven comatose people, only four were still alive, not including the doctor. And with things being what they were, they wouldn't make the night.

Though it had been expected, their deaths shocked the little group the next morning. But, they were somehow able to bury their emotions and concentrate on the most important tasks at hand. Andrew carried the bodies deep into the woods, far away from their camp. He started trembling slightly, so he used his active skill to quell his impending panic.

"Hey, Andrew." Dennis' voice made Andrew realize that he had been silently sitting still for a few minutes. "What did you do before all this?"

This question confused Andrew. "I don't know. Before? Does it even matter?" he asked, feeling a little annoyed.

"Of course it matters," said Dennis. "I mean, I doubt we just started existing all of a sudden. We should have been kids at some point, right? Who are our parents, then?"

These questions made Andrew's head hurt. Dennis was right. Who was he before this? What was his past?

"And since we're talking about kids," Dennis continued, "where the hell are they? Not even to mention, shouldn't there be older people too? I've been asking around, and we all seem to be somewhere between seventeen and thirty years old. And everyone here seems very healthy too. I don't know, but something about this just seems so . . . wrong. And strange."

With the way Dennis was speaking, he must have been making himself crazy about this for days. Andrew empathized. Something about this didn't seem right. He just couldn't put his finger on it.

"I have an idea," Andrew said. "Why don't you start asking people more questions? Find out if anyone remembers anything from before our awakening in the forest. Or if anyone knows where the old and the young people are or what happened to them. Do you think you can do that?" he asked the wide-eyed Dennis, who started to nod.

"If you say so, of course. But many people get strangely irritated if I ask them about stuff like that. That's why I wanted to talk with you about it. If it gets out of hand . . ." He trailed off, head down.

Andrew smiled and patted his shoulder. "I have your back. You can always tell them that I asked you to do it. That should help a little. This group here seems to see me as a leader. And I intend to do my part."

Dennis looked up with motivation in his eyes, nodded, and stood up. Before he left, he turned to Andrew and looked at him seriously. "I see you as a leader too, you know. You are like a pillar of calmness to us. And honestly, I think we would be pretty fucked without you. So yeah, thank you. Really." Dennis blushed slightly and scurried away, walking to the group of people who were making clothes.

Andrew sat still for a while before he stood up and made his way into the woods. It was getting darker, and his face wasn't really visible anymore.

Even though he had his emotion suppression skill, his hands trembled slightly as he held them in front of his face.

"Who am I?"

CHAPTER EIGHT

Rage

Sarah felt like she had been living like an animal for the past few days. She was just eating, drinking, and sleeping. But so far, her plan had worked. As she guessed, whatever she did was connected to one of her abilities, and she leveled up.

By now, she was a whopping level seven, which was huge because she started to feel the magic power in her body. It felt like she was becoming healthier and stronger.

Two of her basic stats, Resistance and Endurance, had even risen by one point each. It was likely due to her eating poisonous stuff nonstop. However, starting a few days ago, no matter how much trash she gorged down, her level just didn't increase.

She mentally summoned her stat screen to try to think about how to level up some more.

Details:
Level: 7
Name: Sarah Anna Fischer
Class: None
Race: Human
Status: Normal
HP: 75/80 **SP**: 40/50 **MP**: 70/70

Achievements:
- How the hell are you still sane?: Resistance to mind damage increased by 10%.
- Poison Gorger: Resistance to orally consumed poison increased by 30%.

Affinities:
Mind (Mid) Body (Mid) Energy (Low)

Specializations:
- Mind (0/2)
- Body (2/2)
  - Adaptation
  - Mutation
- Energy (0/1)

Basic Stats:

Strength: 4

Dexterity: 11

Endurance: 5

Resistance: 4

Intelligence: 20

Force: 1

Special Stats:

Magic Power: 7

Life Force: 7

Active Skills:

None

Passive Skills:
- Poison Body (Adaptation)
- Poison and Acid Resistance
- Walking Hazard
- Metamorphosis (Mutation)
  - Skin:
    - Dense skin
- Bone Structure: None
- Muscles: None
- Brain, Nerve System, and Sensory Organs (not recommended):
  - Predator Eyes
- Organs and Processes (not recommended): None
- Special Mutations (not recommended): None
- Struggle (Conditional Passive)
- Slightly Crazy
- Mean Eye

It was satisfying to see that her HP, SP, and MP seemed to go up in accordance with her magic power and life force. Also, her Walking Hazard skill had been strengthened, going from slightly toxic and acidic to very toxic and acidic.

She knew that this shouldn't be something a normal person would be happy about, but she felt pretty good about it. It was also very funny to just spit on something and see it wither immediately. When she found out about it, she did it for so long that her mouth completely dried out.

She knew that maybe the Metamorphosis skill would help her level up, if she initiated more mutations. But until now, she didn't have an immediate need for new mutations. And she wanted to be able to immediately heal mutilated body parts, like she did with her eyes.

So, mutations were more for emergencies. But as it seemed wasteful to her to only use two out of seven Life Force points, she decided to give her muscles an upgrade. She looked at the other options, and some of the "not recommended" ones looked pretty good. But she just wanted to mutate them if she really needed it. They were not recommended for a reason. Probably.

It was also, sadly, not possible to upgrade or change existing mutations. So her dream of rock-hard skin had to wait for now. But yeah, she still had a lot of potential to mutate, so she wasn't that disappointed.

She grinned widely while she prompted the system to show her the possible mutations in her muscles.

<Mutation: Muscles. Listing available options:
Dense Fibers (1 LF): Increased muscle density. Muscles are tougher and stronger, but they also need more energy.
Strengthened Fibers (1 LF): Strengthened muscle fibers. Slightly tougher and stronger.
Magic Fibers (2 LF): Able to infuse magic power into the muscles to temporarily increase their strength output.
For more options, increase your level and/or heighten your Life Force.>

She was a bit disappointed that the muscle options were so few. And also that she didn't get some awesome options because she had so many free Life Force points. But she probably had to level up to get more options.

She also already knew what she wanted. She didn't want to have a higher energy consumption, so she chose Strengthened Fibers.

When the system initialized the mutation, she immediately fell to the ground. It felt extremely disgusting, like she didn't have muscles anymore but instead a colony of larvae crawling around under her skin. If she still could, she would be throwing up, just to make a point. The system was really sadistic.

While she waited for the mutation to end, something big and furry suddenly sprang into her vision. And chomped down on her. She inwardly screamed as fur was pressed into her face and extreme pain ravaged her left arm. Whatever bit her, it wasn't easy for it to get through her dense skin. But it hurt like hell.

Sarah was furious but couldn't do much except desperately wish for the beast to die. It had seemingly managed to bite through her dense skin. She felt it ripping parts of her skin and her bubbling muscles off. The pain was immense, but so was her rage. She was so furious that she thought she would pass out. She wanted to rip this thing apart and spit on it until it was nothing more than a bubbling mass of goo.

As if just waiting for its chance, the system gave her a notification.

<Specializations Invasion (Mind) and Nerve Control (Mind) unlocked. Acquire specializations?>

With burning eyes, she mentally affirmed the system prompt.

CHAPTER NINE

Mutant

Sarah nearly passed out from the immense dizziness she suddenly experienced. But she held on while concentrating on her pain and rage.

She didn't even have the time to check the system prompts, explaining what her new specializations were and what skills came with them. She just had to trust that the system would give her a solution to her problem.

She concentrated all her mental energy on the furry thing chomping down on her and wanted it to suffer. But nothing happened. With a hollow feeling in her stomach, she realized that nothing had changed. But before she could read the descriptions of her new skills, the bubbling of her muscles died down. She was able to move again. The furry thing on top of her seemed confused. The sudden change in the seemingly near-dead Sarah it had been sitting on alarmed it. Not missing her chance, Sarah grabbed the beast with all the strength she could muster and chomped down on it. The furry thing squealed in her grip and bit into her arms. It was so painful that she wanted to let go, but she held on with an iron will.

She ripped out mouthfuls of fur until she reached soft skin. She sank her teeth deep into the flesh of the thing. This caused it to squeal even louder, and it also started thrashing around in her arms.

Sarah was ripping out the flesh of the thing when she suddenly felt a horrible pain in her back. It felt like something exploding in her guts, as if something had been pushed into her abdomen. A guttural scream left her mouth as she bit even harder into the thing. Her mind was filled with rage, and the only thought she had was to make this thing suffer and die.

Suddenly, it felt like her mind skipped a beat, and she was connected to the beast. She felt its pain, fear, confusion, and rage. She somehow knew that she could use this connection.

While half her face dug into the grisly wound of the thing, she mentally willed it to despair. It gave up any kind of resistance. It was only screaming and flailing around while Sarah ripped out more and more flesh from the thing.

And as suddenly as it attacked her, it stopped moving. Sarah needed a moment to realize that it was dead. She had either bit into something vital, or it had a heart attack from intense fear.

But one thing was for sure. It was dead.

With a groan, she shoved the thing away and immediately regretted it. Whatever was shoved into her gut had been pulled out by suddenly dropping the thing, and with it came pain and blood.

While she pressed her hands on the wound in her back, she heard a slight sizzling sound as her blood dripped onto the ground. She noticed that her left arm hurt, but it was still functional apart from that. That was at least something.

Breathing heavily, she stood up to inspect what had attacked her. She stumbled for a moment before she could get a good look at the creature.

It was a huge rat. Its body was at least as big as her torso, with a weird, bony-looking tail coming out of its back. The tail was sizzling and covered in blood. Which explained what had stabbed her in the back.

Following her initial plan, she spit on the thing a few times, but the pain in her back became too intense and forced her to stop.

With a grunt, she sat back down while still pressing on the wound in her back. She had already started to feel dizzy from the blood loss. If this continued, she would bleed out. The wound didn't seem to want to close.

It was now time for an emergency mutation. But it was problematic that she had already mutated her muscles. She had no idea which mutation would also involve the muscles and tissue in her lower back.

She frantically looked through all the available mutation options, but she found nothing that could help her. Grasping her last straw, she looked into the, until now, empty Special Mutations list. And she was surprised to see that it wasn't empty anymore.

<Mutation: Special Mutations (not recommended). Listing available options: **Mutated Tail** (acquired, 5 LF): A long and flexible tail with an exoskeleton made of spine-like bone segments. Can be stretched over its original length, but will leave the vulnerable muscle and sinew under the exoskeleton exposed. (not recommended) <For more options, ingest the genetic material of other beings infused with magic power.>

"Well, that is new," she said in a raspy voice. Sarah was having a hard time concentrating.

This was her only chance. All the other mutations didn't involve her lower back. And the tail would most likely extend from her lower back. So, there was a high possibility that it would mutate the whole lower section of her back. Hopefully, at least.

With no other choice, she mentally affirmed the mutation choice. Then she waited with clenched teeth for it to begin.

<Initializing Special Mutation Mutated Tail. Ingesting biomass is highly recommended. If not, the biomass for constructing the tail will be taken from the body. Maintaining body structure cannot be guaranteed.>

"Are you kidding me?" she screamed at the system. "Why the hell do you never tell me about these things in advance?!"

<Mutation will start in 10 seconds. Please start ingesting biomass.>

The system was as heartless as ever, not answering Sarah's outburst.

She frantically scrambled to the nearest source of dense biomass in her vicinity. The dead mutated rat.

Just as the timer reached zero, she was able to take her first bite of the disgusting meat and gorge on it.

The mutation was horrible. While feeling like her lower body was melting down and forming new tissue, she had to constantly eat bloody, stinking meat. All the while, nearly falling unconscious from the blood loss and the pain in her back.

It felt like an eternity before the mutation suddenly ended.

She turned away from the now mangled corpse and started vomiting. But hardly anything came out. The system had used up every last bit of biomass.

When she finally stopped heaving, she crawled as far away from the scene as she could. She didn't dare stand up because her legs felt strange. And she tried very hard to ignore the fact that something new was sprouting from her lower back.

"Ohhh, this was horrible," Sarah mumbled to herself while lying in the soft moss. She lay there on the ground for a few minutes, taking deep breaths and trying to get accustomed to the new thing in her lower back.

After a while, she summoned up enough courage and turned her head until she could see behind her.

The wound on her back had closed up, which was really good. But, right above her buttocks, where her spine had ended before, was a long, bony tail.

"Oh, this is so fucking disgusting," she said, closing her eyes for a moment. "I have a freaking tail now. Am I now a monster or something?"

After some more deep breathing, she opened her eyes again and looked at the tail. It was really disturbing that it was just *there*. What was even more disturbing was that it felt like it had always been there. Like a mixture between leg and arm or something.

She quietly swayed it around in the air with some kind of weird curiosity. The longer she looked at the tail, the less disturbing it felt.

"Who's a good tail," she mumbled while lightly touching the tail with her right hand.

It took quite some time, but she started to feel accustomed to her new appendage. Even if it was still kind of gross to have the same tail as a mutated rat.

"Alright," Sarah said to herself, taking a deep breath. "Time to see if my race changed to rat-woman or something."

Details:
Level: 9
Name: Sarah Anna Fischer
Class: None
Race: Mutant
Status: Normal
HP: 10/90 **SP:** 10/60 **MP:** 5/110

Achievements:
- How the hell are you still sane?
- Poison Gorger
- More Than Human: Higher success rate on special mutations.

Affinities:
Mind (Mid) Body (Mid) Energy (Low)

Specializations:
- Mind (2/2)
  - Invasion
  - Nerve Control
- Body (2/2)
  - Adaptation
  - Mutation
- Energy (0/1)

Basic Stats:
Strength: 4
Dexterity: 11
Endurance: 5
Resistance: 4
Intelligence: 20
Force: 1

Special Stats:
Magic Power: 9
Life Force: 9
Mental Power: 2

Active Skills:

Mind Infiltration (Invasion)

Passive Skills:

- Poison Body (Adaption)
- Poison and Acid Resistance
- Walking Hazard
- Metamorphosis (Mutation)
    - Skin:
        - Dense Skin (1 LF)
    - Bone Structure: None
    - Muscles:
        - Strengthened Fibers (1 LF): Strengthened muscle fibers. Slightly tougher and stronger.
    - Brain, Nerve System, and Sensory Organs (not recommended):
        - Predator Eyes (1 LF)
    - Organs and Processes (not recommended): None
    - Special Mutations (not recommended):
        - Mutated tail (acquired, 5 LF)
- Suppression (Nerve Control)
- Struggle (Conditional Passive)
- Slightly Crazy
- Mean Eye

Sarah blankly stared at the status screen. Especially the line describing her race.

"I just hate you," she said to the system, shaking her head.

"Well, at least you were nice enough to call me mutant instead of rat-woman. So, you are just a half-asshole." She sighed loudly. Her only friend and helper in this crazy world had to be an ass.

Trying not to think about being a mutant now, she read the description of the delicious new skills she had acquired along with her new specializations.

Active Skills:

- Mind Infiltration (Invasion): While using magic power, you are able to invade another being's mind. Invasion is facilitated if the being has been poisoned by you. Direct contact is needed.

Passive Skills:

- Suppression (Nerve Control): Your emotions will influence your nerves less. Warning: Instinctual behavior is also suppressed.

She wasn't quite sure about the second one. Was this good? She guessed that it would probably help her hold her shit together if something horrible was happening to her. But it could be a problem that she wouldn't instinctually run from danger anymore.

On the other hand, the first skill was really nice. It didn't really explain in detail what was possible, but Sarah saw it as a good sign. It probably meant that there were a lot of possibilities on how to use this skill.

She now had some weapons to defend herself. A weird tail with a hard, sharp tip, and she also had the ability to inflict severe mental pain on other beings. And last, but not least, she was a walking hazard full of poison and acid.

She swore to herself she would never let anything like this happen again.

The biggest creature she had seen since the creation of this new world was a tall and skinny bird. It looked for food in the shallow water. Sarah didn't know that such animals existed in the swamp. Startled, the bird jumped. It had likely thought Sarah was dying or something. Becoming limp all of a sudden and falling to the ground was not something a healthy person would do.

"Never again." She said it to herself loudly and clenched her fist. "And with that, I guess I have to find out what I can do with my new abilities."

Sarah grinned widely with mad flames burning in her eyes, the dried blood on her face crumbling away.

"Time to experiment."

CHAPTER TEN

The Next Steps

For a few days, Sarah chased after little animals to explore her skills. It actually wasn't easy at all because most of the animals were either fast or slippery. But as she got used to her new tail, the hunt became easier. Eventually, she was able to shoot out her tail, from the length of her legs to double that.

She skewered a lot of little animals this way. The ones that survived had to suffer through being experimented on until they died, but she always ate them, even though they usually tasted gross. The reptiles and amphibians were often poisonous, so those snacks boosted her poison resistance skills.

She found out that she wasn't really able to induce emotions in the animals when she manipulated the minds of insects. They didn't have complex enough brains to really feel anything.

Instead, she stimulated their brains and nerves, sending them into a state of utter chaos. This simulated the reactions to extreme fear and pain. It was enough to make most beings fall unconscious, and many of them even died on the spot when she began her experiments.

Even better, she was able to influence the signals the brains sent to the bodies. Until now, she had only figured out how to make the animals go limp and stop them from breathing. She was also working on stopping their hearts, but it was tricky.

"I kinda feel like I am turning into some kind of nightmarish monster," she mumbled to herself while chewing on a mouse. It had just died because she shut off its breathing reflex. "Naah, that's just my imagination," she assured herself. She had been doing this a lot lately.

While experimenting on the unfortunate wildlife, she scouted her surroundings and tried to figure out what else lived in the swamp.

She was next to a wide stretch of still water, where lots of birds and amphibians lived. Her clearing was one of the dryer regions in the swamp, right at the edge of one. The further she went into the dryer region, the more she began to hear the deep groans and howls of bigger animals. They sounded . . . wrong. She couldn't put her finger on it, but they often sounded more like cries of agony than the normal sounds animals made to communicate.

Being overly aware of her last encounter with a big rat, she'd left the area again. She didn't want to get into unnecessary trouble with the bigger wildlife.

They probably stayed clear of the area she resided in because there were so many poisonous plants and animals there. But that was perfect for Sarah, who was more or less immune by now to most of the poisons that existed in her territory. Only sometimes, her poison resistance couldn't overcome a new threat. But it was always quickly dealt with.

The days flew by as she always did the same things over and over again. Scouting, hunting, eating, drinking, and sleeping. She started to feel like an animal more and more, but she couldn't help that now. At least her hair had begun to grow back, which made her happy. The thought of being bald for the rest of her life had just been horrible.

She would slowly find out more about the swamp until she could find a way out. The problem was that she had no idea what she was looking for. What does the exit of a spatial error look like? Would she even be able to see it? What if the exit was at the bottom of the swamp? She simply had no idea.

By now, she had already checked out a pretty big territory, but an end to the swamp was nowhere in sight. Sarah didn't despair.

"I will come out of this alive," she said into the air. "Just wait, you sadistic system. You will have to deal with me for a long time."

The times when she spoke into the empty air increased day after day. But she guessed it was healthier for her mind to work this way rather than to bury all of her fear and pain inside her.

For now, her goal was to get stronger until she was confident that nothing would be a threat to her in this swamp. But it was easier said than done. She was still at level nine, and that number didn't seem to want to move.

She started to wonder what she hadn't tried until now. Of course, she had two Life Force points left to mutate herself. But the mutations proved themselves time and time again as emergency measures when death came knocking.

The only thing that came to mind was her magic power. She kind of felt it inside of her, especially when she used the Mind Infiltration skill. But she couldn't get a good grasp of it until now.

"Might as well look into this," she mumbled to herself. Then she started to immerse herself in the feeling of the magic power inside her, while going about her usual daily activities.

Some more days went by like this, and she started to notice the effect of the magic. It seemed like it flowed through her whole body, empowering everything she did.

From her breathing to clenching her hand, everything seemed to be supported by this strange energy. She had no idea what exactly it did inside her body, but it seemed to make her stronger, faster, and more dexterous.

The more she focused on this feeling, the more she thought that something was hindering her magic. Like her body was somehow resisting the merge with the new energy.

Sarah was eating some leaves, which were dripping with poisonous goo, when she felt the reason for this resistance. There was some kind of invisible barrier inside her body. No, her whole body seemed to be part of this barrier. She mentally started pushing against the barrier. In the beginning, nothing happened. But after some time, cracks appeared in the barrier.

Invigorated by this new insight, Sarah pushed even harder. The barrier shattered. It was gone, like it had never been there in the first place.

<Congratulations for breaking through the limitations of a normal being. You have managed to merge your body with magic power. The limits of your body have been readjusted.

You are now qualified to experience the first recording of Dr. Alain Becker. Initializing sequence.>

Sarah was still mesmerized by the new feeling inside her body, the magic flowing through her like a strong river current. Nothing like the small trickle she felt before.

Reality came back way too soon when she read the system prompt and saw the familiar timer counting down.

"At least this time I'm not in danger of dying or going crazy," she said optimistically, just before her mind was sucked into emptiness.

For a few moments, there was nothing. She couldn't move or speak. There was no way to tell how much time had gone by or if there was anything around her. Her surroundings weren't even black. They were just . . . empty.

"Recording number one of the incident. Dr. Alain Becker speaking," said a voice out of the nothingness.

After some time, the voice spoke again. "I could never have imagined that." Suddenly, the origin of the voice could be seen. It was a man surrounded by utter nothingness; he was the only thing visible. Dr. Becker was a middle-aged man, with thin brown hair streaked with gray. He seemed haggard, and he wore some kind of white cloak that was ripped in many places. He seemed to be sitting on something, but that was also invisible, like everything else around him.

He started speaking again, this time with a broken and trembling voice. There was nothing left of the calm professionalism of his first words. "None of my measurements indicated an energy of this magnitude. Maybe I should have done more. Maybe I should have, yeah." He shuddered and sobbed a little, and added a few words, almost too quiet for Sarah to hear. "I'm so sorry, Clarissa." For a while, he sat there in the darkness, resting his head in his slender hands.

After some time, he spoke again. "But what can I do now? Our civilization is no more. The fate of humanity is at best questionable, and at worst hopeless. All has gone to shit. So many are dead."

Again, he just sat there, saying nothing and shaking his head at times. He seemed to want to say something at certain points, but he always inflated himself immediately before any sound could come out of his mouth.

This went on for a while until he started straightening his back. It looked like a huge boulder was sitting on his shoulder, making it almost impossible for him to sit upright. Some tears could be seen in his eyes.

"I still cannot believe it. One wish. One tiny little wish made by an insane boy did all of this," he said, while rubbing his eyes. "I always thought that the world would fall apart because of some madman, but I never imagined it to be this way."

He let his hand fall into his lap, looking emptily into the distance. "I guess I should do something." He slowly started speaking again. "I mean, I was the idiot who told the whole world about the energy and led the madman right into its epicenter." He shook his head and paused for a while.

"I still have some of my equipment. Maybe I can repair it somehow. Maybe I can . . . I actually don't know what I could do. I guess I have to find out what can be done."

He slowly stood up, still looking like a huge weight was making it nearly impossible for him to move. He turned around and began trotting into the nothingness until he couldn't be seen anymore.

Sarah forgot where she was while listening intently to the complicated stuff Dr. Alain Becker had said. She was still trying to think through what she had heard when she felt an immense pull in her mind. She seemed to race through the nothingness until she came to a sudden and violent stop.

Her body jerked like it was getting an electric shock, and it made her feel sick. But she couldn't help but feel happy.

While she had no idea what was happening, one thing was for certain—there were still other people alive. She wasn't the only one left.

This fear of being alone had rooted itself deep in her mind, always knocking on her consciousness when she felt exhausted from everything. But with this information, the fear went away like it had never been there. Her struggle had meaning. There were other people. She just had to find the exit.

With newfound hope, Sarah stood up and began to get ready to continue scouting. Then, the system sent her another prompt.

<Congratulations on reaching Level 10. You have unlocked Class.>

CHAPTER ELEVEN

The River

Andrew felt cold. Really cold. It had been raining for days, and the only protection were the trees and the tents they'd all built with branches and big leaves. But the water often found its way in.

His people didn't look good. Many had blueish hands and feet. And the clothes made out of tree bark had begun to wound their skin upon becoming wet and shrinking.

Two people had fevers the day prior. Their bodies were extremely hot, and today they felt even colder than the others. In the beginning, the group tried to help them, but as they lost consciousness and grew colder, everyone else had begun avoiding them. No one had the ability to help them. Like the comatose people that died long ago.

"We can't go on like this," whispered Dennis, who was sitting next to him. "If this goes on much longer, we will all die here."

"The rain must stop eventually," Andrew said. He knew that they had to do something. They had no other option but to wait for the rain to stop, and until then, take shelter under the trees and in the tents. They couldn't even make a fire anymore because everything was drenched in water. It was a pretty gloomy situation.

It was absurd for Andrew to think that they had survived so long only to be brought close to death because of rain.

Just as he was sinking into his thoughts again, the gruff-looking man named Alex, who had become their scout, came rushing into the camp.

"I found caves," he said in a deep and raspy voice. He was one of the few who weren't bothered by the cold and the only person out of the seventy-eight people in their group who had received the Mutation specialization. He had undergone horrible pain when he used the corresponding skill. And he had often been apathetic afterward. But he pushed through it, and it had been worth it.

"Please, not so loud," Andrew said in a hushed voice, looking over to the ragged group of people. They were sleeping tightly packed together on the ground. "What kinds of caves have you found?"

"I'm not quite sure," Alex began, "but they seem pretty big. Big enough for us to stay in."

Andrew's eyes lit up, and Dennis laughed. Alex looked a bit troubled and held up a hand. "The problem is that the caves are located in the rocky hill. On the other side of the river."

Andrew's and Dennis' moods plummeted immediately, thinking about the raging river that separated them from the caves.

"Why have you even told us about this?" Dennis asked angrily. "It is suicide to try to get over the river. Especially now! The current is insanely strong because of the heavy amount of rain."

Alex shrugged his shoulders, looking a bit angry. "Do you have a better solution?" he asked in a tense voice. "Two of us are already dying because of the cold. Another five people lost some toes the other night. And we grow weaker and weaker with each day." Alex looked over at a woman named Karen, who was sleeping with the others. Andrew didn't know what was going on between them, but it was pretty obvious that Alex took a liking to her.

Dennis looked back angrily at Alex, and they started a hushed argument so as not to wake up the sleeping group.

Andrew agonized over the situation, while using his ability to calm the two who were arguing. Dennis was right. It was suicidal to try and swim through the raging river. But Alex was also right. They would get weaker and start dying one by one if this went on much longer. Andrew also felt the toll on his body but tried hard not to show it to the others.

Andrew looked despondently at the sky. It wouldn't get much brighter out, even though the sun would be coming up any moment. There were thick clouds in the sky, spewing out ungodly volumes of rain, as if they were trying to drown Andrew and his people.

"We have to take our chance with crossing the river," he said to the two people standing next to him, and they immediately became silent. Dennis looked at him with fear-filled eyes but didn't argue. He also knew that they had to risk it.

"But we will not just jump headfirst into the water. Let's make a plan."

They went a bit further from the slumbering group and spoke for quite some time. They talked until everyone was awake, and then they began to come closer to the group.

Andrew nodded to the other two and stood up in front of the crowd. Alex went to Karen and took her in his arms, trying to ward off the cold.

Andrew swallowed and took a deep breath. "Alex found some caves," he started explaining, which elicited excited shouts from the crowd. Like Alex did before, Andrew held up his hand and explained the circumstances.

The crowd now looked gloomy and fearful. Contrary to Andrew's expectations, they were also quite determined. They seemed to trust Andrew more than he thought. He felt the weight of responsibility on his shoulders, but he wouldn't let himself get nervous about it.

After the discussions in the crowd died down, Andrew started to explain his plan.

"We will use the ropes Tobias made. We will tie them together, which should give us a rope more or less the width of the river. Alex will swim over the river and attach the rope to one of the trees, while we attach the other end to a tree on our side. With this, you will be able to pull yourself over the river without having to swim."

He waited a moment for everyone to take in what he just said, and then he continued. "We have some people here who won't be able to go over with their own strength. Do we have volunteers who can bring them over?"

The crowd nervously looked at the two ill people, but no one said anything. Andrew guessed as much and steeled his resolve.

"I understand you. I am also not confident enough to do this myself. But we can't just leave them here to be eaten alive by the rats or die from the cold. It is bad enough that this happened to the comatose during the night a while back. Do we have volunteers to give them . . ." He paused for a moment, not wanting to believe what he would say next. "Do we have volunteers to give them a quick death?"

This question shocked the crowd even more. But no one argued against it. Everyone looked to the ground until a woman named Melissa stepped forward.

She looked really afraid, but she held a sharp and pointy stone in her hand. She clenched it so hard that some blood trickled to the ground. "I can do it. I have a skill to temporarily shut off my emotions." Her voice was quiet and shaky. Still, everyone heard her. The crowd gave her thankful and pitying glances. The people closest to her held her shoulders and had their hands on her back, trying to somehow support her.

Andrew nodded to her and spoke again. "Alright everyone, get the ropes and follow Alex to the river. Melissa and I will stay here and . . . give them their well-deserved rest."

The crowd looked nervously at Andrew and Melissa and began to pack up faster than necessary. They didn't have much, so the process went quite fast. As planned, Andrew and Melissa stayed behind, silently looking at each other.

"Let's get it over with," said Andrew, preparing his active skill to calm the unconscious people and himself.

"How . . ." Melissa began, swallowing hard. They were now standing in front of the two pale and unconscious people. "How do you think they would die the quickest? And the least painful?" Apparently, she had initiated her skill; her voice had become monotone and her gaze empty.

"I'm not quite sure myself," Andrew admitted, crouching next to the near comatose individuals and touching their heads. His skill would be stronger like this. "Do you know where the heart is?"

She thought for a moment, then nodded. "More or less, yes. Let's get to it."

She crouched down without hesitation. Andrew hurriedly used his own skill to calm himself and the unfortunate man in front of them, while Melissa rammed a rock into his chest.

He immediately woke up and started coughing blood. He looked shocked and delirious, trying desperately to pull the stone out of his chest. It was no use. He was too weak.

Andrew looked away until the man stopped struggling. He coughed out one last mouthful of blood, and then he died. The whole process took what felt like an eternity. It was horrible for Andrew, even with his calming skill. But they had to keep moving forward.

Melissa's gaze trembled as she pulled out the stone with a sickening sound. Her skill seemed to be reaching its limits as well.

"Quickly," she said, and they moved on to the next man. This time, her aim seemed to have improved, as the man only whimpered and died soon after.

When Andrew and Melissa were finished, they backed away and ran toward the river. Melissa had discarded the stone right away. She was sobbing, making it evident that her skill had completely lost its effect. Andrew was also deeply disturbed by what they had done, but his passive skill didn't allow him to despair like Melissa. His skill often worried him, but in this situation, he was relieved to have it.

After a while, they stopped running. Melissa silently cried for a while, her shoulders shaking heavily. Andrew stood next to her, holding one of her hands. There was nothing that could make this situation better.

Andrew wanted to let her grieve some more, but he knew they were on a schedule. "I'm sorry, Melissa, but we have to leave now. The others are waiting for us."

Melissa nodded and took some deep breaths. "Alright," she said in a raspy voice, and they began walking again.

It didn't take long before they heard the sound of the raging river. The rest of their group stood there, shuddering in the heavy rain and cold wind.

They had already managed to tie the ropes together, and one end was already attached to a big tree trunk on their side of the river.

Andrew pressed Melissa's hand consolingly and approached Alex.

"Are you ready?" he asked the gruff man, who had the other end of the rope tied around his waist. Karen held his hand, looking at him worriedly.

Alex nodded, took a long look at Karen, and took a leap into the river without saying anything else.

Andrew watched him. Alex looked so infinitely small and weak compared with the power of nature.

Alex was immediately washed away in the direction the river was flowing, but he kept swimming, and the rope kept him from being washed away completely.

It took an agonizing amount of time. And sometimes he was pressed underwater by the heavy currents, but he actually managed to do it. He crawled out of the river, breathing heavily for a while and coughing up water.

Andrew was beginning to worry. When Alex stood up and began making his way to the tree closest to the river, he seemed to be limping. Andrew had no way of seeing what was wrong with him from this far away.

Alex fastened the rope to the tree and let himself sink against it, not moving apart from his breathing.

"Alright," Andrew said with a steady voice, "I'll go first."

Everyone looked at him thankfully, apart from Dennis. He eyed Andrew with a fearful but determined expression. Before Dennis could say anything, Andrew ran to the river and began pulling himself through it while holding onto the rope.

"You idiot!" Andrew shouted, but he didn't dare make a move when he noticed Dennis. They had all agreed to allow only one person to go over the river at a time, so they wouldn't overburden the rope.

Even though Andrew had something to hold onto, it was pretty exhausting. Dennis was coughing and struggling behind him. Suddenly, one of Andrew's hands lost its grip., and he could barely hold onto the rope with his other hand.

With a roar, he pulled himself to the rope again, gripping it tightly with both hands. The river hit him so hard that he nearly let go again. It was insanely exhausting, but luckily he now had a good grip on the rope. Clenching his teeth, Andrew pulled himself forward. The water that was nearly ripping him away was so cold that he began to lose all feeling in his body, and his chest was tightening. Every second was complete hell. Right when he thought he couldn't hold on much longer, he felt stones beneath his feet. With the last bit of his strength, Andrew pulled himself out of the river and plopped down to the ground. But he couldn't rest now.

He forced himself to stand up immediately, waving to the crowd on the other side to encourage them. He shot a glance at Dennis, who just smiled at him and kept inching closer. Andrew nodded thankfully and turned his attention back to the crowd on the other side.

One by one, the rest of the group crossed the river. Andrew started to think that they could all manage it. But not everyone was so lucky. Ten people were swept away. They couldn't even scream; the river immediately pushed them under water. Every time this happened, the rest of the people on the other side of the river clenched their teeth and looked down with pained expressions. But it couldn't be helped.

Against Andrew's expectations, the rope held true until the end. Sadly, they couldn't retrieve it right now, but that was the least of their concerns.

Alex seemed to be in better condition again, but he had a ghastly cut on his left leg. "I have no idea what happened," he said, noticing Andrew wanted to ask. "Let's not waste any time. We have to get to the caves. It shouldn't be far."

The tired and silent group began walking behind the limping Alex, who was helped by Karen. Luckily, they didn't need to walk for long before they came out of the woods and saw the caves.

Everyone was cheering and running toward the caves, out of the forsaken rain. Andrew was happy and relieved. He helped the last stragglers to the caves.

It was amazing to have a roof over one's head and not constantly feel the water dripping on it. Even though some of them died, the people who survived were relieved to finally reach their destination. They had survived and now had a dry and safe place to sleep.

As the people started to hug each other, laughing and crying, Andrew went to Melissa. She sat right at the entrance of the cave, holding her knees up to her chest. He took a seat next to her and put his right arm around her.

"We survived," he said to her, squeezing her shoulder tightly.

She nodded and gave him a slight smile, tears in her eyes. "Yeah, we did."

CHAPTER TWELVE

The Path to Walk

<Congratulations on reaching Level 10. You have unlocked the path to greatness and, with it, the Class system. Become the mightiest and stand tall above everyone else. And you will be granted one wish, with which you may have anything and everything you ever wanted.>

Sarah looked curiously at the prompt, not quite sure what to expect. The part about the wish sounded amazing, but it was kind of hard to believe. A wish that would grant anything? Something like this just didn't exist. But what she could believe was the part about Class. She had long wondered what this Class part in her status screen meant. But the system had remained silent about it until now.

<Analyzing Sarah Anna Fischer. Your Race, Specializations, Skills, and Personality will be taken into consideration.>

"Shit." Sarah grabbed her head and groaned. The system already evaluated her as "Slightly Crazy." Not only that, but her race was now "Mutant." And even though the system helped her survive in the swamp, it had a horrible and sadistic sense of humor.

"Please be something . . . normal?" she begged the system, not really believing that it would matter. But she had to try.

<Analysis complete. Listing available paths and options:
Paths of Conflict Available:
Witch
Swamp Stalker
Abomination
Nightmare
Lunatic
Please choose carefully.>

Sarah sat down and held her head in her hands. "These are all insults, you know?" she said to the ever-silent system. She should have known better. "But seriously? Abomination?"

She took a deep breath, took her hands off her face, and looked at the Classes again with empty eyes. She had no idea what to go with. But at least there were also some descriptions of the classes.

<Listing available paths and options (detailed):
Path of Conflict:
Witch: Focus on Magic Power and Invasion specializations.
Swamp Stalker: Focus on Mutation and Poison Body specializations.
Abomination: Focus on Life Force and Body affinity.
Nightmare: Focus on Life Force, Invasion, and Mutation specializations.
Lunatic: Focus on inborn skill Slightly Crazy and Invasion specialization.
Please choose carefully.>

Even though there were some descriptions, they seemed cryptic to her. What was this *focus* exactly? Would it make just these stats and specializations stronger? Would it change them? She had no way of knowing.

She had to guess that Nightmare was her best option. It focused on three different things instead of two like the other classes. And it also focused on two specializations with different affinities.

She was suspicious of the system placing something so good in front of her nose. It was a little scary, to be honest. What if something painful happened to her, or her body deformed even further?

"Oh well, not that I have a choice. I guess it shouldn't be too bad," she said to encourage herself, not believing her own words. "I choose Nightmare. But please don't hurt me," she politely said to the system, which immediately sprang into action.

<You have chosen the Path of Conflict with the class Nightmare. Your body will now undergo a mutation to accommodate the characteristics of the class. Good luck surviving.>

Sarah screamed in anger and frustration. She wanted so badly to swear at the system, but then the mutations hit her.

Her whole body mutated this time. It felt like she was melting and splitting apart at the same time. But she lay still on the ground, trapped in a body that wouldn't listen to her anymore.

Sadly, she didn't pass out because of something like this anymore. She tried really hard, but it just didn't work.

After some time, the agony subsided. She began to suck in air, noticing only now that her body hadn't been breathing through the entire process.

Gasping for air, she looked to the sky and spoke to the invisible system again. "I just hate you."

She started stretching and tried to roll over onto her back so she could rest, but she felt a strange resistance in her head. She instinctively reached for her head and felt something hard stuck to it. She sprang up and tried to pull it off, but she only managed to hurt her neck by pulling so hard.

"What the . . ." she murmured as she gingerly inspected her head with her hands. There were two curved things coming out of the top of her head, just above her forehead. They were solid and had some kind of wavy pattern. They felt like horns.

Sarah pressed her lips together and muffled a frustrated groan that threatened to escape her throat. The tail wasn't enough? Now the system had given her horns. She already felt like an animal, acted like one, and she now looked like one. Great.

"Just please don't give me fur," she begged the system, feeling too exhausted from her transition to get angry again.

"Well, at least it will help me." She opened the status screen to look at the updates.

Details:
Level: 10
Name: Sarah Anna Fischer
Class: Nightmare
Race: Mutant
Status: Normal
HP: 145/145 **SP**: 40/115 **MP**: 20/150

Achievements:
- How the hell are you still sane?
- Poison Gorger
- More Than Human

Affinities:
Mind (Mid) Body (Mid) Energy (Low)

Specializations:
- Mind (2/2)
  - Invasion
  - Nerve Control
- Body (2/2)
  - Adaptation
  - Mutation
- Energy (0/1)

Basic Stats:
Strength: 12
Dexterity: 12
Endurance: 12
Resistance: 10
Intelligence: 21
Force: 10

Special Stats:
Magic Power: 10
Life Force: 20
Mental Power: 5

Active Skills:
- Mind Infiltration (Invasion): While using Magic Power, you are able to invade the mind of another being. Invasion is facilitated if the being has been poisoned by you.

Passive Skills:
- Poison Body (Adaptation):
- Poison and Acid Resistance: You are highly resistant to various poisons and acids. (Overcoming new or stronger poisons or acids strengthens this ability.)
- Walking Hazard: Your body liquids are highly toxic and acidic. You are now naturally producing a strong nerve toxin and acid inside your body. (Consuming new or stronger poisons and acids strengthens this ability.)
- Mutated Glands: Toxin and acid glands are incorporated in certain mutations.
- Metamorphosis (Mutation): You are able to mutate your body. The number of mutations is dependent on your Life Force. Due to your "Adaption" specialization, there will be less Life Force needed, and you will have fewer limitations. Your class, "Nightmare," will influence your mutations.
  - Skin:
    - Dense skin (1 LF)
  - Bone Structure: None
  - Muscles:
    - Strengthened Fibers (1 LF): Strengthened muscle fibers. Slightly tougher and stronger.
  - Brain, Nerve System, and Sensory Organs:
    - Predator Eyes (1 LF)

- o Organs and Processes:
  - ■ Magic Power Nourishment: Able to feed on the Magic Power of other beings.
- o Special Mutations:
  - ■ Nightmare's Tail (class specific, 5 LF): A long and flexible tail with an exoskeleton made out of spine-like bone segments. Can be stretched over its original length, but will leave the vulnerable muscle and sinew under the exoskeleton exposed. Poison gland incorporated into the tip.
  - ■ Nightmare's Horns (class specific, 5 LF): Two large and curved horns are located on top of the forehead. Directly connected to your brain through nerve strings. Amplify mind related skills and enable them to work without direct contact. Warning: strong pain and disorientation if broken.
- • Suppression (Nerve Control)
- • Struggle (Conditional Passive)
- • Slightly Crazy
- • Mean Eye

She gawked at the updated status screen. Her basic and special stats had increased by so much. Some of the skill descriptions had also changed slightly, but it wasn't anything dramatic. What really interested her were her two new Nightmare mutations. A poisonous tail and invading minds without even the need to touch someone?

"Yeah, I kind of get why the class is named Nightmare," she told the system, while stretching her body. It felt like she had been born again.

The strength, magic power, and pure vitality she felt flowing through her body were intoxicating. She was relishing the feeling and didn't really know what she should do with the overflowing energy.

She wanted to analyze her situation better, but she felt like she would burst at any moment if she didn't start doing something. So, she started running through the swamp.

She was more than twice as fast as she was before she leveled up. With a joyful scream, she jumped high into the air, grasping a low-hanging tree branch. After dangling there for a second, she started swinging herself along it.

Like this, she jumped from tree to tree, madly laughing all the while. After some time, she grabbed a branch that felt strangely soft.

Confused, she looked at the branch, and it looked back at her, just as confused. It was a snake. A big and chunky snake.

Still processing what she was holding in her hand, she slammed directly into a thick tree trunk. The heavy impact squashed the unlucky snake.

Sarah tumbled to the ground and landed hard. Her whole body hurt, and she felt like all the air had been pressed out of her. But she still had to laugh. This was just too amazing.

After some time, her body hurt a little less, and she could breathe normally again. She took a bite of the snake as a new idea popped into her head.

She was much stronger now. So something like the mutated rat wouldn't be able to hurt her anymore. It was more the opposite, actually. With her new powers, pretty much everything she encountered thus far was nothing more than prey.

This meant that she could now explore the danger zone, where the bigger animals lived. She hoped that the exit could be found in this direction. If not, she had to start looking deeper into the swamp, which meant she had to wade through murky water with unknown creatures lurking beneath its surface. Just thinking about this made her shudder.

Would she find other people outside of the spatial error? Would she not be alone anymore? With a sinking feeling, she looked down at herself. She was insanely dirty and still naked. Her whole body was smeared in dirt, blood, and unidentifiable goo. Not to mention her messy hair and her visible mutations.

"I guess it would be a good idea to dress myself somehow," she murmured, trying to think about how she could make clothes.

While munching on the snake, the realization struck her. She could just skin everything she found, somehow connect it all together, and then she'd have wonderful clothing. Preferably something that could cover her tail. And her horns. And her whole body. She had a lot of work to do.

She could do two things at once—find materials for her clothes and try out her new abilities. And of course, first came her horns. They were deformations, but at least they gave her a new ability.

Feeling pretty good about her new idea, she stood up, still chewing on the snake, and began testing her horns.

In the beginning, nothing much happened. After some time, though, she started to notice numerous beings around her. They were well hidden by their camouflage techniques.

"So uh," she mumbled, unsure of what to do next, "stop living, I guess?" As soon as she sent the telepathic signal out from her horns, all the beings around her fell to the ground, motionless.

Sarah didn't fare so well, though. An intense vertigo terrorized her head. She tried to sit on the ground but instead fell down, directly on her face. Her consciousness left her before she could think of anything else.

CHAPTER THIRTEEN

The Hunt

Sarah was silently running through the swamp to her destination. For days now, she had analyzed the bear-looking thing that she would hunt today. It often came near the swampy area where she lived. That's how she first noticed it.

When she first saw the creature, she ran away. It was a hulking monstrosity, nearly twice her size. It had stumpy legs and an absurdly big head. It wasn't very good at coordination; it mostly stumbled around and hit its head here and there.

But the thing ate trees. When it found one that tasted good, it just started chomping down. With each bite, big parts of the tree just vanished with a loud crushing sound. She really didn't want to end up like those trees.

But she had to try. She wanted the hide for a cloak, which could cover her entire body. By now, she had managed to at least make some kind of full-body suit from many different snake skins. It was ugly, but at least she wasn't naked anymore.

The downside was that she couldn't undress anymore; the suit was strapped to her body. The trick was to bind the skins together when they were still freshly skinned. Then they would shrink and make the knots even tighter.

She had also learned how to manage her magic power consumption after passing out a few more times. And now she could tell when she was running low.

She started following the pretty obvious trail of the tree-eating bear thing. At the same time, she was going through her plan in her head again, and reviewing what she had learned about her abilities.

It wasn't long before she found it. The creature was happily munching on a tree, stumbling around it in an excited manner. It looked kind of cute, in a very awkward way. But now wasn't the time for these sentiments. It was time to hit and run.

Sarah crept closer until she was a short distance from the thing. It halted its feast, looked up in the air, and began sniffing. It suddenly turned its head in Sarah's direction, looking alarmed and angry.

Sarah didn't wait. She immediately attacked the thing's mind. It winced, and its legs began to spasm uncontrollably, making it fall down.

The magic power consumption was no joke. Sarah reeled for a moment, seeing double, but she pushed through it and sprang forward.

Her tail shot from behind her and stung the thing in the neck. As it was still immobilized, Sarah stung it again and again. What she didn't notice was that it started to gain some control over its legs again.

It cried out and snapped at Sarah. The movement was surprisingly quick, taking Sarah by surprise. She jumped out of the way, but it still managed to rip a nasty gash in her gut.

Sarah jumped into a high tree, wheezing in pain. She checked on her wound and was relieved that her guts weren't hanging out or something. It certainly felt like they were at first. Luckily, it was just a flesh wound, though it was bleeding quite heavily.

She pressed her hands to the wound, holding back the urge to scream out in pain, and kept her eyes on the creature.

It was roaring, but it started to back away, stumbling even more now and fleeing from her. But that wouldn't do the thing any good. She pumped enough poison into it to turn its brain and nerves into complete mush. At least in theory.

Sarah gritted her teeth, took some of the snake skin, and bandaged her wound. It was disgustingly painful, but it managed to hold back the bleeding a little.

Even though it wasn't very fast, Sarah had a hard time following the bear-looking thing. She could only breathe very shallowly, afraid of ripping open the wound even more. It was also very hard to move in her hunched-up position, all the while pressing on the wound with her hands. But she pushed through.

After a while, they were in a hilly area, deep inside the drier part of the spatial error. The thing slowed down more and more, the poison probably starting to do its nasty work.

The thing walked toward a heavily overgrown hill and crawled under a bush. And then it vanished.

Anxious about losing her prey, Sarah came closer and took a good look at the bush. But it was so dense she couldn't see anything. She gingerly pulled some twigs to the side and managed to see some sort of cave behind them. But the thing was nowhere in sight.

She pushed her head a little further inside the bush to see better. It felt like her heart would jump out of her chest.

Trying to make as little sound as possible, she pushed her body inside the bush to be able to see more of the cave. The twigs poked at her wound, causing her to whimper slightly every time.

When she was far enough through, she could finally see the entire cave. It seemed to slightly curve after some distance. And there it was. Half of its body seemed to be hidden behind the curve, only making its lower body visible. It twitched slightly but didn't move other than that.

Sarah pushed herself through the cave entrance entirely, which caused a twig to rip at her wound harshly. Her injury began bleeding more. She couldn't hold back a small scream this time. It burned like hell, and she was dizzy from blood loss.

Afraid of alarming the thing, she bit down on her hand to muffle the sounds she made. Luckily, the thing still didn't move.

She walked inside the cave, her tail at the ready to strike at the smallest movement. But there was no need for that. When Sarah could see the head of the thing, it was clear that it was close to death.

Blood trickled from its uneven eyes, and they were looking in two different directions. It was clear that it had lost the ability to control them. It was barely breathing anymore, and still, it only twitched. Sarah had never killed something in this horrible a manner before. It was disturbing.

With a peculiar feeling inside her, she gently touched its head and slowly shut down its body functions. It was pretty easy now, and she barely used any of her magic power—the thing was filled to the brim with her poison. It wasn't long before the creature stopped moving altogether.

Sarah sighed a breath of relief and knelt down to inspect it further. At this moment, she saw some movement. Startled by the surprise, she stumbled and fell on her back, causing another painful sting in her stomach.

She hurriedly looked back at the thing. But the cause of the movement was something else.

Two horribly deformed beings crawled out from under the dead thing. They began moaning in bizarre voices while patting the dead body with their uneven legs.

The creature had children. But they looked so deformed that Sarah doubted that they would survive. The proportions of their bodies were just so out of sync that it was difficult for them to move.

A scary thought paralyzed her for a moment. They were obviously mutated. And she was too. What if one of her mutations went wrong and she ended up looking like them? Just crawling around in the dirt, barely able to do anything more than wriggle her body. The thought was incredibly disturbing.

With a grimace, Sarah went to the little cubs. She gently placed her hands on them while calming their minds. They stopped moving and fell to the ground. With a hard look on her face, Sarah shut down their body functions. It wasn't hard. In fact, it was even easier to kill them than it was to kill a small lizard. Apparently, their deformations hadn't just impacted their bodies.

Sarah felt a bitter taste in her mouth while she dragged the deformed little bodies deeper inside the cave, so she didn't have to look at them again. They were a reminder to her that her mutation specialization could go horribly wrong. But she didn't have much choice but to push forward in order to survive in this place.

When she had dragged them a sufficient distance away, she returned. Then she lay down right at the entrance of the cave. As the tension faded away, the wound began throbbing wildly, and she felt sick.

The only thing she could do now was wait for the wound to get better. It wasn't bad enough for her to mutate herself, and she wanted to save this ability for emergencies. So she lay on the ground, waiting for the bleeding to stop.

After a while, she fell into a light slumber, having odd, abstract dreams about her recent fight. The two deformed cubs popped up again and again. At some point, she noticed that she *was* one of the cubs, trapped in a horribly deformed body.

This caused her to jump, and now she was awake, feeling a little feverish and weak. After she shook off the dream, she checked her wound.

It had closed up, even though it seemed inflamed. She was amazed that this was even possible with her highly toxic blood. Maybe there were also some mutated bacteria or something. She certainly hoped not.

She dragged herself to the creature's body, which was a little bloated already. She must have slept longer than she thought. She took out a sharpened rock and started to cut off its skin.

It took quite some time, with the rock breaking in half when she was halfway done. But she managed to complete her task. Sarah stumbled out of the bush, holding the bloody fur over one arm and gagging. The smell inside the cave was horrible. She was used to the smell of rotting flesh by now, but it was another thing entirely when something that huge began to rot inside an enclosed space.

"All of this, just to hide my appearance," she said with a sigh, while holding the bloody fur in front of her. She couldn't help but doubt that it had been worth it. But it was done, and she could only move forward.

Leaving the cave behind with the mutated bear-like creatures, she slowly made her way back to the clearing.

The clearing felt like home. It was the place where she collected everything that could be useful. Skins, bones, claws, stones, and other things that could be used to make things. She wasn't quite sure why she was doing it; she had no idea what she would even do with most of this stuff. But it gave her something to do, so she just did it.

After stumbling toward her clearing for a long time, she finally slumped to the ground with a relaxed sigh, starting to feel a bit better about her day. It might have been a nasty experience, but she had managed to do it. She survived and got stronger through it. That was all that mattered.

Her mindset was somewhat restored again, and she started to fashion something like a cloak out of the fur.

The result was pretty crappy, but she was able to tie the cloak around her upper body to hold it in place, and it hid her horns quite well.

"Alright," she said contently. She was finally strong enough to protect herself, and she had something to hide her deformations. Her wound seemed mostly healed by now, only stinging now and then when she made sudden movements.

She took a deep breath and fixed the still-wet cloak around her, hiding her mutations.

"Time to go meet some people."

CHAPTER FOURTEEN

Inspection

"This is it," Andrew said in an excited voice. "I found some."

Dennis came hurrying over and looked down at the ground next to Andrew. But his excited face melted away in seconds.

"They are poisonous mushrooms, you idiot. When will you learn to differentiate them?"

Andrew felt a little embarrassed about his repeated mistakes. He tried to gloss over it with a question. "So anyway, do we have enough for dinner?"

Dennis smiled wryly, knowing Andrew was trying to change the topic. "We should have enough, yeah. I even found some of the tasty herbs you like so much."

Andrew's face lit up with excitement. The mushrooms were good on their own, but the herbs Dennis mentioned made them even better. By far the best thing he'd had since they arrived at the caves.

Andrew felt pretty satisfied with their haul, purposely ignoring the fact that he hadn't contributed anything. He patted Dennis on the shoulder and started to walk back to the caves. Dennis shook his head in amusement and followed him back.

Back at the caves, they gave their haul to the cooking team, who were also pretty excited. After a lot of jokes and handshakes, Andrew and Dennis managed to sneak away into the leader's cave. Andrew hated the name, but others had coined the term.

They made their way deeper into the cave until the group they were meeting with came into view. Andrew couldn't help but glance at Melissa. She was a very beautiful woman with blond hair and a curvaceous body. It was a miracle to him that she retained her curves, even though everyone was a little too thin. There just wasn't enough food.

Melissa noticed his gaze and looked back at him with furrowed brows. Andrew quickly pulled his gaze away. It was annoying that this was the second embarrassing situation he'd been in today.

Andrew sat down on the ground and looked at each member of the small group in the eyes, and nodded. He held eye contact with the still frowning Melissa for as short a time as possible.

He finally turned to Alex and started speaking.

"You wanted to have this meeting. What do you have to tell us?" he asked the gruff man.

Alex swallowed and looked a bit nervous. He always felt uncomfortable when talking to more than two people. "It's getting colder," he said while looking down at his hands. "The leaves are starting to get a little bit brown. The animals seem to be hoarding food. Some of the birds travel downward along the river, which is most likely south."

Most of them had noticed the leaves turning brown at the edges of the forest. And it was also pretty clear that the nights were getting colder. But they didn't think much about it.

Alex continued speaking. "I wasn't quite sure what was happening, so I talked to Tobias about it." With this, he stopped speaking and looked at Tobias expectantly.

Tobias nodded and looked at Andrew with wide and sparkling eyes. Andrew didn't like Tobias very much. While he was a genius and found more and more ways for them to have a better life, he was also kind of creepy. Everything was fascinating for him, even if someone had a horrible wound or got poisoned. He lacked something . . . human.

"The changes in the flora and fauna show a big environmental change," he explained in his erratic voice. "The only thing that changes is the weather. It gets colder at night. So I talked with a few people in the caves, and one was able to remember something very interesting. Winter."

When he said the last word, the whole group grimaced for a moment. They all started to remember what winter meant.

Andrew gritted his teeth in frustration. They had just started to get the hang of their situation. They had enough food, clothing, and even a roof over their heads. People were beginning to accept their situation. And some sort of normality was starting to take root, which gave the people a sense of security. And now they had to deal with this.

"Melissa," Andrew said, not wanting to continue talking to Tobias. "What is the emotional state of the people in the caves?"

Melissa had learned a new skill after the river crossing. She was somehow able to heal emotional wounds and help people get over trauma. She herself didn't know how it worked, but it made her one of the most valuable members of the cave.

Melissa combed her fingers through her hair nervously while biting her lip. "It's okay, I guess. I mean, it is much better than when I first got my new skill."

She took a long pause while thinking about their predicament. "They can take it. But you need to tell them, Andrew. You will be able to think about it in a rational and positive way."

Andrew nodded. He turned his head to tell Dennis to gather the people, but he suddenly wasn't able to speak anymore.

Andrew began to panic when his body stood up on its own and started to walk out of the cave. Judging from the various footsteps he heard, the others were also moving against their will.

Andrew tried his hardest to somehow gain back control over his body, but it was to no avail. It was like someone else had stolen his body, and he was just a passenger now.

While Andrew was still trying his best to somehow get out of this situation, they came out of the cave. What Andrew saw made him forget his efforts for a moment.

Everyone gathered in the rocky clearing that surrounded their caves. They stood in parallel rows and were motionless. Andrew and the other leaders were the last ones to arrive.

"Is everyone here?" said a voice from the front of the group, sounding bored.

"Perfect," the person said, this time with forced cheerfulness. "Thank you for gathering here on such short notice. My name is Detlef, and I will conduct today's inspection. Does anyone have any questions?"

Of course, no one answered him. No one was able to even open their mouths.

"Perfect," Detlef said again. This time, the voice came from Andrew's left. "Alright, what do we have here?" He started mumbling to himself. From what Andrew could gather, Detlef was walking between the rows of people.

"Group of sixty-nine people. Very good survival rate. A few promising individuals. Adaption to magic power in its early stage. Only a few people have close to no chance of completing the adaptation. And . . ."

Detlef entered Andrew's field of vision. He was a tall and very thin man. He wore white clothes made with incredible sophistication. Right now, they could only dream of making clothes like this. Something was very odd about the man. Andrew wasn't sure what it was until he compared him to the ragged group of people. He was completely clean. His dark hair flowed over his shoulders, even shining in the light of the descending sun. Not a speck of dirt stained his clothing. The man looked completely alien in their midst.

When he walked by Karen, he abruptly stood still and looked at her in surprise. "A pregnant woman. How extraordinary. Kai will be very pleased indeed."

The man scribbled something on a plate he held in his hands. While doing so, he analyzed Karen from head to toe, even lifting her hair and clothes up to get a better look at her body.

"This is unprecedented," he exclaimed, almost breathless. He was smiling and shaking his head in disbelief. After he finished checking Karen, he returned to the front of the rows of people and was out of Andrew's view again.

"I want to thank you very much for participating in this inspection. I also want to congratulate you all for your high survival rate and, most of all, for having the first pregnant woman since the integration! This is an amazing achievement. I want to thank you in the name of the Creator and everyone who follows him."

He paused before speaking again. "Alright then. I wish you the best of luck in your endeavors. Hail the Creator, and until next time."

With these words, Andrew gained control of his body again. Then he stumbled to the ground like everyone else. A few screams erupted from the crowd, but Andrew had another priority. Karen. As his knees hit the ground, he saw a flash of light where he had last seen her. That couldn't be good.

He somehow got back to his feet and stumbled toward the spot where he last saw Karen. But he couldn't find her. She was gone.

A breathless Alex came stumbling over. His stoic face was distorted in agony and fear. He wanted to say something, but no words came out of his mouth.

Andrew looked at him and shook his head. He wanted to somehow console Alex, but he stepped away. Alex nodded and bit his lip so hard that it started to bleed. He turned around and started walking toward Melissa. She was already helping the most anxious people.

Andrew also started to use his skill to calm down the people around him, and he managed to ease the unrest, even if just a little. He often glanced at Alex, who was helping Melissa carry the unconscious people back to the caves. Andrew was amazed by how mentally strong Alex was. But then again, maybe he did something so he wouldn't lose his mind.

Andrew couldn't do anything for him at the moment, unfortunately. He was desperately needed here. Dennis would be able to get Alex to talk. He somehow got even the most closed-up people to open up to him.

"What happened just now?" asked Dennis in a tense voice. Andrew turned around and saw him standing behind him, barely able to stay on his feet.

Andrew took him by the shoulders and forced him to sit down. He mulled over the question but only found one solution.

"I guess we now know who put us here," he said silently, looking around to see if anyone had overheard them, "and it seems that we are their guinea pigs."

CHAPTER FIFTEEN

The Border

Sarah had been running through the forest for a while. She had been afraid of the dryer parts of the swamp for nothing. Though she heard and saw a lot of big animals, not one had attacked her so far.

Most of them ran away immediately upon seeing or smelling her. The animals that looked like predators glared at her with fierce eyes but did nothing else.

If she had to make an educated guess, she'd say that she smelled horrible. The animal skins she draped herself with smelled gruesome. The stench of death was her constant companion. And apparently, it was an effective repellent.

She didn't want to attack other animals right now. She was on her way to find the exit. She really wanted to get out of this place.

So she ran. Around ten days had passed since she started looking for an exit. She wasn't even sure if she was walking in the right direction. In the beginning, she attempted to direct herself according to the sun, but that didn't work out at all. She never noticed until now, but the sun seemed to move across the sky in erratic curves.

"This cursed spatial error," she mumbled under her breath, staring up at the sun.

Even though the end wasn't in sight yet, she enjoyed her travels. The cool wind brushing against her skin, the leaves rustling, and the earthy smell of the forest. These impressions seemed to ease a tension inside her that she hadn't even noticed until now. Running made her feel like she was making some real progress, instead of lurking around in the same region day after day.

When Sarah was preparing to stop for the day, she saw something in the distance. She wasn't quite sure what it was, but it reminded her of something. She just couldn't put her finger on it.

Excitement washed away all tiredness, and she ran faster than ever. The closer she came, the more she knew what it was she saw. It was nothingness. The same nothingness she had seen when the system pulled her consciousness from her body to see the recording of Dr. Becker.

She slowed down as she came closer to the border of nothingness. It hurt her eyes, trying to look at the exact border of forest and nothingness. Her eyes simply had nothing to focus on.

The plants, the ground, and everything else seemed to have less substance closer to the border. And everything looked like it was in the process of disintegrating.

When she stepped closer, something primal in her screamed in fear. She had a gut feeling that it would be very dangerous to go any closer than this.

For some time, she walked next to the border. What did it mean? Could this be the exit, even though her instincts told her it would be dangerous to get any closer? Should she try anyway?

She knelt down to pick up a stone, when something hard and heavy hit her in the back.

She heard loud cracks while she was pressed into the dirt. Sarah wanted to scream, but mud in her mouth made her gag instead. The pain was so intense that she nearly blacked out. She wouldn't let that happen.

Like the rat thing that had attacked her in the past, she wildly stabbed behind her with her tail. As a thank-you gift to her assailant, she pumped the maximum amount of poison into the tip.

She felt her tail hitting something. A loud yelp told her that she'd hurt whatever was attacking her. The weight on her back disappeared, and she immediately rolled to the side and stood up. The movement caused her immense pain, but she somehow suppressed it.

What she saw made her want to run away then and there. A huge black wolf stood in front of her, staring with hate-filled eyes. The wolf was so big that it was still taller than her while standing on its four legs. Massive muscles could be seen rippling beneath its fur. The wolf was also twitching in pain and rage.

It was a monstrosity. But she somehow knew why it had attacked her. The beast also followed the Path of Conflict, just like herself. She always wondered what this part meant. Now she knew. The Path of Conflict was more than a categorization of her class. It was a path the system wanted her to walk. And the system wanted them to fight.

The wolf frothed yellow-colored saliva, clearly affected by the poison. But it still seemed full of energy.

Sarah started to walk backward but stumbled over something. The wolf immediately attacked her again.

It slammed into her with so much force that her rib cage caved in, and she was thrown back a few meters.

She could barely breathe. While nearly losing consciousness again, a crazy idea entered her mind. She suppressed the pain as best as she could and took a bubbling breath, before coughing out dark blood. That was not good. She had to hurry.

The wolf backed away again, afraid of her poisonous tail, and waited for its chance again.

Sarah stood up and stumbled to the side, not letting the wolf out of her sight. The wolf twitched and growled in rage, eager to finish her off.

When she was in position, she acted like she had tripped over something again. As expected, the wolf immediately reacted. It jumped at her with insane speed.

Forcing her body to move, Sarah jumped out of the way. The wolf sailed through the air, a hair above her. It leapt right into the border region of nothingness.

Sarah fell to the ground and looked at what had happened to the wolf. It was fascinating. The wolf seemed to rapidly lose substance, while trying its best to leave the border with its disintegrating legs. The wolf even managed to pull it off. But, as it left the border region, its body began gushing out blood like a river.

Even with these horrible wounds, the wolf was still alive. With an evil grin, Sarah walked to the wolf. The beast saw the intention in her eyes and wanted to crawl away. But it was to late.

Even though Sarah was badly hurt, the wolf was worse off. The slow chase would have been comical if not for both participants' gruesome wounds.

When Sarah reached the wolf, she grabbed its enormous head and started punching. With her mutated muscles and increased strength, her punches were no joke. Every time she hit, the wolf's head caved in more and more. She only let go when it stopped twitching.

With a groan, Sarah let herself fall to the ground next to the mutilated beast. She coughed again, and this time there was even more blood. Something was seriously wrong with her insides.

Before she could even think of it, the system reacted on its own.

<Warning. Massive damage to vital organs. Massive damage to the spine and rib cage. Please choose from the following options:
- Acquire Mutations High Density Bones and Magic Power Nourishment System (89% survival rate)
- Acquire Mutation Body Alteration: Four-Legged (91% survival rate)
- Take a bite from the wolf (survival rate unclear)
- Walk into the nothingness (0% survival rate)

Please choose quickly.>

Sarah would have sworn at the system for once again giving her absurd options, but she wasn't able to talk anymore. At least she was still able to choose an option.

<Initializing Mutations High Density Bones and Magic Power Nutrition System.>

The timer in her mind seemed to go down way too slowly, as Sarah literally felt her life flowing out of her.

When the pain from the mutations hit her, she was strangely relieved. Even though it hurt, it didn't hurt as much as her wounds. And the pain meant that she would survive.

A fire burned in her soul the moment she realized this. She had survived against all odds and would once again emerge stronger than before. Wild excitement filled her, making her forget the pain.

This excitement carried her through the mutation until it stopped. It was over. She had survived. It felt like the chaotic emotions inside her would burst out if she didn't do something immediately. So she screamed. It was a scream filled with an insane mixture of excitement, terror, and fear.

Small tears ran down her cheeks, which burned away the caked-in dirt, blood, and goo on her face with their high acidity.

She screamed until her throat hurt, and until she couldn't let out much more than a hoarse sob.

After this, she lay on the ground for quite some time. She felt empty but also relieved. She was finally able to breathe and think again.

So she stood up while cleaning the snot off her face. Maybe it would cheer her up if she looked at the status screen. All this pain should have brought her some nice improvements.

She had leveled up a whopping four levels, bringing her straight to level fourteen. She hadn't leveled up since reaching level ten, so this was very welcome. She also had the usual increase in magic power, life force, and mental power. Even her endurance increased by a whole two points. And there were also new mutations listed on her skill screen.

Bone Structure:

High Density Bones (2 LF): Robust and dense bones. Higher stamina consumption due to increased weight.

Organs and Processes:

Magic Power Nourishment System: Your body is adapted to run only on Magic Power. You are able to sense Magic Power in other living organisms and feed on it. Most substances that enter your digestive system and lungs will be converted into Magic Power. Warning: High potential for cell breakdown if your Magic Power is empty for too long.

The former Magic Power Nourishment had merged with her new mutation. This didn't bother her because she never found out what she should do with it.

But now it would be different; her senses would be focused on feeling magic power and all. It was also great that most things that she consumed or breathed in would be converted into magic power.

She tried really hard to ignore the part about cell breakdown. She just made a mental note to never, ever use up all her magic power. Luckily, her only skill that could use up enough magic power was her invasion skill. But she had it under control.

"Who cares!" she shouted while forcing herself to laugh. "I become more and more like a cockroach. Did I insult myself?" She shook her head at her own stupidity and went to her next point on the program. Taking a bite from the wolf.

The system had proposed it as a possible solution. Of course, it could also be another of its pointless remarks, but she had to eat anyway. After this ordeal, she was insanely hungry.

So she trotted over to the remains of the wolf and kneeled down next to it. She had never eaten anything this big, so she had no idea where to start. She tried to rip out flesh with her hands, but that didn't work out very well. This left her with one option.

"Thanks for the food, I guess," she mumbled while ripping into the flesh with her teeth. It didn't taste particularly different from the other mammals she had eaten. She had expected it to somehow taste better because it had been so strong. She ate the tough meat of the wolf while thinking about what to do next when another system prompt appeared.

<Genetic information for Special Mutation found. Genetic information incomplete due to an unknown cause. More samples needed.>

"A Special Mutation again, huh?" she muttered after cleaning her bloodied mouth. These mutations definitely made her a lot stronger. But they also deformed her. She was somehow happy that it wasn't enough for the system yet. So that was something for future Sarah to worry about.

"So sorry, future Sarah," she apologized to herself, while standing up and pointlessly dusting herself off. Her body was so dirty by now that she couldn't even tell the color of her own skin anymore.

Standing at the border of nothingness, she had no idea where to go. She was clueless about where the exit could be. Her only guess was that it was somewhere along the border.

Not wanting to waste any more time in this godforsaken place, she turned left. With firm resolution, she began walking a safe distance away from the border.

She just hoped that the exit wouldn't be too deep in the swamp area.

CHAPTER SIXTEEN

Do or Die

Sarah searched every inch of the border in the dryer parts of the spatial error. She even ventured a bit deeper into the swampy area.

But she couldn't find the exit. It was maddening. During this time, she also had to somehow get used to her new digestion system.

A weird side effect of this recent mutation was that she didn't have to poop anymore, which was surprisingly unnerving. It just felt wrong. Since it wasn't very comfortable to defecate in this region, she tried to see it in a positive light.

Sadly, she still couldn't figure out how to feed on the magic power of other beings. Even having her new ability to sense the amount of magic power in the wildlife around her didn't do her any good.

The only good thing was that her magic power regenerated incredibly fast, which was pretty important. Her body now constantly consumed magic power to keep her going.

She stood in the deeper parts of the swamp area. It stank pretty bad, and the ground was mostly knee-deep mud or murky water. She had no way of knowing what lived beneath the surface of the water. The only indicators were small ripples that could be seen from time to time, which was horrifying.

The treetops in this region were so dense that nearly no light found its way down here. Not to mention all the spiders, snakes, and other gross stuff that lived in the trees.

All in all, it was a horrible place. And she had to go through it. At least she had her dense skin and poison resistance. But she wasn't quite sure if she should try to swim through the murky water or climb through the treetops full of spiderwebs.

At least she was able to see what she would encounter in the treetops, making it a less awful choice.

She checked one last time to see if her clothes were safely attached to her body.

"Here goes nothing," she said in a forced, happy voice and jumped up into the closest tree. The ground was so mushy that she didn't jump as high as she thought she would. She landed directly in the murky water.

This surprised her so much that she breathed in a mouthful of water. The pain was horrible, and she seemed to feel the bits and pieces sloshing around in her lungs.

She fought her way out of the swampy water, coughing and gagging all the while. Interestingly though, she didn't have the feeling of suffocating, even though the muddy water was still in her lungs.

While still coughing, she concentrated on what was going on inside her. Her new mutation seemed to be able to convert the water and mud in her lungs into magic power. So even though it hurt like hell, it seemed like she wouldn't be able to drown. At least she hoped as much.

"Ugh, this is so gross," she said while coughing out a little leech, which was already somewhat decomposed from her acidic insides. She shuddered, tried not to think about what else she might have breathed in, and prepared herself to go again.

This time she climbed the tree instead of jumping up. There were so many spider webs that they were constantly getting in her way. They were just everywhere.

She started to climb from tree to tree. It was surprisingly hard for her to navigate herself because her sight was permanently disturbed by the webs. She felt countless little things crawl on top of her, which gave her the constant urge to brush off her body.

But she knew that this wouldn't change anything. Just by climbing onto another tree, she would have a colony of spiders and other things on her again. At least they wouldn't be able to bite through her dense skin.

She progressed horribly slowly, and it was exhausting to deal with the constant irritation. She was very tempted to use her invasion skill to kill everything around her. But she knew that with the immense amount of wildlife around her, this could empty out her magic power. That would be much more dangerous than any kind of little insect.

While climbing, she tried to motivate herself. "Alright, Sarah, you just have to go through with this, and—Oh shit, it's in my mouth!" she cried out in a disgusted voice. She gagged and spit out a spider and its web. So no more talking.

Now silent again, she climbed further and further until night came. It was dark. Really dark. Even with her mutated eyes, she was barely able to see her hands if she held them in front of her face. Luckily, she stopped early enough and cleared out the crown of a tree from webs and snakes. It wouldn't be comfortable here, but the dense canopy would prevent her from falling down while she was asleep.

She tried to sleep, but it was hard with all the buzzing and the cries of unknown animals.

Restless in the unnerving environment, she tried to find a comfortable position—sadly, without much success.

Frustrated by her situation, Sarah looked down from the tree. She was trying to somehow see the nocturnal wildlife around her.

She was staring for a while when she suddenly thought that her eyes must have played tricks on her. There seemed to be a small, turquoise light hovering above the surface of the water. She rubbed her eyes, but the light was still there.

A short moment later, hundreds of these lights began to emerge from the swamp. No, there had to be thousands.

The colors ranged from turquoise to dark blue and gave the whole area a surreal and mysterious glow.

Sarah looked at the scene in awe. It was the most beautiful sight she had ever seen during her time in the swamp.

The lights flew around, seemingly in disarray. But, after watching them for a while, it became apparent that they were flying around in a pattern. They appeared as wind that had become visible, flowing around in gentle streams. It was mesmerizing.

Sarah was so immersed in the spectacle that she didn't notice the sound of something big swimming through the murky water. And it was coming closer to her.

Only when she saw something huge being illuminated by the lights did she notice it.

It was a gigantic lizard, barely able to fit through the gaps between the trees. The lights reflected from its scales, making them shine like crystals.

When it came close to her tree, the lizard stopped moving. Sarah tried to breathe as little as possible, not moving at all.

The lizard erected itself out of the swamp, nearly reaching the treetops with its huge frame. And it looked her directly in the eyes.

Turquoise flames began to erupt from the back of its body, flowing along its frame. Sarah froze in shock at the sight of it. But there was something even worse. This huge lizard was also on the Path of Conflict. She could feel it.

With its huge eyes, as big as her head, it looked at her curiously. There was some intelligence in them.

It narrowed its eyes at Sarah, who didn't know if she should attack or run away.

For some reason, though, the lizard seemed to have lost interest in her. It slowly let itself sink back into the water, its flames now extinguished. And it carried on.

Sarah's heart seemed to explode with each rapid beat while she waited for the lizard to leave her sight.

A while after the lizard had disappeared, Sarah could finally relax again. That had been seriously horrifying.

She wondered why the lizard had not attacked her. The only explanation she could give herself was that she was probably like an insect to it. Not even worth the effort to kill.

She shuddered at the thought of a creature so strong. And she hoped she would never encounter it again.

Sleepy from the intense fear she felt before, she was lulled by the gently flowing lights.

When the sun rose again, Sarah woke up from her dreamless sleep. She stretched, ate a snake for breakfast, and went on her way again. She tried really hard to ignore the thought of the lizard coming back to kill her, so she concentrated on climbing to forget.

Feeling a little more accustomed to the environment, the struggle was a little less horrible. But still, who wanted to climb through a myriad of spiderwebs?

Her only motivation was to find the exit. And at least her surroundings had changed somewhat by now.

The trees were sparser, and the swamp beneath her looked less muddy. She could even see . . . weird things moving around under the surface of the water. She really shouldn't look too hard.

And finally, she could see the border again. With excitement, she climbed faster and soon reached the edge of the trees. Some distance away, the nothingness began. It was hard to tell, but it was quite a distance away. And seeing how there were barely any patches of grass or mud around, she would probably have to swim. Only if she had to get close to the border, though.

Invigorated by reaching the border, she climbed along the edges of the trees, looking for the exit again. It was much easier here because there weren't as many spiderwebs as before.

She climbed for some time until the sun went down again. Luckily, it wasn't as dark here thanks to the stars, and she was able to continue.

She was so full of energy, thinking of getting out of here, that it chased away any semblance of tiredness.

While reaching out for a long hanging branch, she felt something so weird and alien that she nearly fell down again.

She looked toward the border in excitement, and she couldn't see anything. But she felt it.

Somewhere around here, there was something fundamentally different. She had never encountered something like this before.

"It has to be the exit!" she said in a breathless voice, and she started climbing down.

She gingerly stepped onto a more or less solid patch of mud on the edge of the water and looked toward the border.

It was hard to tell at which point the exit could be. Her gut feeling indicated a general direction but she couldn't pinpoint it. She noticed that the border wasn't a straight line here, like it was in other places, but was more erratic. There were spikes of nothingness that swallowed part of the swamp. She would have to be careful. One false move, and she would end up disintegrating like the wolf she had fought.

While trying to guess the exact direction of the exit, a section of the border began to light up.

A small sun seemed to shine through it, bathing the entire region in intense light. All kinds of colors drew arcs in the air, making the scene seem like a dream.

Through this radiating light, it became clear where the border was. And also where the exit was.

For a moment, she just stood there, amazed by the spectacle in front of her. It reminded her of the lights she'd seen in the swamp the previous night. But the little lights couldn't even compare to the glory unfolding before her. Everything around her was bathed in radiant light, which continually changed colors.

Even though it was mesmerizing, she didn't forget why she was here. This was her chance to get out or die trying.

Without further hesitation, she jumped into the water and started to swim. She felt various things brush against her, some even biting her.

Shockingly, some beings even got through her skin. But they let go of her immediately when her blood began to poison them. Nonetheless, it was a horrible feeling, not knowing what was attacking her.

The contrast between the insane beauty around her and the horrors beneath her was just bizarre.

She came closer and closer to the exit. Nothing was attacking her anymore. The beings probably didn't want to get too close to the border.

She was only a short distance away from the exit when something grabbed her leg, and she got pulled underwater.

Horrified, she looked for her assailant. The sun lit up the water underneath her, so she was able to see what had grabbed her.

It was an enormous thing, seemingly only made of tentacles. The various colors shining upon it made it look like something straight out of a fever dream.

With a guttural roar, Sarah ripped apart the tentacle that was pulling her closer to the monstrosity. She immediately started to swim in the direction of the exit again.

Uncountable tentacles snatched at her, trying to pull her closer to it. She ripped apart as many as she could, but there was seemingly no end to them. She also tried to poison it, but that didn't seem to bother the aquatic creature at all.

With no other option, she activated her invasion skill. She had no idea what kind of magic power consumption would await her after trying to attack something this huge. But it was her only way out.

She barely overcame its resistance and sent it into a world of pain.

The water rippled because of the thing's contractions. It seemed to lose all control over its limbs.

This expenditure nearly drained all of her magic power, making her nearly lose consciousness. But she wouldn't let that happen.

With newfound hope, she started swimming toward the exit again. But the monstrosity didn't want her to leave.

Even though it was in immense pain and couldn't fully control its tentacles anymore, it followed her.

When Sarah looked over her shoulder, she immediately regretted it. The thing had somehow opened up its main body, and she could see a cavernous mouth, eager to swallow her whole.

Sarah tried to swim even faster, already painfully breathing in the water. She was in desperate need of the magic power it would give her.

The exit was just in front of her, when she felt a pull on her waist again. She turned around, only to see that the thing was right behind her, its mouth wide open.

With her last ounce of strength and magic power, she attacked its mind and body at the same time. She pushed herself off of it with her legs, propelling herself toward the exit.

After exhausting all of her magic power, unconsciousness overwhelmed her. The last thing she saw was iridescent light all around her.

CHAPTER SEVENTEEN

First Contact

"Are you sure this is a good idea?" asked Dennis in a nervous voice, forming tight fists at his sides like he always did when he was afraid.

They stood next to the river, as they had been following it for quite some time now. The raging river almost drowned their voices.

"It will be fine," said Alex in a raspy voice, void of any emotion. He looked at Dennis with empty eyes and turned around to lead their group ahead.

Andrew looked at Alex with worry written on his face. He patted Dennis on the shoulder and started walking again. Alex was walking so fast that they were starting to lag behind quite a bit.

"You know this isn't a good idea," Dennis said next to him in an angry voice while trying to stare a hole in Alex's back. The river was behind them by now, and they walked deeper into a forest with dense undergrowth.

"And you know why I am doing this," Andrew answered in his typical calm voice. "He hasn't spoken much since Karen's . . ." His voice choked for a moment before he continued. "Since Karen's disappearance. You know we have to engage him somehow. And if this is what it takes, then so be it. He is the strongest person in our group; he will keep us safe."

Dennis didn't seem to agree with him. "Like Monica?" he spat out in an angry voice.

Andrew sighed in response. He didn't know what to say. Monica had terrible wounds when Alex brought her back from their hunt. Her wounds would heal in time, but they didn't know if she would ever be able to run again.

"This time, we are prepared," Andrew said, looking at the gear the group had prepared for them. It was plain wood that was formed to fit their arms, legs, and torsos. It was strapped to their bodies with a simple rope. They also had spears with stone tips and heavy wooden clubs.

Dennis swallowed down his comment on the questionable defensive qualities of the equipment.

"I honestly don't know what we will find, but Alex seems to be convinced that it is somehow a . . . doorway to the inspectors. To Karen," Andrew said to Dennis, who now crunched up his face in guilt. Dennis nodded again and said no more.

After more walking, they saw Alex waiting for them. He was holding his finger to his mouth, indicating for them to be quiet.

"What is it?" asked Andrew in a hushed voice as they came closer.

"Here is the part where the animals are going crazy. It isn't far now. Follow me, don't stray off, and for the damn Creator's sake, don't make a single sound." Alex turned around again.

Andrew frowned and continued following him. A few people had a theory that this Creator the inspector talked about was actually a god. A god who sent the inspector to look out for them. That he gave Karen the honor to follow him as a reward for her achievement in being the first pregnant woman in the new world. They'd begun praying to the Creator in the hope of getting out of this crazy situation they were in.

It seemed very problematic to hope for an unknown entity to get them out of their misery. And as far as Andrew knew, this Creator had probably put them in this situation in the first place. At least if he really was a god.

Strangely enough, Alex also participated in their prayer, even though the inspector had kidnapped his lover and unborn child. He never said what he prayed for, but it was very clear to everyone.

Putting those troubling thoughts aside, Andrew started concentrating again. He didn't want to step on some dry wood and get the attention of the crazed wildlife.

While they heard disturbing howls in their surroundings, they didn't encounter anything. Andrew wasn't quite sure if Alex was a very good guide or if they were just lucky.

With every step, they started to feel why the animals had gone crazy. There was such an insane amount of ambient magic power around them. And this energy somehow entered them, energizing them. Andrew felt like the energy would violently burst out of him if he didn't do something.

But Alex had already warned them of this phenomenon. So Andrew and Dennis controlled themselves, also thanks to Andrew's emotion manipulation skill.

After some more walking, the forest ended abruptly. And in front of them, the ground was plain stone and led to a steep cliff. Dennis wanted to get closer, but Alex held him back.

"Look," Alex whispered, pointing at a part of the cliff some distance to their right.

"I can't see anything," said Dennis, narrowing his eyes to slits in order to see into the distance.

But Andrew saw it. No, he felt it. There was . . . something. He couldn't explain it, but it seemed like the place where Alex pointed didn't really fit. It felt like space itself was somehow misplaced.

It was a very disturbing feeling, like something that shouldn't be possible. Like being controlled against one's will.

Andrew now knew why Alex suspected the inspectors were behind this. It was just so alien, exactly like the inspector they encountered.

They moved closer to the spatial oddity while the sun began to set to their left. It would have been a beautiful sight, but Andrew was so focused on what was in front of him that he didn't notice it.

When the sun reached the horizon, the last rays of sunshine lit up the spatial oddity. It started to shine brightly in thousands of colors. It was so bright that all three of them were momentarily blinded.

Without anyone saying anything, they all ran behind a big bush to hide themselves.

"Do you think they noticed us?" asked Alex. This time, he sounded slightly agitated. At least that was better than his empty, emotionless voice.

"We don't even know if it's them. Just wait and see. It doesn't seem all that dangerous," answered Andrew, who was still rubbing his eyes. He could still barely see anything.

"What was that?" asked Dennis in a frightened voice, while grabbing his spear tightly.

Alarmed, Alex and Andrew turned their heads to the spatial oddity again. Right at this moment, the sun completely set and the iridescent glow of the oddity ceased.

But there was something lying on the ground. Or rather, someone.

Alex jumped up and ran toward the person before Andrew and Dennis could hold him back. The only thing they could do was try to catch up to his inhuman speed.

"Alex, wait!" Andrew shouted, throwing any caution to the wind. But Alex didn't listen.

He had already arrived at the person's side and grabbed them by the throat. The big, furry cloak slid back, and he saw what seemed to be a woman. A woman with horns. Alex let go of her immediately, stepping back with a frightened look on his face.

The woman's head hit the hard stone when Alex let her go, which woke her up.

Andrew and Dennis weren't quite caught up to Alex yet, but they couldn't get any closer. There was such a foul stench that Dennis started gagging.

The woman got on her wobbling feet and looked around with unfocused eyes. Her eyes were glowing red in the last light of the setting sun. Her hair, skin, and whatever she was wearing were covered in so much dirt and blood that it made her look like a walking corpse. She looked like a monster straight out of a nightmare.

Her gaze landed on Alex, and she jumped into action faster than anything Andrew had ever seen. She punched him unconscious and bit him in the neck. She made a weird motion, like breathing something in. Then she let the poor man fall to the ground, where he lay motionless.

The monster woman sighed happily and patted her stomach. "So that's how this works," she said in a content voice.

After rubbing her belly for some time, she looked at Alex again. "Oh shit, what have I done?" she screamed and grabbed her dirty head with her hands.

"Hey, wake up! Wake up! Wake up!" she started shouting, while kicking the unmoving Alex with her feet.

"Stop!" screamed Dennis, pointing his unsteady spear at her. His whole body was shaking like a leaf in the wind.

The woman turned around and looked at them with wide, open eyes. Her hands were still clasped around her head. And her right foot was frozen in motion, just before it could hit Alex again.

"Is there any chance that you haven't seen all of this?" she asked with a bloody smile. Andrew had never seen a more horrifying sight than this.

Dennis thought the same, apparently, because he started shaking even more. Andrew pulled himself together, held his hands up, and took a step in the direction of the monster-woman.

"Sure, we haven't seen anything. If we can just take the man lying there, we will leave. Right?" said Andrew, and he gave Dennis a slight kick.

"Yes, sure!" he answered in a high-pitched voice.

The woman looked at him for a moment and then buried her face in her hands. "Shit! I know you're lying!" she screamed in an ashamed voice.

Andrew froze in place, not knowing if he would get knocked out next. He swallowed nervously and tried again. "Okay, you're right; we have seen it. But we don't want any trouble, alright? We will just leave and forget everything."

The woman looked straight into his eyes. "How about you forget about everything and also take me with you?"

Andrew's and Dennis' mouths gaped wide open at the shamelessness of this person.

"Please?" she said, trying to give them a cute smile.

"We can talk about it, but please just stop smiling," Andrew said, as he protected his eyes from the horrible sight.

After a moment, he dared to look again. What awaited him was the woman pointing her thumbs up and smiling as wide as possible without opening her mouth. That wasn't better.

"Andrew," Dennis said in a suppressed voice. "Have you gone mad? What are you doing right now? This . . . person is clearly insane! And dangerous!"

Andrew glanced at the woman to see if she'd heard him, but she just looked at them with a curious expression.

"Just bear with it for a moment," Andrew whispered back, and he turned around with a kind smile.

"I'd really like to help you, but . . . you attacked one of us. I cannot overlook that." He spoke cautiously. His heart was pounding so hard in his chest that he thought that it would jump out of his chest.

She looked at the ground and started explaining herself in an insecure tone. "I'm really sorry about that. I was dying of magic power depletion, and I just had to replenish myself." After this sentence, Andrew looked at Alex in alarm. But the woman hastily held her hands up. "Everything's fine, it won't kill him. He'll just be out cold for a while. You could say I have a . . . special body."

That was quite clear to Andrew. But he wasn't insane enough to comment on it.

"That might be true," he said, lowering his hands, "but how can I be sure that you're not lying? That you won't plan to attack us?"

The woman looked at him with clear, sad eyes. "I am really sorry. I wasn't in my right mind. And I really, really just want to have someone to talk to. I've been alone since the beginning. Please let me come with you."

For a moment, Andrew was moved a little by the sad emotions he felt inside of her, until the woman spoke again. "And don't worry, I won't hurt you. If I wanted to, you'd be dead by now."

Andrew pressed his lips together. He tried hard to look past this weird and threatening comment.

He didn't want to invite her to their caves. The woman seemed insane. He was pretty sure she would just follow them if he refused anyway. It would probably be safer to be on her good side. At least he hoped so.

"Alright," he said with a sigh, "but if you come with us, we need to know more about each other. My name is Andrew. What about you?"

The woman stood up and beamed so brightly that he could almost overlook the blood and dirt on her face.

"My name is Sarah."

CHAPTER EIGHTEEN

A New Beginning

"I'm outside!" screamed Sarah while jumping high in the air. "I'm outside!" She was so incredibly happy to finally be out of that damned swamp.

Her whole body still hurt like hell from the fight, even though she was reenergized through the absorption of the magic power from the poor guy.

But that couldn't diminish her joy. She had dreamed for so long of this moment that nothing could dampen her mood.

"Could you please not scream so much?" asked the lanky teen named Dennis. He had an insecure voice.

She looked back with an annoyed glance. The two men who were carrying the unconscious one flinched for a moment and stopped moving.

They were both pretty skinny and looked like they hadn't eaten in a while. The taller one, Andrew, had a pretty sharp face with a square chin. His face looked nearly overgrown with light brown hair and a beard. While he had broad shoulders and good looks, his expressionless face ruined all that. He constantly seemed to be either tired or bored, which made it kind of weird to talk to him.

The younger one looked like a puppy, with his brown, wavy hair and beardless face. His big brown eyes looked at her in fear.

She involuntarily had to grin. Dennis paled immediately and held his free hand protectively around his throat. Such a cute boy.

Andrew cleared his throat and asked in Dennis' stead, "Could you please not make so much noise? The animals in this region lose their minds and sometimes attack."

He seemed to add some more, but Sarah just lifted her head. "It's fine," she told them. "Whenever one of those gets too close, I knock them out. No need to be afraid."

Andrew looked at her skeptically, but didn't say anything else.

They walked quite a distance like this. They were very slow because the two had to carry the unconscious one. Sarah had offered to help, but they resolutely refused. Their loss.

After a while, they encountered a river, which made the other two relax. Apparently, it wasn't very far to their home from here.

Sarah suppressed her incredible urge to bathe in the water. She settled for drinking to her heart's content and scrubbing a little of the dirt from her face. It was amazing.

The water was so fresh and clear. After all the disgusting water from the swamp, the river's water tasted almost sweet. She drank until her stomach started to hurt, forcing her to stop.

With a refreshed feeling, she stood up and turned around to the other two guys and gave them a happy smile. They didn't look afraid anymore when she smiled, which was a big plus.

After some more walking, Andrew told her to stop for a while.

"We are close to our settlement, you see," he started explaining. "And honestly, you stink very, very bad. And you look horrifying with all the blood and . . . other dirt you have caked on your body."

Sarah was initially a little offended. But then she compared herself to the three guys and had to accept that maybe he was right.

With a disgruntled face, Sarah nodded. Andrew let out a quiet sigh, stepped toward her, and stretched out his hand. In the middle of it, though, he seemed to have changed his mind and hastily pulled his hand back while gagging a little.

It couldn't be that bad . . . right? Sarah thought to herself and quickly sniffed at her arm. She couldn't find anything amiss.

"I will send someone with new clothes," he said while holding his hand in front of his nose. Sarah just nodded again, and Andrew and Dennis basically fled from the scene.

A little sullen, Sarah went into the river, right behind a big tree that had fallen into the water, which had calmed the raging current.

While sitting on the stony riverbed, she let the gently flowing water brush away the dirt on her skin and clothes. The water that flowed away from her was nearly black. She was so dirty that it would take quite some time to get herself clean like this.

This place was so peaceful. With the clean river flowing through the land and the wind that moved across the trees and meadows, she knew she was out of the spatial error, but only now could she fully realize this fact.

"Excuse me?" asked a quiet voice behind her.

Sarah was so surprised that she immediately jumped to her feet and turned around. In this process, she somehow managed to step on her coat, ripping it off of her. She wanted to catch it, but the river pulled it away faster than she could react.

The woman looked at her in shock for a moment and started speaking again. "Andrew and Dennis told me that you have horns, but . . . you even have a tail."

Sarah pressed her lips together and nodded in resignation. The woman didn't look frightened, though.

"Did it . . ." she began and hesitated. "Did the mutation hurt a lot?"

This question hit Sarah squarely in her suppressed emotions and trauma.

With burning eyes, she looked down at the flowing water and nodded slightly. She heard the woman come closer and step into the water.

When Sarah felt the woman's arms around her, her first instinct was to defend herself. But that only lasted a moment, and she let herself fall into the warm embrace.

"It must have been difficult all alone," the woman said in a gentle voice while patting Sarah's back. "But it's okay now. You are not alone anymore."

Sarah just nodded and sobbed. She felt like the pain and suffering from her time in the swamp were beginning to wash away, like the dirt from her skin.

The woman held her in her arms for quite some time, so Sarah could let out all the emotions she had been suppressing all this time.

Sarah reluctantly stepped away from her and gave her a crooked smile. "Thanks," she said with a raspy voice and sniffed a little.

The woman nodded understandingly and then looked down at herself with a frown.

"And they didn't exaggerate." She looked up at her while laughing a little. "You really do stink horribly."

Sarah also had to laugh, and the heavy atmosphere fell from them. Only now could Sarah clearly look at the woman.

She was really beautiful, with blond, wavy hair and a gentle face. In contrast to the three guys, she didn't look skinny. She had, in fact, a rather curvaceous body.

Sarah noticed a moment too late that she had been staring and quickly looked up into the woman's eyes again. Luckily, she'd been busy inspecting the dirt on Sarah's clothes.

"Can't help it," she said with a sigh and looked at Sarah with resolute eyes. "Let's get to cleaning."

For a moment, Sarah was strangely excited about washing herself with this beautiful woman. But that didn't last long.

"Come on! You need to get this dirt off you!" the woman shouted at Sarah, who was now sitting on top of a tree.

"No way! That brush is a torture instrument!" she shouted back, not intending to come down any time soon.

The woman sighed heavily and rested her face in her hands. "Listen. You look and smell like a monster straight out of a nightmare. If you want everyone to run away screaming at the sight of you, then be my guest."

Sarah was very uncomfortable; the woman's words were so close to the truth. Her class was already Nightmare, so she saw no need to make it even worse. With a yielding expression, she climbed down the tree and took the brush from her.

"Thanks for coming down. If you need help with your back, come get me. I will wash myself behind the bushes over there." She pointed to dense greenery some distance away.

With this, she walked away and left Sarah to herself. With a sigh, she started peeling the snake skin off and cleaning her body.

It was surprisingly hard to get herself clean. The dirt and blood were not only completely caked in, but the stuff was literally everywhere. So gross. How had she lived like this for so long?

With a disgusted shudder, she began scrubbing herself even harder until her skin was completely clean again. With some hesitation, she decided to throw away the snake-skin suit. For one, the woman had brought her new, strange-looking clothes to wear. And the snake skins were in tatters by now, not to mention extremely dirty.

With a sigh, Sarah started dressing herself in the new clothes—a simple shirt and trousers, which seemed to be made out of an elastic material, woven together in thick cords. It wasn't very comfortable because it was pretty rough and way too tight. It felt more like it was made for a skinny man than for a woman. The only good thing was that her tail wasn't obstructed by the clothing.

While inspecting herself some more, she noticed something else. Her skin was way too pale. It seemed like being caked in dirt and blood makes for good sun protection.

"Ready to meet everyone?" asked the woman from behind her.

Sarah turned around and nodded. When the woman began walking, Sarah grabbed her arm and held her back for a moment. "What's your name?"

The woman smiled apologetically and gently removed Sarah's hand. "My name is Melissa. Yours?"

"Sarah," she answered, smiling.

Without saying anything more, the two made their way uphill and through some woods.

As they approached their destination, Sarah could hear what sounded like various people speaking in loud voices. She gulped and was suddenly nervous.

Until now, nobody had shunned her because of her monstrous looks.

"Something is weird," Melissa said, looking worried. "Let's walk faster."

Sarah tensed up and readied herself for conflict. She couldn't have her new potential friends die before she had the chance to meet them.

The forest cleared, and they came to a wide and stony clearing. All the plant life that had lived here had been trampled on so often that the whole clearing was barren.

A bit further uphill, she saw a steep cliff with numerous caves in it. And in front of the largest cave was a big crowd of people. They were shouting in excitement and cheering.

Now very curious, Melissa and Sarah ran toward them and joined the big circle of people. The crowd was so focused on what happened in front of them that nobody noticed Sarah.

"Do it again!" shouted one of the guys, standing closest to a man, who was sitting on the ground in front of a smoking pile of wood.

Melissa tugged at the shirt of one of the women nearby. "What is going on here?" she asked.

"He got an energy specialization. You will not believe what he can do," she replied in an excited voice without taking her eyes away from the man in the middle of the crowd.

The man smiled widely and held his hands near the pile. The crowd held their breath while watching intently. Sarah was also overcome by the tension and watched in silence.

After a few moments, the air around the man's hand started to shimmer, and the wood began to glow red from the heat. Soon after, it started burning.

"That is so awesome!" shouted Sarah, before the crowd could start with their usual round of cheers.

Drawn to the unfamiliar voice, everyone looked at her, and simultaneously took a step back in shock.

While the crowd looked at her either fearfully or curiously, Sarah only had eyes for the little flame burning in front of her.

She always wondered what she could do with her empty energy specialization slot. She already saw herself burning the disgusting tentacle monster with hot flames and then eating the well-cooked meat.

She only had to find out how to unlock this specialization and how to get the monster out of the water to burn it.

With a mad smile, she grabbed the shocked man by the shoulders and looked him deep in the eyes.

"You and I are gonna be good friends."

CHAPTER NINETEEN

Revelations

"What is going on here?" said a neutral and calm voice over the shellshocked crowd. With only these few words, the people seemed to calm down quite a bit.

Andrew gently pushed people aside so he could see the reason for the commotion. Sarah realized at this moment that her holding the lanky man by his collar couldn't look too good. But it was too late.

Andrew looked at her with a resigned face and lifted an eyebrow. Sarah wanted to speak up, but he held up a hand and shook his head.

"I want you to welcome Sarah," he shouted to the still-quiet crowd while pointing at her. "She was alone for a long time. She had to undergo even harsher mutations than Alex. And she is just very happy that she is among fellow humans again." He turned his head to her and nodded encouragingly.

"Yeah, that's right," Sarah said while still trying to wrap her mind around how Andrew calmed the crowd so fast.

Even though a few gave her suspicious looks, most of them nodded in understanding. Some around her even patted her back and shoulders and murmured some encouraging words.

Andrew nodded again and spoke to the crowd. "Alright people, there is still a lot to do. Our supplies for the coming winter will not come by themselves."

The crowd booed a little and threw some jokes at Andrew. But they almost immediately went to work again. This demonstrated how much they liked and respected him.

The fire-guy, who had long since freed himself from Sarah's grasp, also tried scurrying away.

"Stay," Andrew said to the man. He froze like someone who had been caught while doing something forbidden.

Andrew closed to the distance between him and Sarah and had a slightly worried face. "I hope I won't regret this. And please stop attacking my people."

"I didn't attack him," Sarah replied, her eyes narrowing. She really didn't like it when someone assumed things. "He happens to have an energy specialization, and I have an open slot. So, I got a little excited."

Andrew seemed like he wanted to start arguing with her but let it be.

Instead, he patted her shoulder and walked up to fire-guy. "Xavier," he said, addressing the man, who was trying really hard not to look into his eyes. Andrew put a hand on the man's shoulder and spoke to him in a soft voice. "I'm proud of you."

Xavier let out a small laugh and scratched his head in embarrassment. "Thanks, Andrew," he said in a choked-up voice.

Andrew waited for a moment and said, "Explain."

The lanky man brushed his black hair out of his pale and haggard face and began telling his story with some hesitation. "So, you know how I need to do the odd jobs for the kitchen, right? They . . . um . . . they just let me do the fire now because . . . Well, it doesn't matter. You see, I hate making fire above all else. It is so exhausting and frustrating. So after what felt like one hundred tries, I really, really wished for the fire to start burning. And then it just . . . happened."

Andrew turned to the side to hide his consternation and massaged his temple. "So, basically," he began, holding his hand over his eyes, "you were so lazy and extremely bad at something that it awakened a big enough wish in you to gain this ability."

Xavier, who had stretched out proudly until now, slumped down in shame.

Sarah, on the other hand, felt her heart burn up. That made so much sense. Whenever she awakened to a specialization, she felt an intense desire. The only question was how she could manage to awaken this desire to make fire.

Andrew took a deep breath and turned to Xavier again. "I know it has been hard for you to find your place here, but you can do something nobody else can. For now, help out the kitchen staff with your abilities. And tomorrow, go to Tobias. You can make an important contribution to our group."

Xavier nodded without speaking and stood up on shaky legs. He suddenly hugged Andrew and then ran off.

Andrew let out an exhausted breath and turned to Sarah. "You see what we have to deal with here. The people seem fine on the outside, but most of them are afraid, and they struggle." He paused for a moment, searching for the right words.

"Just don't do things that frighten the people. We need more trustworthy and strong people like you to protect us and hunt for us. Can you do that?"

Sarah felt a small sting of yearning for belonging somewhere in her heart. So, she resolutely nodded in affirmation.

"Then, welcome to the caves," he said and patted her shoulder. "And now," he said suddenly, startling her a little, "we will go meet up with the leaders. I've seen how strong you are, and these mutations . . . You must be quite a bit stronger than our hunters. And we think you might help us break through a bottleneck. Are you willing to talk about it?"

Sarah had a feeling that they were probably stuck at level nine for a while. She knew all too well how frustrating it was not to be able to advance anymore. "Sure. But I really want something to eat. All this talk about kitchen stuff made me realize that I've only eaten gross stuff until now."

Andrew looked at her in bewilderment and laughed out loud. "No problem. You can have all the food you want tonight. The kitchen staff will bring it over once it's ready. Let's go."

Sarah was looking forward to seeing more of their camp, but they went straight to the biggest cave, which was only a short distance away. It was dimly lit by torches along the walls at various intervals.

A few people were silently waiting for them, their features barely visible in the dim light.

Sarah recognized Melissa, Dennis, and Alex. But she hadn't seen the fourth one until now. He had straight, black hair and very bad posture. His skinny body rested on the ground, looking frail and weak. His appearance seemed unkempt and fragile, but his eyes were completely different. There seemed to be a fire burning in them as he stared at her without blinking.

His gaze was kind of burdensome, so she sneaked a peek at Alex. He was the large and burly man she had knocked out and bitten in the shoulder to feed on his magic power. He also stared at her, but with a lot of suppressed anger in his eyes. This would be fun.

Andrew stepped closer to them and waved his hand at Dennis. The lanky teen stood up hastily and left them with quick steps.

"Why is he leaving?" Sarah asked curiously.

"He volunteered to help hunt some nocturnal critters. I'm pretty sure that one of the reasons he didn't want to be here was you. You should apologize for your behavior toward him later." Andrew answered her in a subdued voice while guiding her to sit on the ground. "The person you don't know is Tobias. He is our . . . researcher, you could say." He nodded at Tobias, who didn't do anything in response.

Andrew didn't let himself get irritated by him and cleared his throat. "Thank you for coming," he said loudly, addressing the small crowd. His eyes rested longer on Melissa than the others, without letting it be too obvious. Sneaky guy.

"First of all, let me introduce Sarah. We found her next to the oddity and brought her with us. She initially attacked Alex, but it turned out to be a misunderstanding." At this point, he stared into the eyes of the agitated Alex. "And she will apologize and answer questions later."

Alex tensed up but said nothing. Andrew breathed a sigh of relief and continued. "First and foremost, it is important that we break through the bottleneck. So, do you mind sharing your status screen with us first, Sarah?"

"Sharing my status screen? That works?" she asked in a skeptical voice, but wanting to try it out. As always with the system, this intent, plus her vocalization of it, seemed to suffice for it to spring into action. And it promptly showed her status screen to the group.

Details:
Level: 14
Name: Sarah Anna Fischer
Class: Nightmare
Race: Mutant
Status: Normal
HP: 205/205 **SP**: 150/175 **MP**: 300/310

Achievements:
- How the hell are you still sane?
- Poison Gorger
- More Than Human

Affinities:
Mind (Mid) Body (Mid) Energy (Low)

Specializations:
- Mind (2/2)
  - Invasion
  - Nerve Control
- Body (2/2)
  - Adaptation
  - Mutation
- Energy (0/1)

Basic Stats:
Strength: 13
Dexterity: 13
Endurance: 15
Resistance: 10
Intelligence: 22
Force: 10

Special Stats:
Magic Power: 14
Life Force: 32
Mental Power: 17

Active Skills:
- Mind Infiltration (Invasion)

Passive Skills:
- Poison Body (Adaptation)
- Poison and Acid Resistance
- Walking Hazard
- Mutated Glands
- Metamorphosis (Mutation)
  - Skin:
    - Dense Skin (1 LF)
  - Bone Structure:
    - High-Density Bones (2 LF)
  - Muscles:
    - Strengthened Fibers (1 LF): Strengthened muscle fibers. Slightly tougher and stronger.
  - Brain, Nerve System, and Sensory Organs:
    - Predator Eyes (1 LF)
  - Organs and Processes:
    - Magic Power Nourishment System
  - Special Mutations:
    - Nightmare's Tail (class specific, 5 LF)
    - Nightmare's Horns (class specific, 5 LF)
- Suppression (Nerve Control)
- Struggle (Conditional Passive)
- Slightly Crazy
- Mean Eye

The whole group was looking at her status screen with gaping mouths. For a few seconds, Sarah asked herself if they had collectively experienced some kind of brain seizure. But then they began bombarding her with questions.

For what felt like hours, she explained every little detail about her experiences with the system. How she got the specializations, achievements, class, and everything else. Somewhere in between, a sweaty, smelly guy pressed a plate full of food into her hand, which she absentmindedly ate while talking to the group. What interested the group the most was how to break through to level ten. They also talked a lot about the skills and specializations the group had achieved, which was also very interesting for Sarah. Apparently there was an absurd amount of options. And practically everyone seemed to have skills that gave them some sort of resistance against poison and against fear.

"I still don't understand it," Alex said in a grumpy voice. He had been quiet most of the time, apart from a snarky remark about her race being mutant instead of human. Luckily, the others didn't seem surprised or deterred by it.

"You expect us to simultaneously tear down a so-called resistance and accept the magic power to fill our bodies? How do we know it won't kill us?" he asked in a threatening voice, a vein bulging on his forehead.

"It won't," said Tobias with a trembling voice. "I just did it."

Sarah looked at him in amazement. He was literally trembling on the ground, like a leaf in the wind. His eyes also seemed to glow a little bit.

This time, everyone looked at him with gaping mouths.

"Are you serious?" asked Andrew, flabbergasted.

But before anyone could pry further into the overloaded Tobias, someone came running into the cave.

"Dennis and Vanessa!" the woman shouted when she came to a sliding stop.

"They didn't come back from their gathering trip, and we can't find them!"

Andrew stood up immediately and held the heaving woman by her shoulders.

"Tell me everything."

CHAPTER TWENTY

Scum

Sarah was running through the woods, trying to find the tiniest trace of Dennis and his companion, Vanessa.

She still vividly remembered the rage in Andrew's normally neutral face. When he asked her to go, a strange and fierce urge to help him rose from within her.

This feeling had ebbed down by now, and she began to wonder if Andrew might have a skill that let him influence other people's emotions. That would explain a lot of the things that had happened around him. And also why she had such a strong urge to please him.

She was very, very sure that this wasn't what she would normally be like. Even if he was one of the few humans she had talked to since waking up in this strange world.

If he really had done that, she would need to have a rather intense discussion with him. But still, she couldn't just ignore the group of people who had accepted her. They seemed pretty nice so far.

Suddenly, Sarah's head turned around like it was pulled by a magnet. There were traces. A path was carved in the undergrowth, and pretty violently. Animals didn't do something like this.

Like a specter, Sarah sped silently through the dimly lit forest. After a few minutes of full-speed running, she heard voices.

With a triumphant feeling, she was looking forward to bringing back the lost people. That would enhance her social standing, and maybe even Alex wouldn't scowl at her anymore. One has to have dreams.

With one last jump, she flew above some tall bushes and landed near the voices. "Your savior is here, Dennis!" she shouted while landing graciously.

She looked up with a confident smile, only for it to freeze on her face. Three men were sitting next to each other on a fallen tree trunk and were in the middle of eating.

One of them looked at her with an open mouth, the dried meat half-way inside it. The other two apparently forgot to chew as they stared at her for a few moments.

The moment didn't last long, as they sprang up simultaneously and pulled out weapons from behind their backs.

"Puff youw hawds in we aiw!" screamed the biggest and ugliest of them all, while spitting out big chunks of food. He had greasy, dirty skin and a very nasty aura around him.

"So gross," Sarah said, her face contorted in disgust. "Have you never heard of closing your mouth while eating?"

"Shut up!" screamed the big, ugly one, now with an empty mouth. "Who are you?"

He looked at her more closely and went pale when he looked into her eyes. He froze for a moment before he was able to speak again. This time, his voice didn't sound as confident. "Answer us if you are sentient! We are armed and ready to use violence if necessary."

Sweat was running down his greasy forehead. The two smaller guys next to him didn't fare any better. They looked at her in utter horror, gripping their weapons tightly.

Sarah crossed her arms and looked at the thugs with contempt. "I am sentient, sweat-face. There's no need to get violent. I am just looking for someone."

She was pretty surprised. There were other people in their surroundings who didn't belong to the caves.

The three guys exchanged quick glances, and the biggest one swallowed nervously. Sarah looked at them with squinted eyes, not quite sure what was happening. "What are you . . ." she began to ask, but was interrupted by a sudden system prompt.

<Emergency Quest (Path of Conflict exclusive): You have the following options:
- Kill your enemies
- Run away
- Fall to your knees and beg for mercy
- Die

Rewards are based on which option you choose.>

"What the . . ." Sarah began, but was interrupted by a large stone that was suddenly hurled at her.

She was too slow to react and was hit on the side of her head, even though she tried to turn away as fast as possible.

A dizzy spell nearly made her fall down, but she gritted her teeth and focused on the men in front of her, who were now running at her.

"Guess it's the first option."

She raised her arms just in time to block the first two hits. It hurt, but her arms were so extremely sturdy that the two clubs bounced back like they had hit solid rock. The two smaller guys whined in pain when their wrists were sprained from the unexpected resistance.

The bigger guy, on the other hand, tried to grab her and lift her up. He didn't expect her to be as heavy as she was, given her objectively slender build. He couldn't have known Sarah had mutations that made her bones and muscles extremely dense and heavy.

He grunted in exasperation and only managed to lift her up about an inch before tumbling to the ground. The problem was that she was also falling down.

She tried her best to use her invasion skills, but the injury from the stone prevented her from utilizing them properly. She couldn't connect with their minds.

As she lay buried under the colossal guy, two clubs began hammering down at her. They mostly hit her arms and horns, but it started to hurt more and more.

She desperately tried to free her tail, which was buried beneath her; the guy was too heavy to lift without her arms.

Intense rage bubbled up inside her over this ridiculous situation. With a roar, she grabbed the thick head of the ugly guy on top of her, and twisted it around. Ugly cracks and snaps could be heard, and the man died immediately.

The two clubs, which were still on their way down, hit one of her horns in quick succession. A crack appeared in it, and with it, unimaginable pain in her head.

The two guys roared in anger and fear upon seeing their comrade die such a gruesome death.

Sarah dizzily grabbed the man on top of her and threw him off. Before the other two guys could pummel her again, she sprang up and created some distance between them.

She had some difficulties staying conscious with the pain of her fractured horn, but she had been through worse.

One of the two guys tried to come at her from behind, but she wouldn't let that happen.

With a mighty jump, Sarah was on top of the one who was standing still in front of her, and she punched into his chest with all she had. With a loud cracking and popping sound, the man flew back some distance and didn't stand up. He was coughing and barely breathing, with bloody bubbles coming out of his mouth.

The other guy screamed in terror and tried to run away, but he was too slow. It didn't take much effort to catch up with him. Sarah grabbed him by the neck and pressed him down into the mud until he passed out.

With an exhausted sigh, she let herself sink to the ground and tried to wipe the blood out of her face. She had no idea if it was from her or one of the other two guys.

The dizziness calmed down to a stinging headache, so she stood up and lifted the unconscious man onto her shoulders.

With tired steps, she returned to their encampment. For a moment, she looked at the two motionless bodies on the ground. The other one had apparently died too.

Somehow she knew she should feel guilt or something similar. But, she felt the same thing she always felt after having survived a brush with death—elation and excitement.

They'd tried to kill her and paid the ultimate price for it. And she would live another day.

She quickly looked over the corpses to see if she could find anything useful, but their clothes were even more rudimentary than her new ones. And their clubs were just rough-cut wood.

The only thing useful were their sacks of provisions, which she planned to take with her.

Suddenly, she heard a soft whimper. At first, she thought that the guy with the caved-in chest was still alive, but the whimper came from another direction.

She cautiously stood up and approached the place where the sound was coming from—behind a bush.

She carefully pushed away the twigs to sneak a peek.

A woman lay on the dirty ground. Her hands and feet were tied together behind her back with what seemed to be the remains of her tattered clothes. Her naked body was covered in bruises, and she was sobbing quietly.

Sarah looked back at the last living guy with murder in her eyes, but she held back. She had some questions for him. The other two had definitely died too quickly.

Sarah sat down next to the woman, who was most likely Vanessa, and lightly touched her shoulder. She immediately started to scream and sob, probably thinking that Sarah was one of the guys. Her eyes were so swollen that she couldn't see anymore.

"Everything is fine," Sarah spoke in a soft and soothing voice while gently untying her. "The men are incapacitated. Andrew sent me to save you and Dennis."

Vanessa held her breath for a moment and started crying. "Thank you," she mumbled through her swollen lips and grabbed Sarah with her now-freed hands.

"You're safe now," Sarah told her while holding her in her arms. "Tell me, where is Dennis?"

Vanessa tensed up in her arms and tried to steady her breath. "They beat him brutally. I don't know how far from here, but he didn't look good when they . . . We need to help him."

With a nod, Sarah stood up again and grabbed the last man alive by his clothes to lift him up with one arm before returning to Vanessa. "I'll give you a piggyback ride," she told her while crouching down next to her.

When Vanessa was secure on her back, she let out a frightened sound. "What is with your head?"

"Ah, it's just a special hat. Don't mind it," Sarah answered, still with her soothing voice.

The woman on her back started repeating, "It's just a special hat," while Sarah started to run through the forest, along the trails of the trio.

It didn't take long before she found the scene of their assault.

Dennis lay on the ground without moving. She could feel with her magic power that he wasn't alive anymore.

She stepped closer to inspect him and immediately regretted it. His body was horribly mangled. If she didn't know that this was Dennis, she would never have been able to tell.

She looked down in disgust at the unconscious man in her hand. What kind of monster would do something so cruel?

"Did you find him?" asked a weak voice from behind her.

Sarah didn't know how to say this. She opened her mouth a couple of times without any words coming out.

"He's dead, right?" asked Vanessa. Her voice was still soft and quiet, but trembling.

"Yes," Sarah said and heard Vanessa start crying again on her back. "Can you hold on by yourself? I need both arms to carry one guy each now." Vanessa didn't say anything, so Sarah took it as an affirmation.

With some hesitation, she grabbed Dennis' already somewhat stiff body and began her journey back to the caves.

CHAPTER TWENTY-ONE

Crossing the Line

Andrew used up a lot of magic power to suppress the anxiousness inside him. Death wasn't new to their group, but Dennis was loved by all of them. He was always able to put a smile on everyone's face and didn't hold back when he thought that Andrew had made a bad decision.

Only now had Andrew noticed how much he had relied on his assistance.

So it was all the more shocking when he saw a bloodied Sarah come up the slope to the caves.

In one hand, she held an unfamiliar man. In the other, the mangled remains of a human. With Vanessa's red hair visible from behind Sarah's back, this left only one conclusion.

The shock left Andrew breathless for a second, and he felt like his heart had fallen out of his chest. But, in a timely manner, his skills suppressed the heavy feelings to a somewhat bearable degree.

Everyone who stayed back at the caves looked at Sarah without moving. The scene in front of them was just too shocking.

"What have you done to him?!" screamed a woman named Sofia.

The whole crowd became restless, and murmurs started to emerge. This wasn't good. Andrew prepared to interfere when Sarah spoke up.

"What I have done to him? Don't you see what I am doing, you stupid piece of shit? I have saved Vanessa, picked up the remains of Dennis, and let one of the perpetrators live so that we can question him." With her bloodied face and a cracked horn, she appeared pretty insane when she looked at the crowd with wide, open eyes. "You are welcome."

At these words, the murmurs died down, and some people even apologized in quiet voices. Sofia started sobbing and fell to her knees, her face clutched in her hands.

Andrew nodded to her friends, and they took her away from the scene.

Sarah came closer and threw the stranger unceremoniously to the side, where he lay motionless.

The mangled remains of Dennis, on the other hand, were set down carefully. Sarah then gently took Vanessa from her back and gave her unconscious body to her friends, who had come rushing over.

Everyone knew what to do. This wasn't their first death since they'd arrived at the caves. But it was by far the most horrible one.

"Sarah," Andrew said, turning to her. "Can you try to find out more about this guy?" he said, while looking at the motionless stranger with anger in his eyes.

"Sure. He might scream, though. Anywhere it won't disturb the others?" she asked him in a neutral voice. Andrew got the chills when he heard the insane woman talk about something like this so casually.

"There is a cave some distance away to our left. The distance will be enough. I will come later." Andrew turned to leave when a stone-hard grip on his arm held him back.

"Don't do the emotion thing to me anymore, or I will rip you a new one," Sarah whispered in his ear before letting him go and dragging the stranger away.

Andrew broke out in a cold sweat. The people more or less knew what he was doing. But until now, nobody had complained about it because it was always helping them. He had never thought about a situation like this. Maybe he needed to be more careful.

With a heavy heart, Andrew turned around to see Dennis' remains. Some of the people had already lifted him up and were waiting for Andrew.

He nodded to them, and they started their silent march to the graveyard. It was a small clearing some distance away, where five mounds could already be seen.

Still completely silent, they began their arduous work of digging a hole big enough for Dennis.

It was extremely difficult to penetrate the hard ground with nothing but sharpened stones, but the pain helped Andrew forget who he had lost.

When the hole was big enough, they let down the remains and quickly closed the grave again. Nobody wanted to look at Dennis in this state any longer.

When they were finished, they all stood silently in front of the grave while tears trailed down their dirty faces. They had cried so much already over their lost companions, but it didn't get any easier.

Andrew wanted to say something, but he had no idea what. He had a lump in his throat that made it impossible to say anything. He had lost his best friend, his reliable supporter. From the beginning, Dennis had been by his side. And now he was dead.

Realization crept in. Dennis was no more. Murdered in cold blood by some strangers. And one of them was here. Cold rage was now bubbling up in his chest. Andrew turned around and ran toward the cave where Sarah would be.

He heard some shouting behind him, but he ignored it. He needed to do something, anything to somehow make the situation bearable. To avenge his friend.

Through a veil of tears, he nearly fell down a couple of times, but he somehow managed to get to the cave.

When he approached the cave, he could hear Sarah and the stranger talking.

"How about we make a deal, scum?"

A male voice laughed and asked, "What are you offering, bitch? Your body looks nice."

"My offer is this. You tell me everything."

"That's not a deal!"

"Another beating then."

"You lunatic!"

Right when the man started screaming in anger and pain, Andrew reached them and saw Sarah kicking into . . . places.

"What are you doing?" asked Andrew, a clear look of disgust on his face.

"What does it look like?" Sarah said with a raised eyebrow. "After what he did to Dennis and Vanessa, I thought I wouldn't have to be gentle. And we have to know if there are more of these bastards."

Andrew had to remind himself that he had asked her to do this. But it was extremely hard to witness what it really meant.

"The problem is just that he has some kind of skill to numb his body or something like that. It doesn't matter what I do; the bastard won't tell me much," she said, lightly kicking the man again.

"Hell no, I won't!" the man screamed with rage and just a hint of fear in his eyes. "I can withstand everything! And, at some point, Kevin will find you. And he will kill you all!"

Irritated, Sarah looked at the man and kicked him again. "Do you think you can do something about his emotions?"

Andrew nodded and swallowed down the sick feeling. He braced himself to use his skills to damage someone for the first time.

<Condition fulfilled. Unlocked the following skill:

Emotion Overdrive: You are able to overdrive certain emotions in another being. This might permanently cripple their mind.>

Andrew stared at the message for a while and then went into action. He didn't want to chicken out at this point.

He grabbed the protesting man by the head and activated his skill.

The man immediately started laughing wildly and trembling, his body jerking up and down as if having a seizure.

"What the hell are you doing? Are you seriously giving him a good time right now?" Sarah asked in disbelief.

Andrew looked back for a moment to meet her steely gaze. "I have seen people live and smile with horrible emotions deep inside them," Andrew said while draining his magic power to keep his skill activated. "But, what really breaks people is if you take from them what makes them happy."

Sarah nodded in approval and rubbed her chin. "I didn't think you'd have it in you, Andrew. So evil," she said, looking him up and down.

"I am not evil," Andrew replied, turning back to the laughing man. "I am necessary."

It didn't take long for Andrew's magic power to run dry. He stopped before it emptied completely and looked down at the stranger.

He was just lying there with empty eyes and an open mouth, his breathing shallow. "Are there more of you?" Andrew asked with an emotionless voice.

The man focused his empty eyes on Andrew, and a small hint of hope could be seen in them. "If I tell you," he began speaking in a hoarse voice, "will you give me this feeling again?"

Sarah whistled and patted Andrew's shoulder. It was disgusting to be complimented for something like this.

Andrew focused on the matter at hand. "That depends on your answer." His voice was cold, and he took a step back as a demonstration.

This seemed to give the man his energy back.

"There are more," he said hastily, nearly biting his tongue. "We have a campsite, about two days up the river. We were sent out to find more . . . women."

Andrew looked at the man in disgust, who had started to drool a little. "Please give me the feeling again!" he screamed in a hoarse voice.

"Details."

It appeared that there was another settlement close to them. It was led by a small faction of brutal men with an even more brutal leader named Kevin. They had killed most of the other men in their group and taken the women hostage. And when they started to get bored of the women they already had, they began looking for new ones.

"That is so messed up," Sarah said, shaking her head. "And this Kevin guy. You say he is the strongest and your leader. How strong is he?"

"He can punch through a tree trunk like it's nothing."

"I can deal with that," Sarah said, scratching her chin in thought. "It doesn't matter how strong someone is when I pump them full of poison."

She looked over to Andrew, who was silently contemplating what he had just heard.

"So now what do we do with him?" Sarah asked him.

Andrew looked away from the man and took a deep breath. "A quick death," he said, steeling his resolve.

"Better than he deserves, but I guess it's your call," said Sarah. She shot forward faster than Andrew's eyes could follow, and punched the shocked man's neck.

With a sickening crunch, his neck was bent out of shape, and he fell to the ground lifelessly.

Andrew stood there, shocked to his bones. And then he threw up.

"So gross," Sarah said.

Andrew snorted and looked up at her. "You are stone cold," he said with contempt in his voice.

"I am not," she retorted, lifting an eyebrow. "I am necessary. Could you have given him a quick death?"

Andrew had nothing to say to that, so he turned around. He needed to leave this cave as fast as possible.

Without saying anything else, Sarah followed him outside.

CHAPTER TWENTY-TWO

The Way of the Mutant

Sarah was washing herself in the cold, raging river in a frenzy. She had expected that killing the guy in the cave would give her the same rush as the fight in the woods, but she just felt dirty. She also realized why. The rush didn't come from killing, but from fighting to the death, and surviving it. What she had done in the cave was just cold-blooded murder.

At least she didn't feel guilty about it, as the man had been scum through and through.

After a while, she realized that she couldn't get any cleaner. So, she dressed again in the uncomfortable clothing and went up the hill again.

While running silently through the woods, she thought about the fight with the three men again. Her reactions had been way too slow. She now realized the downside of her suppression skill.

<Suppression (Nerve Control): Your emotions will influence your nerves less. Warning: Instinctual behavior is also suppressed.>

She hadn't paid the warning any mind, as it hadn't been apparent to her what it meant. But now she knew.

Her suppressed instinctual behavior also influenced her reaction time. It seemed to her that she had to consciously think about doing something before her body followed suit. That led to her reacting slowly to threats, resulting in her being caught off guard again and again.

Luckily, she had a solution to her shortcomings. Her Mutation skill.

Now that she wasn't alone and didn't live in a deadly spatial error anymore, she could fully utilize the Mutation skill.

The process of mutating had its merits, as it could heal potentially fatal wounds. But there was no guarantee she would be able to mutate exactly in the place where she would get a critical wound. And if she were stronger, the likelihood of her getting such a wound would decrease.

More power meant less danger to her life, but more danger to everyone else.

When she got to the caves, she didn't join the busy crowd. Instead, she sneaked around the edges of the clearing, not wanting to be seen.

People had been tense around her after what happened with Dennis and Vanessa. And she really didn't want to deal with it right now.

She silently went to the foot of the cliff and began climbing, after making sure that nobody was paying attention in her direction.

"Don't look down, don't look down," Sarah mumbled to herself while climbing further up. Her goal was a cave located much higher than any of the trees around them. There, she would undergo the mutations.

But it was so damn high up. "Don't look down, don't look—" Her mantra was interrupted when a part of the wall she had just grabbed broke off.

With the other hand, she gripped the stone wall so hard that it actually cracked. She was free-falling for one second until her right hand stopped her fall. For a moment, she made the mistake of looking down while dangling from her right hand.

With a groan, she tightly clung to the wall again and calmed her breathing. She really wasn't good with heights.

The last leg of the climb wasn't far, so she got to the elevated cave without further issue.

With a contented sigh, she walked deep inside the cave and sat on the ground.

First, it was time to check what she had gained from the so-called quest the system had given her.

<Emergency Quest (Path of Conflict exclusive): Kill your enemies (complete)
Rewards:
Unlocked: Mutation extensions (partially)
Achievement: Junior Reaper (upgradable): You are able to slightly sense weak points in your enemies.>

Sarah was very content with her rewards. Not only did she get a new achievement, which would most likely help her in battle, but she also got an addition to her Mutation specialization. Furthermore, the completion of the quest pushed her to level fifteen.

This meant that she had 35 Life Force points, but only twenty had been used so far. It was time to get even more freakish.

With some excitement, she opened up the mutation screen. A flurry of new options greeted her, and she didn't know where to start. But the new options in Organs and Processes were the most interesting:

<Mutation: Organs and Processes. Listing available options.

Acid Gland (not recommended, 4 LF): A gland located in the throat that produces highly corrosive acid. Can be spit out with moderate pressure.

Extension: Gaseous acid (1 LF)

Poison Gland (4 LF): A gland located in the throat that produces potent poison. Can be spit out with moderate pressure.

Extension: Gaseous poison (1 LF)

Poison Concentration Organ (not recommended, 7 LF): A special organ located underneath the heart. Collects highly toxic waste and concentrates it. The product can be injected into the bloodstream for a short burst of lethality.

For more options, increase your level and/or heighten your Life Force.>

That was really awesome. These mutations would be invisible but would give her fighting power a huge bonus. She was very tempted to immediately choose the Poison Concentration Organ, but she didn't have that many points left; she had to take a closer look at every option she had.

<Mutation: Skin. Listing available extensions to Dense Skin (0/3)

Oily Film (1 LF)

Contact Poison Film (1 LF)

Acidic Film (1 LF)

Magic Signature Suppression (2 LF)

Mutation: Bone structure. Listing available extensions to High Density Bones (0/3)

Predator Teeth (1 LF)

Poison Teeth (1 LF)

Vital Organ Shielding (2 LF)

Retractable Claws (2 LF)

Mutation: Muscles. Listing available extensions to Strengthened Fibers (0/3)

Short Fibers (explosive strength) (1 LF)

Medium-Length Fibers (strength + endurance) (1 LF)

Long Fibers (endurance) (1 LF)

Magic Power Reinforcement (2 LF)

Mutation: Brain, Nerve System, and Sensory Organs. Listing available options.

Protective Brain Webbing (2 LF): Protective webbing surrounding the brain. It cushions it and protects it from impacts.

Optimized Brain Structure (Battle) (not recommended) (6 LF): Optimized structure, focused on movement and decision-making.

Sturdy Nerve System (3 LF): Impacts and wounds will impede the functionality of the nerve system less.
Decentralized Nerve System (10 LF): Signals can be transmitted, as long as one nerve-string still connects the brain to the respective body parts.>

Those were some nice options. She thought she had a lot of Life Force points, but seeing that one of the options used up ten of them, what she had didn't seem like much anymore.

"But seriously, oily film? How gross do you want me to become?" she asked the system in a perplexed voice and looked at the extension options for her skin in disgust. Apart from the magic signature suppression, every other option would guarantee that no sane person would ever touch her again. No thanks.

But at least the optimized brain structure was exactly what she needed right now. It sounded like it would counter the deficit she gained from her nerve suppression skill.

Other than that, she wanted to increase her lethality. As tempting as the poison organ was, the immediate gain wasn't as apparent as the glands. Even more so because she could add an extension to make the poison or acid gaseous. She would be able to melt her enemies just by breathing.

But what else should she choose? Natural weapons such as claws and teeth were certainly useful. But what about the more exotic options? Or should she take the Magic Signature Suppression?

Ah, fuck it," she said, scratching her head in frustration. "I am not made to think too much about stuff like this. Give me the murder brain, the acid breath, and the claws and teeth."

Sarah smiled at the notification, telling her about the mutations that would start in a few seconds.

"Oh wait," she said in shock, her eyes widening. "Was it a good idea to do everything in one go?"

<Answering your question: No.>

"Why don't you ever tell me that beforehand?!" she screamed at the system in frustration. It was the first time it had actually answered her, and of course, it had to be something like this. But before she could swear at the system, she blacked out.

With a cough, Sarah woke up as suddenly as she lost consciousness. She was lying face down on the ground, and a lot of dirt had gotten into her mouth.

Her whole body hurt, and her brain felt like it was splitting apart. Not to mention the weird foreign feeling she had in her throat. She started to gag, and a stream of slightly turquoise gas exited her mouth. The dirt in her mouth immediately melted into goo, and the stone and dirt in front of her didn't fare any better.

A bubbling mess lay in front of her, which quickly vaporized and filled the air with an acrid stench.

"Awesome." Sarah coughed out the goo in her mouth and tried to suppress the reflex to gag even more. She would have to get this new gland under control before she accidentally melted one of her new friends. She was pretty sure that they wouldn't be too happy about that.

Her head was throbbing like it would burst any second, but she wanted to check on her body before she went to sleep.

With some hesitation, she held her hands in front of her face. Luckily, the worst hadn't come to pass. She still had her normal nails, but right underneath them, a small vertical slit could be seen.

She needed a few moments to figure out how to extract her claws. The small, bony claws slid out of her finger tips, and she shuddered in disgust. That was a really horrible and wrong feeling.

The claws were disappointingly small, but it made sense that they weren't too big, considering they were retractable. Where would long claws go without stiffening her fingers completely?

At least they were very, very sharp. She applied a little bit of pressure, and they cut through her dense skin like it was a thin leaf. They would rip normal skin to shreds in seconds.

As she had no possibility to check on her teeth visually, she had to make do with checking them out with her tongue.

"Ow!" she screamed in fright as a slight brush against her improved, sharp, and long canines ripped a wound in her tongue.

With an annoyed sigh, she tested her teeth with her fingers. It appeared that all her teeth had changed. The basic structure of her teeth was still the same, but her canines were far longer now, and each tooth had gained one or more very sharp tips.

As long as she didn't accidentally bite her own tongue, this was also a very good weapon.

Lastly, she opened up her status screen to see if her mutations had changed anything in her stats.

Details:
Level: 16
Name: Sarah Anna Fischer
Class: Nightmare
Race: Mutant
Status: Disoriented (50% higher magic power consumption. 80% slower reaction time)
HP: 200/235 **SP**: 40/205 **MP**: 100/390

Basic Stats:
Strength: 13
Dexterity: 20
Endurance: 15
Resistance: 10
Intelligence: 21
Force: 10

Special Stats:
Magic Power: 16
Life Force: 38
Mental Power: 23

In the beginning, she was elated to see that she had received six extra points in dexterity. And she had even leveled up from the mutations. But then she noticed with shock that the mutation of her brain had taken away one point from her intelligence.

"Oh, come on!" she shouted in the empty air. But, the system seemingly didn't want to answer her anymore. She let it go with a sigh.

The throbbing in her head got worse and worse after she concentrated on figuring out the changes in her body.

With a pained groan, she let herself sink to the ground. Even though she was in a lot of pain, she couldn't help but smile a toothy grin.

It didn't matter how strong this group of brutal men were. If they attacked her new friends again, she would rip them apart and melt their remains.

Very pleased with this outlook, she let herself glide into a deep slumber. And the whole time she was asleep, a happy smile was on her face.

CHAPTER TWENTY-THREE

Confrontation

Sarah woke up feeling like she had been hit on the head, just like she had the other day. She felt groggy and weak, and just wanted to go back to sleep to recuperate from her brain mutation, but her stomach was grumbling like it would soon start to digest itself. A look at her near-empty magic power told her that this was actually not that far from reality. With her constitution, empty magic power led to her digestion system consuming her own body. Pretty nasty way to go.

So, even though she felt like lying on the ground for at least another day, she had to stand up. Contrary to her expectations, she didn't feel any vertigo at all. Moving also felt entirely different than before.

She couldn't put a finger on it, but it definitely had to do with her mutated brain and raised dexterity. She felt like, up until now, she had been moving like a duck with no legs.

This strange but enticing feeling made her forget her muddled state, and she wanted to experience more. She ran to the exit of the cave and made her way down the steep cliff.

It was amazing. Climbing down the cliff was completely effortless. She felt every movement of her body and somehow knew exactly how to shift and position herself.

"That's definitely worth the lost point in intelligence," Sarah told herself, trying to somehow see the positive side of this particular position on her status screen.

She jumped down the last few meters and landed with a loud thump on the ground. She heard a shocked gasp and noticed a guy on the ground beside her, who had a basket full of mushrooms next to him.

Sarah gave the man a smile, which she thought should be very friendly. "Mind if I snag a few of those?"

Humming happily, she left the exhausted looking man behind while holding the basket of mushrooms in her hands.

"You mustn't eat them raw!" The man shouted behind her, but she just ignored him.

"So delicious," she mumbled with a full mouth, already gorging on the raw mushrooms.

Though she had already made the effort to collect some food, she went to the kitchen area anyway. She was looking forward to eating something cooked.

The people she encountered while walking through the camp had mixed reactions. Some seemed afraid of her and hurriedly moved out of her way. Others respectfully nodded, and some even came over to thank her for what she had done. It felt really good to be appreciated.

To her disappointment, it seemed like the last mealtime was already over and the kitchen team was taking a break. But not everyone.

Xavier was sitting next to a large pot made out of stone, heating it up with his bare hands.

Even though she wouldn't get something cooked right now, she would get something else.

"Hi, Xavier," she greeted the lanky man, standing directly behind him.

He shot up with a high-pitched screech and nearly toppled over the big pot.

"H-h-hi, S-Sarah," he said, stuttering and trying to back away. "You see, I h-have something important to do. See you around."

With these words, he turned around, but Sarah grabbed him by his collar and held him in place.

"Where are you going, my friend?" she asked the gagging Xavier, who was dangling in her grip. "You still have to show me how to do your fire thingy."

She put down the struggling man, who rubbed his sore throat with a despondent look on his face. "Can I go after I show you?" he asked with uncertainty in his voice.

"Sure!" Sarah promised and put an arm around his shoulders.

Xavier surrendered to his fate and led her to a pile of wood some distance away from the kitchen area. He took one large piece and laid it down in a circle of stones.

He sat down with a sigh and held his hands above the wood. "What do you want to know?" he asked in a lifeless voice.

"So, I already know that you really wanted to make fire. Is it always necessary to have a strong wish to be able to do something to gain a specialization?" Sarah asked.

"According to Tobias, yes. But I am really no expert in this area. I just know how it was for me, and it is just as you described." Xavier said, a bit more lively. He seemed to like to talk about himself. "And when I use the skill, I kind of . . . channel the magic power through my hands outside of my body. I also change the . . . um, how to say this." He scratched his head and squinted his eyes in concentration. "I guess you can say I change the . . . structure of the magic power somehow. Before I use the skill, the magic power is raw, like before you cook something. And with the use of the skill, I refine the magic and change what it does. Does this make sense to you?"

Sarah thought about it for a moment, then nodded in understanding. She knew this feeling very well from her invasion skill.

"Now show me," she demanded and fully concentrated on her magic sense. A second layer of reality seemed to superimpose itself over her vision, and she began to feel the errant energy around her.

Xavier nodded and started using his skill. Sarah could see that something was happening. Colorless energy gathered in his hands and began to press out of his palms, taking on a dim shade of red. The energy then disappeared, and instead, the air distorted, and the wood started to heat up.

When the wood started burning, Xavier got ready to stand up, but Sarah grabbed his arm and held him back. "Do it again."

Xavier held his hands up with a sigh.

She made him do it over and over again, but she wasn't able to understand what exactly happened with his magic power. She tried a few times but only managed to gather a miniscule amount of magic power in her palms.

"Can I go now?" Xavier asked in a weak and raspy voice, after having used his skill for the twentieth time. He looked pretty pale and had difficulty staying upright.

Just as Sarah wanted to demand that he do it one last time, another voice interrupted her.

"You can go now, Xavier. The kitchen team will need you later."

Sarah looked to her right and saw Andrew walking toward them. Xavier didn't wait. He scrambled to his feet and staggered away as fast as he could.

"You can't just do things like this to the people here," Andrew said, frowning.

"But you can do to them what you want, it seems, including ordering me around every time you see me," Sarah retorted, standing up to face him.

Andrew flinched and averted his gaze. "This is different—" he started but was interrupted by Sarah.

"How is this any different? Explain to me how you think what you are doing is okay."

Andrew sighed and rubbed his tired eyes. "Listen, why don't we talk about it some other time? I have—"

"Now listen, fish-face." Sarah had interrupted him again. She wasn't going to listen to him make excuses again.

"Fish-face?" Andrew asked, flustered, but she didn't care to answer.

"You are super sketchy. Objectively, it seems like you are helping everyone, but you are manipulating everyone's emotions behind their backs. Give me a good reason not to believe that you are some power-hungry pervert."

Andrew opened and closed his mouth a few times, unintentionally giving his new nickname credibility.

His expressionless face seemed to crack when he sighed and sat down on the ground. His shoulders were hanging down, as if a large weight was pressing down on him.

"Everybody knows what I am doing. They trust me, and I only use this ability to calm them down or to help us get through difficult situations."

"And do you only use it for that?"

Andrew looked up at her, a pained expression in his eyes. "I'd love to say yes, but honestly? Sometimes I use my skill without knowing it, like when I want someone to feel a certain way, it activates itself. Apart from that, I have another skill that is always active—passively influencing the people around me. And I can't turn this one off."

He held up his hand, just as Sarah wanted to say something in response. "I know that this is not a justification for doing it. I am doing my best to avoid situations like this. But I am only human. How am I supposed to just . . ."

He looked at his hands, trying to somehow find the answers he was looking for. "How am I supposed to lead these people? How can I avoid abusing my skills? And these questions only matter if we survive winter."

Sarah looked down at the slumped-down figure before her. Andrew looked so small and frail. If she hadn't known it was him, she would have never recognized him.

Sarah sat down next to Andrew, who was still looking at his open hands.

"I know that these are not the answers you want, but I honestly don't have any good ones for you." Andrew let out a joyless laugh. "I don't even have the answers for myself." He hesitated for a moment, then let out a small chuckle. "You know, this is the first time I've told someone about these thoughts of mine. And, it honestly feels good. You are the first person I met who doesn't expect me to be a perfect person and to have all the answers."

For some time, they just sat silently next to each other until Sarah punched Andrew in the shoulder.

He shouted in surprise and held his aching shoulder. "What was that for?!"

Sarah looked at him with squinted eyes while rubbing her chin. "You see, I first thought you were just a sly goody two shoes. But you seem to honestly care about the people who trust you. So, now you are a slightly likable fish-face."

"Thank you . . . I guess," Andrew said with a crooked smile. "But, why fish-face?"

"I cannot help you if you don't know for yourself," Sarah answered with a sigh, shaking her head.

"You are very strange; you know that, right?"

"Oh yes, I know that."

The two of them looked at each other before laughing out loud. They laughed a little too much for a situation that wasn't very funny to begin with. They'd both had a lot of tension built up inside them, and the laughter lessened their burden.

When their laughter had died down, Sarah reached out a hand to Andrew. "Let's be friends."

Andrew nodded with a slight smile and shook her hand. "I'd love to."

"So, now that we have that out of the way," Sarah said, pulling him closer. With their faces very close now, a blush crept over Andrew's face. "Show me your status screen."

"My . . . my what?" Andrew stuttered while trying to gain some distance from her.

"Show me your status screen."

"I don't . . ."

"Status screen."

"Can't we talk about . . ."

"Status. Screen."

Andrew gave up his efforts to free himself of her grip and sighed. "Alright, alright. But please let go of my hand. It feels like you want to squeeze the blood out of it."

Sarah let him go, and she saw another person's status screen for the first time.

Details:
Level: 9
Name: Andrew Gruber
Class: None
Race: Human
Status: Equilibrium (Permanent)
HP: 120/120 **SP**: 30/50 **MP**: 110/130

Achievements:
- Medicine Can Be Poisonous

Affinities:
Soul (High) Body (Low)

Specializations:
- Soul (2/3)
  - Equilibrium
  - Domination
- Body (1/1)
  - Adaptation

Basic Stats:
Strength: 6
Dexterity: 9
Endurance: 4
Resistance: 4
Intelligence: 26
Force: 11

Special Stats:
Magic Power: 9
Soul Power: 11
Life Force: 4

Active Skills:
- Emotion Manipulation (Equilibrium): With moderate Magic Power consumption, you are able to influence another person's emotions to a certain degree.
- Emotion Overdrive (Domination): You are able to put another being's emotions into overdrive. This has the potential to permanently cripple their mind.

Passive Skills:
- Equilibrium (Equilibrium): You are unable to feel extreme emotions and are always in a state of balance. In a localized area around you, people will be slightly influenced by this skill.
- Poison Resistance (Adaption): You are slightly resistant to various poisons. Higher effectiveness if the substance is in your digestive system.
- Fast Recovery (Adaption): You need less sleep and rest to recover from mental and physical fatigue. Regeneration is also slightly increased while sleeping.
- Struggle (Conditional Passive)

Sarah looked up from the status screen after studying it for some time. Andrew stood there and scratched his head in embarrassment.

The basic stat Force that had confused her for so long finally made sense to her. While she only got more points in this category after reaching level ten, Andrew already had eleven Force points. So logically, it must have something to do with the soul. Or, in this sense, with the strength of the soul. Whatever that meant.

Sarah forcefully ignored the fact that Andrew's intelligence was a few points higher than hers and moved closer to him.

"Domination sounds really badass. You've got some nice skills there."

"You don't think it sounds too . . . evil?" Andrew asked her with an atypically insecure voice.

"Ohhh yes, it definitely sounds evil," Sarah said with a wide smile, which prompted Andrew to press his lips together in frustration. "But that's not bad. I seriously doubt you would come far in this world without having the means to scare the shit out of everyone who wants to harm you." Sarah explained to him. For some reason, though, he still didn't seem all that happy with her view. "And I also don't trust people who are only good. There is no bright side without a dark one."

Andrew finally smiled and patted her shoulder. "Thanks . . . I guess. I feel a little less like a hidden villain now. Or no, scratch that. I don't feel bad about it anymore."

"That's my boy!" Sarah shouted and slapped his back so hard that he nearly fell over.

"You really have to work on that," Andrew said, reprimanding her while coughing and wheezing.

"You're fine," Sarah said absentmindedly, looking for her mushrooms. But, they were nowhere to be seen. That sneaky Xavier must have taken them when she wasn't looking.

"You can't just . . . You know what? It doesn't matter." Andrew resigned himself and looked at her with a complicated expression. "I was actually looking for you before all this. I need to ask for your help. We are in a really desperate situation, and no one else is as strong as you are."

"Let's hear it," Sarah said, intrigued.

"I want to ask you to find Kevin and his men. And I want you to kill them."

CHAPTER TWENTY-FOUR

Overload

Andrew looked Sarah in the eyes, anxious about how she would react to his request.

The scary-looking woman stared at him with a troubled expression for some time and seemed to ponder his request. Just as Andrew opened his mouth to speak again, Sarah nodded.

"I guess I'm the best option for this job. I cannot help but feel kind of dirty. Do you really think this is the best choice?" Sarah asked him with a little hope in her voice.

"Remember how the guy we interrogated reacted. Remember what he told us? They are not humans anymore. They are animals," Andrew said. He didn't even see for himself what the man had described. Just imagining the cruelties committed by this group turned his stomach. "They will find us. And I don't want to expose my . . . no, our people, to this risk."

"That's true . . ." Sarah relented and let out a loud sigh. Then she smiled. "I just wish we could leave them be, but I guess we would be doing humanity a favor. Especially the women."

Andrew nodded and laid his hand on her shoulders. "I know it is a lot to ask, but you are the deadliest person we have here. And Alex is too . . . unstable for this job."

With some worry, Andrew thought about the once-stoic man who'd become more and more violent and hot-tempered.

"I understand," Sarah told him and patted his hand, which was still on her shoulder. "I guess it will take some more time before I can rest a little. Make sure to cook me a feast when I get back."

"I'll even cook it personally. I can't guarantee it'll taste great, though."

"That's fine. After what I ate in the beginning, everything tastes divine." Sarah gave him a crooked smile and turned to leave.

"Can we somehow support you? Do you need any people to go with you, or food, or—"

"It's fine. Honestly, apart from Alex and Melissa, everyone here looks like they'd snap apart if I so much as breathe too hard next to them."

Andrew was offended. But it was true. And it showed that she was starting to care about them.

"Take care of yourself!" Andrew shouted when she was already some distance away.

"Don't shit yourself!" she called back, and Andrew chuckled a little.

He watched her walk away until she disappeared into the dense forest. It seemed very quiet and lonely now that this rude and loud person wasn't around. So, Andrew found something to keep himself busy.

It was time for him to get to level ten. Tobias had already managed it, but he was secretive about it. He didn't want to share anything about his gains before looking into them himself. So Andrew would have to see for himself what it would be like.

He would go into their off-limits cave. Alex and Tobias had scouted it out and noted that this cave had a stronger concentration of ambient magic power. Because of their horrible experience with the crazed animals around the spatial oddity, they didn't want to take a risk. Who knew how people would react when they were subjected to it for a long period of time.

But Andrew was confident that this was exactly what he needed for his break-through. Since Sarah told them what they needed to feel in order to break through, he had tried numerous times to do so. But he had failed miserably until now.

Every time he thought he was close to feeling the presence of the barrier inside him, it got away like a slippery fish. So, he theorized that with the help of a surplus of magic power, this barrier might be easier to find.

As the cave was some distance away from their camp, nobody saw him as he entered it. He felt kind of guilty because he hadn't talked to Tobias about this, but in the end, Tobias was just as new to all of this as he was.

Everything was normal at first, but the deeper he went inside the off-limits cave, the more he began to feel the chaotic, ambient energy. It really was very dense here.

He thought it might even be possible that the energy was denser than it had been around the oddity where they found Sarah. Luckily, there weren't any animals down here, or else they would have a big problem.

When Andrew started to feel like he would burst from the surplus energy inside him, he sat down on the dirty ground. It was so dark this deep into the cave that he accidentally bumped his head quite painfully on a wall.

Andrew shuffled around for some time until he found a more or less comfortable position to concentrate.

He closed his eyes and began to concentrate on the world within himself. Like always, he only saw the back of his eyelids in the beginning, but more and more, he started to feel and see the magic power.

Normally, it was a small trickle, which was barely visible. But now, it felt more like a blocked river, which tried to burst the obstruction out of the way.

He followed this feeling until he found what was holding it back. And to his surprise, it was different from what he had imagined. He envisioned the blockage as some kind of wall he had to break through. But it was in fact more of a subconscious resistance against the magic power that wanted to flow into his body.

So, he mentally relaxed himself and let it flow. The resistance was gone, as if it had never been there in the first place. For a moment, Andrew was elated. The magic power vigorously coursed through his body, and he felt like he could rip trees from their roots with his bare hands.

But soon, the energy got to be too much. His body felt stuffed, and it became painful. With a coughing groan, Andrew hurriedly got up on his feet and began staggering out of the cave.

His sense of balance was completely off, and he saw double. He stumbled and fell to the ground, but he didn't stay put. With a ragged breath, he pulled himself out of the forsaken cave. All the while, he felt like not only his body but his very being were being ripped apart.

When he finally got out of the cave, the feeling got a little bit better, and he was able to walk again. But he was still in a lot of pain.

"Melissa," he mumbled and focused on the only person who could help him.

He stumbled along the stone wall, not sure if he was walking in the right direction. His body was pulsating with every step he took. He felt like he would shatter at any moment.

<Warning: Magic Power overload, your body is in danger of breaking down. Warning: Through your skill, suppressed emotions have accumulated and are in danger of breaking out.

You are in mortal danger. S*5rching for opti?ns.>

The system warning didn't register with Andrew right away, but even without the warning, he knew all too well that something was seriously wrong with him.

He suddenly felt himself being lifted from the ground and heard dull screams around him. He saw a few figures through his waning sight that were carrying him somewhere.

"Melissa," he called out, but he wasn't sure if anyone heard or understood him.

<Yo(a/& i8 &%*)^ danger. S6"%78d fpa (Uwnksd>

In his dizzy state, he wondered if the system had somehow broken or if what he was seeing meant that he was too far gone to make sense of it.

By now, he didn't even notice what was happening around him. He was floating in an endless space of pain, with only nothingness surrounding him.

Somebody was talking to him, but he understood nothing.

Suddenly, extreme pain erupted in his chest. He roared but couldn't hear himself.

And as suddenly as the pain had come, it disappeared again, and with it, the stuffy feeling inside him.

"Hold him down!" he heard a female voice shout somewhere to his left.

"Melissa?" he asked in a hoarse voice, finally able to hear something again.

"Can you tell me what happened, Andrew?" she asked immediately, while laying her hands on his chest.

"I . . . went . . ." Andrew croaked, but he couldn't get much more out because of his sore throat.

"Shit!" Melissa shouted, but calmed down again. "Listen, you had way too much magic power in your body. I have no idea how, but I managed to let it out. But . . ."

She hesitated and put her mouth closer to his ear. "There is . . . something in your soul. Like a big lump of darkness. And it is spreading. It is damaging your soul, Andrew. Do you know what it is?"

"Emotions . . . suppressed . . ." Andrew croaked out, happy that he got the general message through.

Melissa looked at him for a moment with a confused face, until she lit up with understanding.

"Hold him down!" she commanded the people surrounding them with a powerful tone. Andrew was pressed down by heavy weights.

"What . . . ?" Andrew was afraid of what would happening next.

"I have to let it out somehow, Andrew. It is destroying you from the inside. But . . . it might hurt. Stay strong," Melissa told him while pressing his shoulder gently, and then she closed her eyes.

Her hands lay on his chest, but he could feel them reaching deeper inside him, directly into his very being. It was a horrible experience.

She rummaged through his soul for a few moments, which nearly made Andrew faint again. Then she caught a hold of something. Searing pain shot through him as she gripped a part of him in her metaphysical grasp.

"Don't . . ." Andrew wanted to warn her, realizing what it was she held. It was what the system had warned him about. Every emotion that his skills had suppressed until now had somehow sedimented into his very soul.

They were mostly horrible emotions like fear, panic, terror, and dread. And Melissa was about to pull all of this out of him.

"Are you ready?" Melissa asked him in a loud voice, but Andrew couldn't answer anymore. His voice had given out.

"Hold him down! I'll take it out in one, two, three!"

She ripped her hands off his chest, along with the part of her that had rummaged through his soul. And the lump of darkness inside him spilled outside.

First, nothing happened, and Andrew thought that maybe nothing would happen. But then he felt it. A scream from deep within his primal self escaped his lips, carrying with it immeasurable terror.

With his last bit of sanity, Andrew heard everyone around him scream just like he had.

And then everything went black.

CHAPTER TWENTY-FIVE

The Purge Begins

Sarah silently ran through the forest, by now so used to her stealth that not even animals sensitive to noise noticed her until she was right next to them.

She was running along the river in the direction of the camp where the scum supposedly resided. She had been traveling for nearly a full day, but she hadn't seen any activity.

"Did this dirtbag lie to us?" she murmured, while looking for any tracks humans might leave behind.

Frustrated, she decided to climb a tall tree to get a better look at her surroundings. With quite some shock, she noticed that not only her fingers but also her toes had gained claws. She felt more and more like a feral animal.

The claws were extremely useful for climbing trees. It didn't even matter anymore when there were no low-hanging branches. She could run up a tree trunk like a feline predator.

Sarah gracefully climbed the tree in no time and sat down on the highest branch, which was surprisingly able to hold her weight.

"Wow," Sarah said in a flat voice. "I see a forest, and a river. That was really helpful."

She sighed and was getting ready to climb down again when she noticed something out of the corner of her eye. She turned her head around but couldn't see anything.

"Strange," she muttered, furrowing her brows. After thinking about it for a moment, she focused with her magic power and was rewarded with the location of the dirtbags.

Some distance away, there was a cluster of dense magic power, which reminded her of the camp by the caves. "I guess I have to get to work."

She was quite nervous. Sure, she had killed people before, even one of them in cold blood. But, it was different attacking an entire group of violent scum. She didn't really want to think about what they would do to her, if they managed to capture her.

This thought made her shudder in disgust but also steeled her resolve.

Like a ghost, she rushed through the forest toward her destination. It wasn't long before she began hearing the sounds of people busy with work. Unlike the group in the caves, no one seemed to talk here.

Before she moved closer, she smeared her unusually pale skin with dirt.

"Ugh, that's so gross," she murmured in disgust as she covered herself in the slimy mud. She really had no other choice, as it was still daytime. She pulled a wriggling caterpillar out of her hair and ate it before she moved even closer to the camp.

She somehow imagined horrible scenes of mutilated people lying on the ground. All of this, with the dirtbags doing horrible things to women out in public. But, the bustling crowd of people didn't look all that different from the one at the caves.

The most glaring difference was that they were even thinner. They looked so starved that Sarah expected them to fall over at any moment. And they were also barely dressed.

The other stark difference was that the overall mood was dark and ominous. Everyone was silent and appeared apathetic. They were doing various odd jobs, from cooking to building tents and working on equipment.

In the middle of them all sat the only well-nourished and armored man. He watched over them like a hawk and was chewing on some dried meat.

Sarah watched them until night fell, but nothing out of the ordinary happened, apart from the armored man slapping a few of the women on their butts.

When the sun went down, everyone breathed a sigh of relief and took a pathetically small portion of food from the cooking team.

They wolfed it down in an instant and went into different tents to sleep immediately afterward.

The armored man held one of the women back, who wanted to go to sleep. She struggled a little, but when the man hit her, she went with him, her entire body shivering. They left for the woods, where they disappeared.

Sarah struggled within herself, not really knowing if she should do something right now. She knew that she had around twelve opponents. Her initial plan was to whittle down their numbers before she confronted their leader.

She had hesitated too long. The armored man came back alone, stretching out with a content smile on his face.

He walked into the middle of camp again, hesitated for a moment, and then began to walk in Sarah's direction.

Sarah panicked, but the man didn't seem alert. So, she climbed a tree in silence and watched.

The man went some distance into the woods and started peeing with a happy sigh. This was her opportunity. But first . . . she would wait until he finished.

She sneaked behind the man, who froze in the middle of pulling his pants up. He turned around with an angry look on his face, only to look Sarah straight in the eyes.

A look of utter horror appeared on his face, and he had opened his mouth to scream. But Sarah shut his mouth with so much force that she heard a few of his teeth shatter.

The man was knocked out cold and fell to the ground. Sarah didn't wait. She snatched the unconscious man and ran away.

After she was a good distance away, she found a tall rock formation with some shrubbery on top of it. With some effort, she managed to climb it with the man slung over her shoulders. This was the perfect hiding place. Close enough to the camp but out of hearing distance. And on top of that, the dense shrubbery hid her well.

After she made sure that no one was around them, she started slapping the unconscious man in the face. The shattered teeth crumbled completely, and he woke up with a muffled groan. He coughed out blood and the broken pieces of his teeth.

"My teeth!" he shouted in horror, picking up the pieces from the ground.

"No biggie," Sarah told him in a soothing voice and laid her hands on his shoulders. "You won't be needing them anymore."

The man looked up at her, terrified. He apparently wanted to scream but was only able to open and close his mouth like a fish on land.

After a few moments, the man realized he was able to defend himself. He pulled out a crude stone knife and stabbed at her. Sarah evaded his clumsy attack without much effort, grabbed his elbow, and shattered it in her grip. The man screamed and tried to free himself from her. But Sarah didn't budge.

"No can do. You first have to tell me a few things before you can go," Sarah said with a smile.

"You will let me go when I tell you what I know?" he asked with a shaky voice, fully ignoring her earlier comment about his teeth.

"Of course I will let you go," Sarah assured him, pulling him closer. "I am not a monster."

The man spilled the beans faster than she was able to process anything. She didn't learn a lot of new information, but a few things were quite helpful.

Right now, only six of the twelve dirtbags were in the camp, the rest out looking for new "material," as they called it. But still, five people were a lot to go up against. Especially when Kevin was as strong as described. And the other six could return at any time.

As she watched the shivering man in front of her, she gained some inspiration.

"Fear," she mumbled with a hard face, knocking the man out cold before he could say anything else. "Those dirtbags will get to know fear."

She grabbed the unconscious man and climbed down the rock formation again. When she was right next to the camp again, she began looking for a fitting place.

After some time, she found what she was looking for—a tree with some sharp pieces of wood sticking out of the trunk.

Sarah gathered her resolve and lifted the unconscious man high in the air. With a grunt, she slammed him down on the trunk. The sharp wooden remains penetrated his body with ease, and a fountain of blood streamed from him.

To her surprise, he didn't die immediately. He even woke up and began screaming in a weak voice. Panicked, Sarah punched him in the face again. This time, though, she couldn't rein in her strength, and his head caved in with a sickening crunch.

She immediately turned around and gagged a little, but she had no time to lose. She heard some shouts coming from the camp, and she knew she didn't have much time left. She darted away as fast as she could.

Not long after, she heard angry and fearful shouts coming from behind her. She had done something really gruesome and it had the intended effect. In the end, her class was called "Nightmare." So, that's what she would deliver.

Sarah heard hurried footsteps and heavy breathing in front of her. With a sad smile, she readied herself to make another spectacle.

She sneaked into a bush and waited for the man to come closer. When he was right next to her, she got ready to punch him in the face and knock him out.

But the man reacted lightning fast. Before Sarah realized what was happening, the man had taken out a stone knife and attempted to disembowel her.

Luckily, her dense skin lessened the impact, but he still got her. With a shocked face, the man tried to pull the knife out again, but it was stuck inside her tensed-up muscles.

With a pained groan, Sarah grabbed the throat of the horrified man and started pressing. He struggled for some time but fell limp soon afterward. She dropped his unconscious form and pulled the knife out of her midsection with a grunt and threw it away. Sarah quickly checked her wound and focused on her next move.

After some thought, she crushed the man's neck with her hand, and her face distorted in disgust. At least he wouldn't have to go through this alive. They were dirtbags, but she wouldn't put them through unnecessary pain.

She dragged his lifeless body near the campfire and then used her new acid gland.

The turquoise fog quickly covered him. The sizzling sound and acrid smell told her that it was working. She didn't really want to see the aftermath, so she turned around and left the scene. Maybe she would be able to find the woman who had been left alone somewhere in the woods.

Not long after Sarah fled, the man's body was found by her three remaining adversaries. They shouted in anger and horror while looking fearfully into the dark and silent forest.

They felt like a demon had come to get them.

CHAPTER TWENTY-SIX

Not as It Seems

Sarah was fucked. As long as there were only three guys remaining, she could take them out without much issue, but the morning after her attack, the six other guys came back. And they somehow seemed to be able to communicate with each other over great distances.

The guy her new group had captured and tortured came to mind. In her opinion, it was unlikely he had sent some sort of warning to his camp. They had been way too relaxed for that.

Now they were on high alert. They took shifts guarding their camp and only went hunting in groups of four. Sarah was somewhat confident that she could take four on at the same time, but she didn't want to risk getting into a pincer fight if the others got wind of it.

She also couldn't find the woman who had been left behind by the dirtbag. She must have gone back to the camp during the course of the fights. Sarah wasn't sure about that, though, as everyone in the camp looked kind of similar with their haggard and apathetic faces.

Sarah had been staking out the camp for the last few days, and every now and then, she left claw marks on trees and mutilated corpses of various animals around the campsite. The dirtbags were visibly spooked by it. They were so tense and tired by now that they didn't even have the energy to molest the women in the camp.

They could only stare with wide eyes into the forest, flinching at every rustle of the leaves. Sarah still hadn't been able to catch a glance at their leader. He always stayed in the biggest tent, and only his hand was visible when he let someone inside.

At one point, Sarah considered throwing stones at the group to freak them out some more, but when she picked up a stone and held it in the air, it somehow managed to fall on her foot.

"What the hell?" she cursed, not realizing what she'd done.

<Bug detected. Mutation in the brain caused loss in ability to throw. Searching for options.>

Sarah looked at the status screen with an open mouth and a vein popping up on her forehead. She had to wait a few minutes until the system spoke to her again.

<Solutions found:
- Live with it.
- Get angry, and then live with it.

Please choose carefully.>

While Sarah tried her best to suppress the furious scream that was coming up her throat, the vein on her forehead seemed it would pop any second. She pointed her finger at the screen with burning eyes and insulted the system until she felt somewhat satisfied.

She didn't know why the system had shown her the first option in the first place.

While shaking her head in resignation, she went back to observing the camp.

Luckily for her, some of the guards fell asleep for a while. They were snoring without a care in the world until one by one they snapped awake again with panicked looks on their faces. Sarah was attempting to use these small windows of time to kill them one by one.

At least that was the plan. A very risky plan. If she was caught, they would all attack her at once. No matter how strong she was, Sarah wasn't confident fighting against nine men at once.

So guerrilla warfare and fear it was.

She waited another two days, until the dirtbags were so tired that they sometimes even fell asleep while standing.

And then an opportunity presented itself. One of the guards walked around the camp, believing that his partner would cover his back. His partner, on the other hand, was sleeping soundly at his post. Sarah waited in a bush on the edge of the camp, watching the guard get closer and closer.

She could hear his tense breathing and see a thin layer of sweat covering his forehead. He held his big wooden club so tightly in his hands that thick veins bulged on his forearms.

Sarah held her breath when he was only a few steps away. He abruptly stood still, looking around him in alarm. Sarah knew that she had to act now.

When he looked behind him for a moment, Sarah jumped out of the bush and punched him in the throat.

Contrary to her expectations, his neck wasn't crushed by her punch. He spat out a mouthful of blood, and a dark bruise began forming on his throat, but he was still able to breathe.

He stumbled backward and tried to scream, but only a coarse and quiet sound could escape his lips.

Sarah swore and pounced on him again. The man desperately hit her with his club, but she deflected it with her forearm.

Ignoring the sharp pain, she ripped his club away and was upon him. The man looked at her in utter horror as she punched him in the face and made him stumble. But he still didn't die. He was absurdly sturdy.

The man still tried to call for help when Sarah changed her tactics. Her tail shot forward into his neck. The sharp tip barely penetrated his skin, but it was enough. She pumped him full of her poison, and she saw his skin blacken around the sting mark.

It took only a few seconds for the man to start frothing bloody bubbles from his mouth and for his whole body to spasm. His skin began to darken, and he was bleeding from his orifices. It was a gruesome spectacle.

Sarah was horrified for a moment because of the unexpected potency of her poison. She knew that she had some pretty horrible stuff in her tail, but this was beyond her expectations.

She soon snapped out of it and disappeared into the forest again.

When she heard the horrified screams coming from the camp, she couldn't suppress an evil grin. It was strangely exciting to play the invisible monster.

Sarah lay low for another day after this because the dirtbags were on edge again. Even though they looked more tired than before, they wouldn't close their bloodshot eyes again.

Sarah had to wait two whole days until she saw another chance. Much like the first time, one of the guards started to fall asleep while the other guard walked around the edge of the camp.

She sneaked up on the poor sap and waited, like the first time. The guy seemed to be pretty nervous. Sweat was pouring down his face, like there was a river flowing over his head. He was constantly looking toward certain tents in the camp instead of the forest.

He also seemed familiar for some reason. After a few moments of thinking, Sarah noticed that this was the guy who was sleeping while she had killed the other one. She couldn't put a finger on it, but something seemed fishy.

She already wanted to back off when she heard rustling sounds around her. They were coming from all sides.

"Shit!" Sarah snarled in anger over her own stupidity. How had she not seen it coming? In any case, she would reduce their numbers as long as they were far apart.

With this conclusion, she jumped out of her hiding spot and directly onto the shit-scared guard.

He was screaming his lungs out, but Sarah couldn't care less. She had to kill him quickly and make a spectacle of it.

So, she slid her claws out and began slashing at the poor sap. His screams soon turned into gurgling sounds. She'd probably ripped open his lungs in the few seconds she assaulted him.

"Stop!" she heard a man with an imposing voice shout behind her.

Sarah held onto the near-dead man, lifted him up, and sank her teeth into his neck, all while looking the man in the eye who had shouted at her. She sucked the man's magic power from him, not leaving a smidgeon of energy behind, while his skin grew even paler. Soon after that, he stopped breathing.

Sarah let the body fall to the ground while trying to ignore the fact that she had human blood in her mouth. She smiled at the man who had spoken to her with her bloodied teeth, and he was visibly shaken, but not as much as the other guys around her. Every one of the dirtbags was shivering like leaves in the wind. Two of them had even wet their pants.

The guy who had spoken to her was most likely their leader. He tried to put up a hard front, but Sarah could clearly see his fear. He was walking closer to her and was flexing his massive muscles while holding a giant club in his hand. Upon further inspection, it was closer to a tree trunk than anything else.

"You will die at my hands, monster!" he shouted in a thundering voice while swinging the trunk in a threatening manner. Sarah knew that she should be intimidated by this show of insane strength, but for some reason, something was strange about this scene.

The men around her seemed to find their spirits again, and were starting to cheer on their giant leader.

"I will strike you down with this massive club!" he shouted again and started walking faster.

Right at this moment, Sarah noticed some kind of incongruity in the man's appearance. It looked like two different images were superimposed on top of each other.

One image was that of the hulking man with the tree trunk in his hand. The other was of a lanky, hunched-over man holding a rather sharp stick.

Sarah felt a sting in her head, and her horns vibrated. The image of the hulking man was shattered. Now she only saw the hunched-over man, shouting with a voice quivering in fear.

An evil smile crept over her face as she realized what was going on. This guy was somehow able to create illusions.

Not hesitating any longer, she leapt forward and stabbed her right hand into the man's stomach. Her hand, aided by her claws, effortlessly dug into the unprotected belly of the man, and he let out an agonized yelp.

He looked at her in utter confusion, not realizing what was going on. "How?" he asked her before Sarah lifted him up with a roar, grabbed him with both hands, and ripped him apart. Her muscles ached horribly afterward. She had overexerted herself to show the men her absurd strength.

She tried her best to ignore the gruesome scene beneath her and looked at the other men with an insane smile.

For a few moments, they looked at her with open mouths. As if they had decided the same thing simultaneously, the men all began running away in different directions.

Sarah didn't dare follow them. While she was strong, she wouldn't dare fight that many of these guys. Even though she could take a few with her to the grave, someone might be able to land a deadly blow. She would have to hunt them down one by one later.

When she was sure that the guys had run away, she tried to wipe away all the blood that had landed on her. She shot a quick glance at the mutilated guy on the ground and immediately regretted it. That was a sight she wouldn't forget for a while.

With her complicated feelings, Sarah turned toward the camp. A crowd of utterly terrified people stood some distance away from her. And right at the front, there stood an absurdly beautiful woman who would make even Melissa look like a formless rock.

She had flowing red hair that looked like fire in the wind and a slender body with pale and flawless skin that sparkled in the moonlight. It was simply unreal. It came to Sarah's mind that someone in the caves had gained the ability to make himself more beautiful. This was most likely something similar.

The woman ignored the gore on the ground and stepped toward Sarah with a wide smile.

"Thank you so much for liberating us!" she shouted, beaming at Sarah with tears in her eyes. "You don't know how we have suffered because of them!"

Sarah looked into the teary face of the woman, and an intense desire to protect her and make her happy overcame her.

The woman was still smiling at her when Sarah slapped her so hard in the face that the sound echoed over the silent clearing.

CHAPTER TWENTY-SEVEN

Out of Control

Andrew woke up with a horrible headache and a fuzzy mind. It took some time before he was able to orient himself and realize that he was awake.

He looked at the dimly lit ceiling and noticed that he had to be in one of the caves. His memory of what had happened was unclear at best.

He sat up with a groan, and his body was stiff. He looked around the silent cave and saw a row of leaves around him, with Melissa lying in one of them. He was in the nursery.

He leaned over, all of his joints cracking from not moving for a long time, and gently touched Melissa's shoulder. She immediately jumped up, now awake, and looked at him with a fearful expression for a moment and laid a hand on her heart.

"By the Creator, Andrew. You scared the shit out of me." She looked at him with a discerning eye, and a little smile appeared on her face. "But it's good to see you awake. How do you feel?"

"I feel . . . okay," Andrew answered her in a coarse voice and coughed. His throat was utterly dried out.

Melissa gave him some water, and he accepted it with gratitude. After wetting his throat, he was able to speak again. "What happened? How long have I been out?"

Melissa looked at him with a complicated expression, and she nervously began fumbling with her blond hair. "There was an . . . accident. Something happened to you. And when I wanted to heal you . . ." She paused for a moment, and a look of horror crossed her face. "I pulled something out of you. I cannot describe it other than to say it was the essence of fear and despair. I activated my emotion suppression skill in time, but . . . Derek and Till weren't so lucky."

Andrew felt a sinking feeling in his chest, guilt overcoming him. His memories started to come back. How he tried to break through to level ten with the help of the higher magic density in their off-limits cave and how it went horribly wrong.

Andrew sighed heavily and rested his face in his hands. "What happened to them?"

"They went mad," Melissa replied in a quiet voice. "It's like they lost their conscious minds and are only acting on instinct. They are not dangerous, just . . . more like animals than humans."

When Andrew didn't respond, Melissa continued explaining. "We have isolated them in one of the caves, far away from the others. It's too difficult to let them live with us. I try every day to somehow heal them, but without success."

The guilt that had been building up inside of him reached new heights. Two of his people had lost their sanity because of his greed.

"What will happen to me now?" Andrew asked, ready to accept any verdict.

"Nothing," Melissa replied.

"What do you mean, nothing?" Andrew exploded and sprang to his feet. "I more or less erased the minds of two of our people! How can nothing happen to me?"

"Because this group needs you." Melissa's voice was calm, but her hands were trembling due to his outburst. "I told the people that you three went into the off-limits cave to investigate. And that your minds got hurt by it, just like the animals close to the oddity."

Andrew deflated and sank onto the bed of leaves again. "That's not right. You shouldn't have done this for me," Andrew said with an empty voice.

"Not right?" Now it was Melissa's turn to explode, and her hands were shaking even more. "I cleaned up this mess! Not for you, but for all of us! What do you think would happen to this group if they knew you had the power to cripple minds? What would happen to us without a leader to hold us together?"

Andrew could only stare at this otherwise calm and gentle person in front of him while she was screaming.

"And yes, you shouldn't have done what you did. But how is this any more your fault than mine? I was the one to rip out these emotions! I was the one who released it! So don't come at me with your self-pity. Deal with it and do your best." Her voice had calmed by the end of her outburst. She also carried guilt with her.

"I'm sorry," Andrew said with a downcast face, and Melissa nodded slightly. He pressed his hands on his eyes and took a deep breath to steady his mind. "Alright, let's do this," he mumbled, looking at Melissa again.

"I will come with you to Derek and Till to take a look at them. But first, I'll have to check my status screen. The system sent me illegible messages when I suffered from the overload."

He furrowed his brows while thinking about it. He was strangely afraid that his system was now broken. It took a few moments before he had the courage to open his status screen.

Details:
Level: 10
Name: Andrew Gruber
Class: None
Race: Human
Status: Soul injury (Effects currently unknown)
HP: 130/130 **SP**: 5/55 **MP**: 50/145

Achievements:
- Medicine Can Be Poison: You are able to overload emotions easier.
- Closer to Death is Not Possible: Your Resistance is increased by 33% in dire situations.

Affinities:
Soul (High) Body (Low)

Specializations:
- Soul (2/3)
  - Equilibrium
  - Domination
- Body (1/1)
  - Adaptation

Basic Stats:
Strength: 17
Dexterity: 11
Endurance: 11
Resistance: 19
Intelligence: 21
Force: 21

Special Stats:
Magic Power: 10
Soul Power: 13
Life Force: 5

Active Skills:
- Emotion Manipulation (Equilibrium): With moderate Magic Power consumption, you are able to influence another person's emotions to a certain

degree. Warning: Suppressed emotions collect over time in your soul and can break out if they reach a certain threshold.

- Emotion Overdrive (Domination): You are able to put another being's emotions into overdrive. This has the potential to permanently cripple their mind.

Passive Skills:
- Equilibrium (Equilibrium): You are unable to feel extreme emotions and are always in a state of balance. In a localized area around you, people will be slightly influenced by this skill. Warning: Suppressed emotions collect over time in your soul and can break out if they reach a certain threshold.
- Poison Resistance (Adaptation): You are slightly resistant to various poisons. Higher effectiveness if the substance is in your digestive system.
- Fast Recovery (Adaptation): You need less sleep and rest to recover from mental and physical fatigue. Regeneration is also slightly increased while sleeping.
- Struggle (Conditional Passive)

The good news was that his system wasn't broken. He'd even managed to cross the barrier to level ten and gain an achievement. Even though the name of the new achievement was pretty weird, it gave him an amazing effect. Everything that helped him stay alive had indescribable worth for him.

The bad news was his soul injury and the updated descriptions of his abilities. He wondered if they changed because of the incident or if the system just hadn't known about it before. And it was even more disconcerting that not even the system knew the repercussions of his injury.

All in all, he had a serious problem. Andrew wasn't the only one who relied heavily on his skills. He wouldn't be able to offer unlimited help like he had up until now.

Melissa seemed to have noticed his distress and laid a hand over his own. "What is it? Is everything okay?"

After some hesitation, he decided to tell her about his predicament. Contrary to his expectations, she offered him a crooked smile.

"The people are stronger than you think, Andrew. And what is even more important is that they won't be able to handle difficult feelings if you always take them away. It was fine for the chaotic beginning, but I think this might actually be for the best."

The heavy weight on Andrew's heart was lifted with Melissa's words. He had subconsciously assumed that without his abilities, everything would break apart. In hindsight, those were some pretty silly thoughts.

"Thanks, Melissa," Andrew said with a small smile on his face. "This was more important for me to hear than you know."

"Oh, Andrew," Melissa said with a laugh. "Believe me. I knew."

Andrew looked at her with a frown, which made her laugh even more.

"You are so dense, but that's maybe for the better," she told him between her laughs.

He honestly felt a little hurt, but he couldn't hold back his own laughter. He had to admit that she was right. Maybe.

She wiped away a small tear and took a deep breath, serious again. "I guess we should get it over with. Can you stand?"

Andrew shrugged his shoulders and stood up slowly. He was still stiff and weak, but he could manage. Seeing his struggles, Melissa took his left arm and laid it over her shoulders.

Feeling the warmth and softness of her body caused heat to rise up in Andrew's body and his mouth to dry out.

"Everything okay?" asked Melissa.

"I'm fine, just a bit dizzy," he replied while waiting for his passive ability to kick in and calm him down. But it didn't happen.

"Melissa, let go of me," he said in a frightened voice. There were even more feelings welling up inside him. He tried to let go of her, but she instinctively held his arm tight in her grip, thinking that he was falling down.

Andrew didn't manage to free himself before he felt something break out from deep inside him. He felt a sharp pain in his chest and sank with a groan.

Melissa also fell, her knees giving out. She had an intense blush on her face and was breathing heavily. She looked at him with quivering lips, and he didn't know if he should run away or stay right where he was.

She leaned closer to him with a deep hunger in her eyes. And then she slapped herself.

"Damn it, Andrew!" she shouted, still breathing heavily. "Don't you know how to . . . help yourself? How much have you suppressed up until now?"

He looked to the ground, deeply ashamed of this outburst and her words. And even more about his subconscious decision to not back away. He felt completely helpless; his feelings and skills were out of control.

"It's fine, Andrew. Those are natural feelings," she said in a calmer voice, pulling him to his feet again. "But we shouldn't touch like that anymore."

"Agreed," he said hastily, happy she was forgiving him, and let go of her hand as fast as possible.

"We should probably call over a guy to help you walk. Unless you also . . ."

"I'll be fine," Andrew answered her while feeling the strange need inside of him to assure her that he was interested in women. He slowly realized what that meant. He liked her. And he really was dense.

While thinking about this new revelation, Melissa brought over one of the guys, and he helped Andrew stand up. Andrew was still dazed and didn't dare look at Melissa when she stepped in front of him.

She cleared her throat and crooked her neck until she could look him in the eyes.

"Are you ready to go see Derek and Till?"

All other thoughts left his mind when he thought about the two guys whose minds had been destroyed because of him.

He nodded, and they slowly started walking.

CHAPTER TWENTY-EIGHT

Something Like Home

Sarah was annoyed. She tried to flee from her pursuer with quick steps, but she worried the group might lose sight of her if she overdid it.

"So tell me, what is this new place like? Who is the leader there?" asked the red-haired beauty with a crooked smile. Denise's smile looked a bit strange because her cheek was still swollen from Sarah's slap.

Remembering this sweet moment, Sarah smiled at the annoying woman. Denise flinched out of reflex and stumbled over a thick root coming out of the ground. She fell to the ground unceremoniously, displaying a surprising lack of reflexes. Denise noticed halfway down that she was falling, so her hands were only raised to her hips awkwardly, which caused her to fall right on her face.

Sarah stood still for a moment and looked at the fallen woman with a gentle smile. "If you could stay like this, it would be perfect."

Denise looked up at her with a dirt-smeared face, and for a moment, Sarah saw burning rage deep in her blue eyes.

Sarah's face changed immediately and took on a hungry look. "Bring it, bitch."

The enraged look on the woman's face faded as fast as it came. It was replaced by her usual, unwavering smile.

With an exhausted groan, Sarah turned around and resumed walking. She decided Denise was insufferable. She didn't know why, but Sarah's gut instinct told her to rip that poop-face's heart out.

Denise seemed to have accepted that this wasn't the time to sweet-talk Sarah into giving her more information. So, she started limping some distance away from her, and everyone else.

For some reason, the rest of the group typically stayed a safe distance from Denise, but nobody would say why. This was unsettling to Sarah. Maybe she needed to have a more intimate talk with one of them.

The ragged group of people barely had the strength to walk. They were emaciated because they had had just enough food to not die from hunger. They were also carrying everything they were strong enough to carry, which was mostly food and some furs that were in surprisingly good condition. These people would make good additions to the caves with their skills.

Without any forewarning, a particular memory of the dirtbag camp came to mind. This memory made Sarah feel sick to her very core.

In the aftermath of her fight, Sarah had tried to hunt down the rest of the dirtbags, but she only got one of them. She had heavily overestimated her tracking abilities.

When she'd come back to the camp, she'd had to convince the people for hours that she wasn't there to eat them or something like that. When she finally managed to convince them of her good intentions, many broke down crying.

Sarah had begun to help them gather their belongings when one of them came to her with a disturbing request. It was to help them bury their dead.

She'd followed them, not knowing what to expect, and witnessed the most horrific sight of her life. A large pile of decomposing human bodies was located some distance away from the camp. Most of their remains had been eaten by wild animals, but there was still enough left for them to smell extremely repulsive.

Two of the women had begun pulling the remains down from the pile one by one without even showing a smidgeon of emotion. Sarah later learned that they had been forced to carry the corpses to this place and strip them of their belongings. But, it wasn't only corpses that were taken to this place.

To punish troublemakers, they first crippled their limbs and then threw them on the pile, so they would be eaten alive by the wild animals. Sarah had a hard time accepting this reality. This was a level of perverted cruelty that was outside of her scope of understanding.

She forced her consciousness to come back to reality. This memory would haunt her for her entire life.

She moved the big pile of stuff on her back to a more comfortable position and resumed her march. The group wasn't very fast, but they would reach the caves in the next hour or so.

Her estimation turned out to be right, as they arrived at the caves when the sun began to set.

The group behind her fearfully stayed some distance away, too afraid to experience a new kind of hell. They still didn't fully trust her.

The busy people in front of the caves soon noticed their approach and started gathering in front of Sarah.

They greeted her as one of their own, albeit sometimes with suspicious looks. Nonetheless, it felt really good. She hadn't been with them long, but it was the place that had come the closest to home since this nightmare began.

"Where's Andrew?" she asked the noisy crowd, who were asking her who all the new people were.

Before anyone could say anything, Andrew was front of the crowd. Sarah had to look twice when she saw his face. His usually stoic and neutral face seemed a bit more . . . alive.

"Nice to see you again and alive. Welcome back," he said to her like he wanted to give her a hug.

Sarah hastily grabbed his outstretched right hand and shook it in an awkward manner.

"Not much of a hugger, huh?" Andrew asked with a chuckle and patted her shoulder. "Are they from the other camp?" he asked with a more serious tone.

Sarah nodded and came closer to whisper in his ear. "Beware of the red-haired bitch. I think she has the same abilities as you, but . . . something is wrong with her. I cannot explain it, but be careful. My gut tells me she is bad news."

Andrew looked at her with a surprised face. "I am honestly surprised that she is still alive."

"Do you think I am a monster or something?" Sarah asked with anger in her eyes, only to see a mischievous glint in Andrew's eyes. She hit his chest, which nearly sent him tumbling to the ground.

"Damn, that hurt Sarah, but I guess I deserved it," Andrew said with a pained groan, finding his balance again. "Go rest up. I am pretty sure you had it rough. And let Melissa take a look at you. This mission might have damaged your emotions."

Sarah wanted to protest at first, but then the scene of the mutilated pile of corpses came to mind again. So, she nodded and swallowed down her angry response.

"I'll deal with these people for now. Go with Melissa to the woods behind the kitchen area. I'll cook for you, as promised." He pointed in the general direction where Melissa could be found.

Sarah gratefully accepted, threw her backpack to the ground, and got away from the clearing as fast as possible. She didn't want to deal with this walking mass of trauma anymore. She had no idea what to say or do to help them.

She had to admit that Andrew wasn't completely useless; he was able to handle situations like these pretty well.

Sarah had been searching for some time but wasn't able to find Melissa. She soon became frustrated and started looking for her using her magic sense.

"Found you," she said with a glint in her eyes. She was looking forward to seeing the gentle beauty again after having the red-haired bitch around her for days.

When she came closer, she heard the sounds of chewing. She was hungry and would have to eat something before Andrew cooked for them.

When she moved the last obstructive bush, she saw Melissa crouching on the ground, her hands full of half-rotten food. Melissa was looking up at her with a shocked face, her mouth stuffed full. She coughed and spit out the food and hastily came to her feet.

"This isn't what it looks like!" she said in a desperate voice.

"So you didn't eat half-rotten leftovers?" Sarah asked with a raised eyebrow.

Melissa's shoulders slumped, and she let her head sink in shame. "I am so sorry you had to see that," she said in a quiet, quivering voice.

"Eh, it's no biggie," Sarah replied and sat next to the pile of leftovers, which had probably put here by the kitchen crew. It was mostly spoiled food, like bones and inedible plant and animal parts. At least they were inedible for most people.

Sarah took something out of the pile and began eating. "It's actually not that bad," she mumbled with a mouth full. "I have eaten much more disgusting things in the swamp. Do you know how utterly horrible acidic snails taste?"

Melissa looked at her with a priceless expression. "I did not expect that."

"So, what did you expect?" Sarah asked her with a frown.

"To be . . . rejected." She fumbled with her curly blond hair and continued speaking. "I am a stress eater, you know. I have to deal with so much shit here, and I can't help myself. And it helps conserve our food reserves when I eat this stuff. I am the only one who has strong enough poison resistance for this."

It was as if Melissa had wanted to tell someone about this for a long time. And suddenly, Sarah had an epiphany.

"So that's how you stay so curvy!" she said, nodding in realization. She felt a cold chill run down her spine.

She turned her head with an apologetic smile, only to see Melissa's cold smile. "Watch your mouth."

"Yes ma'am."

Melissa sighed and sat next to her. "I guess there's no point in pretending anymore. Might as well resume eating."

"Oh, but don't eat too much. Andrew will cook for us tonight," Sarah said with a smile. She was looking forward to eating cooked food again.

Melissa, on the other hand, started stuffing food into her mouth even faster than before.

"Why are you doing this?" Sarah asked through squinted eyes.

"No reason," Melissa replied as best she could with her mouth full.

While shrugging her shoulders, Sarah also ate one or two things. She didn't want to spoil her appetite too much. She thought about asking Melissa to take a look at her soul, but somehow she couldn't gather the courage for it.

When Melissa seemed to be finished eating, she said, "Thanks a lot, for accepting me, I mean. I am always afraid to show this side of myself to other people."

"Don't worry," Sarah told her, caressing her head. "You are lovable enough to have more than a few quirks."

Melissa looked up at her and said, "You think I am lovable?"

Sarah felt the blood shoot to her face, and she hastily stood up. "I think I heard Andrew! Let's go look for him."

Melissa stood up with a giggle and followed her into the woods. Even though Sarah had lied, they found Andrew not far from them, sitting next to a small campfire.

"I thought you might like some distance from the others," he told Sarah with a smile, not the least surprised at her finding him there. When he looked at her face, he started frowning. "Why is your face so red?"

"It is not." Sarah looked at him with murder in her eyes. Melissa giggled a little next to her.

"But I clearly see . . ."

"It. Is. Not."

After giggling some more, Melissa showed mercy on the flustered Sarah. "It's probably from the fire. The light makes her pale skin seem red."

Andrew still looked at her with a raised eyebrow, but then shrugged his shoulders.

Sarah was still embarrassed but grateful for Melissa's intervention. They sat together on the ground next to Andrew, who was busy stirring some kind of stew inside a stone bowl.

"You want some too, Mel—?"

"No thanks." Melissa spoke as fast as lightning, without giving Andrew the chance to finish his sentence.

"More for us then," he said with another shrug and scooped Sarah and himself wooden bowls full of stew.

Sarah couldn't help herself. She grabbed the offered spoon and took her first bite with a delighted expression, which crumbled soon afterward.

"What the . . . ? Andrew? What is wrong with you?" Sarah said with a full mouth, not really daring to chew anymore.

"Why, what is it?" Andrew asked in a bewildered tone, already happily eating his meal.

"I don't know how you did it, but this is by far the most disgusting thing I've ever had. How did you even manage to do this? There is nothing that even remotely tastes as horrible as this."

"Uhhh," Andrew said with an irritated look. "I think it's fine."

He was looking so lost with his half-full bowl in his hand that Sarah began laughing wildly, spitting out the food that was still in her mouth. Melissa started laughing too.

"Oh, Andrew, you are so useless, apart from leading people," Melissa cackled while wiping away a few joyous tears.

Andrew's face was resigned, which caused even more laughter from the two women.

The evening went on like this, with Sarah and Melissa making fun of Andrew and him making horrible comebacks. It was the first lighthearted moment Sarah had had since waking up in this strange world. And a lot of heavy feelings inside her started to melt away.

With a happy smile on her face, she watched Melissa argue with Andrew over whether the mushrooms he had gathered were poisonous or not. This moment was so light and comfortable that she didn't want it to end.

And soon after, she fell into a deep and comfortable slumber.

Torn

"I got to level ten!"

Sarah heard an excited shout from outside. She groggily opened her eyes and stretched like a cat. A quick glance outside told her that it was already late in the day. Once again, she had slept for a very long time.

With practiced ease, she left her cave and climbed down the steep wall. She was quite curious about who had reached level ten.

She walked toward the big clearing and saw a group of people standing in a big circle around someone. She even saw some of the refugees she had brought with her. After two weeks of lots of healthy food, they looked way better.

Sarah couldn't help but smile a little. They were all afraid of her, but at least she had managed to save them from their precarious circumstances. She went toward the crowd, and when the people noticed her, they made space for her to take a look. Maybe a little too much space.

In the middle of the group was one of the kitchen crew. She always forget his name somehow. Was it Norman? Or Neil?

The sight of bright red hair ripped her from her thoughts. There she was, the hateful bitch, acting all nice and friendly with the people. Apparently, she hadn't noticed Sarah's arrival yet because she usually ran away when she even saw Sarah's shadow.

The bitch even went as far as hugging the blushing man, which caused him to stutter and flail around helplessly with his arms. While the gathered crowd started to laugh and whistle, Sarah felt her horns vibrate.

She looked around in alarm, focusing her senses. With suspicion in her eyes, she walked toward the forest while the crowd was still joking around. The vibration of her horns became weaker the further she went, until it broke off completely.

"What the heck is that?" Sarah cursed and tried to look into the forest with her magic sense. But there was nothing. Uncountable times, she had had this vibrating feeling in her horns, and it gave her the creeps. She somehow knew it meant danger, but she had no idea why. Was it possible that something invisible was stalking their camp? Something that messed with their minds so they wouldn't notice it?

She worriedly shook her head and went back to the crowd. There was no point in looking for something invisible anyway. She just had to stay alert at all times in case it decided to attack their camp.

As she got back to the crowd, she noticed that the red-haired bitch was gone.

"Hey Neil!" She called for the guy who got to level ten.

He looked at her with dejection and frustration in his eyes. "My name is Norman. As it always is. What is it?"

"Sheesh, no need to get that worked up," Sarah said with furrowed brows. "Tell me what your path is. I'm curious." She noticed how different his facial expression was toward her as opposed to his demeanor toward the beautiful bitch. So superficial.

He clenched his teeth and looked at her with anger in his eyes. A few of his colleagues seemed to notice this and stepped forward to calm him down. Sarah looked at him in bewilderment. She knew that she sometimes annoyed people, but to get so angry about something so small? What was up with that?

Another of his friends went over to her and smiled forcefully. "He got on the path of craftsmanship. Happy now? We need to get going." With these words, the crowd started to disperse and leave Sarah behind.

She knew that some people were still suspicious of her, but in the last two weeks, more people had started accepting her. Sarah was puzzled and dejected.

She was still standing there when she noticed an unwelcome presence come closer to her.

"Harassing our people again, I see." She heard the hateful voice of Alex from behind her.

"I swear, Alex, one day I will rip your tongue out if you keep spouting shit like that," she said with an irritated look on her face. This wasn't her best moment, and she really didn't need another scumbag to annoy her right now.

Alex just looked at her with furrowed brows. "Is this a threat? Are you threatening me right now? I wonder what the folks would think about this."

Sarah clenched her teeth in frustration. She had tried hard to be accepted, but this guy wouldn't leave her alone. She wouldn't be surprised if he was responsible for the rejection she experienced before.

Her leg muscles had already flexed, and she was ready to jump at him, but she forcefully suppressed her instincts. If she gave in, he would only have more ammunition to rally the people against her. The best way to prove him wrong was to simply not care about his antics.

Alex's eyes had an expectant glint, which quickly faded when he saw Sarah smile at him. He snorted and walked away.

Sarah was proud of herself. She had endured this crap for a few weeks, and she still hadn't ripped him apart. "Good girl!" she said, while patting her own head.

She felt somewhat better, but she didn't want to encounter anymore people right now, so she decided to do something she had wanted to do for a long time. Climb the cliff.

With excitement bubbling up inside her body, she looked to the top of the cliff. It was far above any treetops, and a fall from so high up would mean death.

As long as she didn't look down, she'd be fine. She stopped by her cave to grab a few slices of dried meat and began climbing higher.

She carefully went up bit by bit, always looking for the best place to go. It took longer than she had expected and was also exhausting. After she had to climb down a short distance for the second time now, she decided to take a break on a small outcropping. She turned around and sat down, and the view was amazing.

The forest reached as far as Sarah could see, with a glittering band of water flowing through the middle of it. Sarah thought that she was able to see the spatial error she had come out of in the distance. And even further than that, she could spot high mountains with white peaks.

"Snow," she whispered in amazement as the memory of this substance came back to her mind. This scene was so uplifting and exciting that she wanted to see what was on top of this cliff.

With newfound vigor, she climbed further up. After some more time, the wind began to get more and more violent. It ripped at her harshly and threw her tail around, which impacted her sense of balance. But something like this wouldn't stop her.

With gritted teeth, she started to use her tail as another limb to grab the steep stone wall. It wasn't that effective, as her tail wasn't able to support her weight, but it was better than nothing.

The wind grew colder the further she climbed, and her hands started to get stiff. "Not good," she murmured and started to climb a little faster. If she lost feeling in her hands, she'd be done for.

The stone up here was less stable than at the bottom, and it crumbled underneath her grip more than once.

She was already starting to feel anxious when her outstretched hand wasn't touching cold stone anymore, but air. With a surprised look, she saw that she had managed to reach the top of the cliff. She leaped up the last stretch and rested on the ground.

"Why the heck did I even do that?" she asked herself. It had looked so easy from down below. If she had known about the violent, ice-cold wind, she would have thought twice about doing this.

"Or maybe not," she mumbled and stood back up on her feet. She massaged her cold, aching hands and took in the view in front of her.

It was breathtakingly beautiful. She was on the edge of a plateau that was leading down in the distance on a gentle slope. Waist-high grass was dancing in the strong winds, and further down the plateau, Sarah could see woods flanking a glistening lake.

At the edge of the horizon, towering white clouds were drifting through the sky with golden sunlight reflected in them.

Sarah could feel an intense desire inside her to just walk away. Exploring this unknown, beautiful landscape and leaving all the problems with this community behind.

The urge was so strong that she took a few steps forward without even realizing it. The tall grass was tickling her legs, and she could smell fresh and unknown scents coming from the forest.

"Another day," she mumbled to herself. It wasn't in her nature to give up. And if she left, she'd be all alone again, and she definitely didn't want that. She felt like she'd lose her remaining humanity if she wasn't surrounded by other people.

With a deep sigh, she turned away from the sight of the majestic landscape. She had to concentrate on the good. Even though she had difficulties bonding with the people here, she at least had two friends, Melissa and Andrew. That was enough for now.

She had planned to scout out the region on top of the cliff for a few days, but she feared she wouldn't come back if she did. With a heavy heart, she turned around and started climbing down again.

Just before her head disappeared beneath the cliff, she took one last look. "Another day," she whispered before she began climbing down again.

CHAPTER THIRTY

Juicy Prey

Sarah was sneaking through the ever more colorful forest. Even the red and yellow leaves falling from the trees were louder than she was.

A group of absurdly tall deer looked up from where they were feeding, and into the forest with irritated gazes.

Before they could realize why exactly they were afraid, Sarah disturbed their nerve functions. They began wobbling. This would only last a few seconds at most, but it was all she needed.

With a swift and flowing movement, she jumped from one deer to another and slit their throats with her sharp claws.

She managed to kill seven deer before the rest of the herd managed to gain control over their legs again and ran away. Sarah didn't follow. The team would have enough to do as it was.

"I'm done!" she shouted into the seemingly empty forest, and a group of ten people emerged. They were the ones who would carry the carcasses to the caves.

After even more time had passed, Sarah was becoming even more accepted by the cavers. With a few exceptions, she didn't want to think about that.

"Should I come with you guys?" Sarah asked the group, who were wrapping the carcasses in carapaces and tying them with ropes.

"I think it should be fine," said the biggest man in the cavers group, Bertrand. He had gained some skills in his adaptation specialization, and his build and muscles had begun to grow. He was even taller and stronger than Alex. Heck, he was stronger than her by now.

The giant of a man bound two deer on his back and took another two in each of his arms.

"You are just not normal," Sarah told him with a small shake of her head.

Bertrand laughed very loudly with his deep voice. The people surrounding them covered their ears with annoyed expressions. "You are one to talk. Ever seen your reflection?"

Sarah grinned at him with her sharp teeth. "No idea what you could be talking about."

Bertrand shook his head with a smile and started walking in the direction of the caves. "Just don't stay outside too long. The days are getting shorter."

With these words, he gave her one last nod and walked away.

The rest of the group was still busy tying up the deer and began shouting after Bertrand to not just walk away alone again. They groaned frustratedly and threw their hands up in the air when the giant ignored them.

Sarah smiled and turned around to leave. "Bye, guys!"

They were all complaining about her getting the easy job and letting them do all the heavy lifting, but not really with anger in their voices. This had become more or less a ritual of theirs.

The smile quickly faded from Sarah's face when she delved deeper into the forest. For a few days now, she had been on the cusp of reaching level twenty. The fight with the dirtbags had pushed her to level nineteen, and her intense hunting had done the rest.

But no matter how much she used her abilities and hunted prey, she couldn't level up. She wondered if she would need to overcome another barrier inside of her, but she couldn't detect anything.

While looking for a stronger beast to fight, preferably a predator, she fell into deep thought. Maybe it was because she was so distracted, but she didn't notice that someone else was already in this area.

Only when she saw a movement out of the corner of her eye did she notice the presence of the other person.

A hand shot out from behind a bush and tried to grab her shoulders. Sarah swiftly dodged, jumped to the side a few meters, and readied herself.

"Why so nervous?" Alex asked her with a dead expression on his face, as he was coming into view from behind the tree.

"What's the matter with you?" Sarah hissed, fury burning in her chest. "Just back the fuck off, if you know what's good for you."

Alex had pestered her at any opportunity he got. She didn't know why, but he seemed to have it out for her.

"You are dangerous. And nobody else can see it," he said with a resolute voice. "You are an animal. And you need to know your place."

Alex flexed his enormous muscles underneath his now scaly skin. He had also undergone a lot of mutations, and while he still looked more human than Sarah, his eyes had lost more and more emotion.

But Sarah wouldn't let herself get provoked like this. She knew that if she gave in, she would prove his point about being aggressive and dangerous.

So she suppressed her rage and settled for spitting in his face.

"Ahhh, you crazy bitch!" he screamed while holding his sizzling face.

With a grin, she felt his magic power well up and soon noticed that it was stronger than before. This idiot had apparently managed to get over level ten. But there was something else.

A feeling. Or rather, a calling. He was also on the Path of Conflict.

"You juicy, juicy prey," Sarah said with hunger in her voice. Alex stopped screaming for a second and looked at her with apparent shock on his face.

"What did you just—" He began to speak but was interrupted by a fist slamming into his jaw.

Sarah's fist hurt pretty bad from the impact, but she didn't stop there.

Before the hulking man could regain his balance, she began pummeling him with her fists. She could feel it—the unsurmountable wall to level twenty crumbling bit by bit.

When he tried to grab her with his big hands, she interrupted the signal from his brain for a moment, and he lost control of his arms and legs momentarily.

Sarah immediately felt dizzy. This had drained nearly all of her magic power. But she had a solution for that.

She grabbed the falling man and bit into his shoulder with gusto.

"Not again, you freak!" he roared and tried to pull her head away, but he stopped with a loud scream when he felt her teeth ripping at his muscles.

Sarah inhaled deeply, and his magic power flowed inside her like a strong river. This definitely felt different from the last time.

Her reserves filled up instantly, and Alex fell unconscious. She quickly opened her mouth so as not to accidentally rip out part of his shoulders with her sharp teeth.

"This is it!" Sarah shouted in excitement when she felt the wall to level twenty shatter completely.

It didn't take long for the system message to pop up.

<Congratulations on reaching Level 20. You will now witness the second recording of Dr. Alain Becker. Please brace yourself.>

As soon as she realized what this meant, she felt the horrible pull on her mind again. Before she could lose consciousness, though, she kicked Alex's unconscious body one last time.

"Damn, I missed his balls," she mumbled before her consciousness left her body.

Just like the first time, she seemed to fly at extreme speed through pure nothingness. When the feeling of motion stopped after some time, nothing happened for a while. Then the hunched-over figure of a lanky man came into view.

"Recording two, Dr. Alain Becker," he said in the emptiness, in which he was standing with his dry and professional voice.

Dr. Becker didn't seem downcast anymore. He had a rather fanatical expression burning deep in his gray eyes.

"This energy. It changes everything," he began speaking in a breathless voice. "It does . . . things our science cannot even begin to explain. It is outside of every possibility we could even imagine."

He started walking around, his hands clamping together like claws. "The damage is regrettable, but . . . humanity can ascend from its ashes. It will be worth it. It will definitely be worth it."

While speaking those last few words, Dr. Becker's voice began quivering, but he soon composed himself.

"We will ascend like the mythical phoenix out of the ashes. Humanity will be reborn. We will be more."

His fanatical rambling came to a stop, and he cleared his throat with a surprised look on his face. He looked around him as if astonished by his location.

He cleared his throat again and continued speaking. "It seems like not only were a number of humans not able to survive the initial impact of the energy, but from visual observation, a lot of flora and fauna also perished. This needs more research."

He started walking again, and the glow started to come back into his eyes. "But the humans who survived . . . they started changing. It wasn't quite apparent at first. Objects breaking without any reason, people disappearing without a trace. But the boy. He showed us all. The true potential of the energy."

His voice got louder and louder, as if he could barely control himself. "We haven't found any limits to the application of the energy. The only limitation is the extent of what and how much can be done. But this limitation is also slowly disappearing. We are getting stronger."

He stopped walking around and shook his head for a while, as if to somehow shake off errant thoughts. He rubbed his face and stepped closer. Now Sarah could see deep, dark circles beneath his eyes. His skin was pale, and he seemed very ill. Something was definitely wrong with him.

"I cannot say for sure right now, but . . . humanity will take the next step. We will become gods."

With his last words, his image disappeared like smoke, and his voice echoed through the endless nothingness.

Sarah started racing through the nothingness until she violently connected with her body again.

She heaved for air as her body spasmed like it did the first time.

"That's seriously horrible," she groaned, trying to regain control over her body. When she managed to do it, she looked over at Alex and noticed he was still unconscious next to her.

She lay down on her back and rested for a while. She was so exhausted, like she had been awake for three days straight. Why the hell did the system show them such visions? And what did they mean?

The system said that they were recordings. She wasn't quite sure what that meant, though. Something in the back of her head told her that she should know what that was. She just couldn't pinpoint it.

With a frustrated groan, she sat up. Although she hadn't seen much of Tobias during her time in the camp, he was well known for being pretty smart. Also for being pretty weird, but who was she to judge? She would have to ask him about these visions. Maybe he would be able to gain some insight into them.

Sarah grabbed Alex by his neck and started pulling him back to the caves. Even though he was an ass, she wouldn't let him get eaten alive by wild animals. He didn't deserved that. Yet.

On her way back, she mused some more over this Becker guy. Most of what he had said made no sense to her. It was just too different from what she had experienced. Either this was a scene from a long time ago or from a very different place.

But one thing was for sure—the energy he described was definitely magic power. Why he didn't call it that was another mystery. A lot of things just didn't make sense.

It didn't take long for her to reach the caves. It was close to nighttime by the time she got back, so hardly anyone was around. She threw Alex into the dirt and noticed that he was naked and badly scratched on top of that.

"Whoopsie," Sarah said, looking around. Luckily, she was alone.

Without waiting any longer, she ran away in a hurry, leaving the naked Alex lying in the dirt. Seeing as everyone was most likely already asleep, she would talk to Tobias in the morning.

"This is a problem for the tomorrow-Sarah," she mumbled, still running to her personal cave. Well, it was mostly her personal cave because no one else dared to climb so high. But it still felt good.

After she finally reached her home, she made herself comfortable on her furs. The new people from the other camp had some serious skills in tanning the hides of animals. And, as Sarah was the one who hunted most of the animals, she was given the honor of receiving the first fur-blanket. With a satisfied sigh, she let herself sink into its soft embrace.

She tried to switch off any thoughts she had and get some sleep, but it took a long time for sleep to come.

One thought just didn't leave her alone—something was seriously wrong with this Dr. Alain Becker.

CHAPTER THIRTY-ONE

The Calm Before the Storm

Andrew was ripped from sleep by a horrible scream. He jumped to his feet and looked around in panic. Before long, he realized that he had screamed in his sleep.

With an exhausted groan, he let himself sink into his bed of leaves again. He had been haunted by bizarre nightmares since his soul injury. It seemed like his skills didn't work properly while he was sleeping.

What was really disconcerting was that he still hadn't received a system prompt about achieving a class. Andrew and Tobias had talked a lot about this phenomenon and came to the conclusion that the system had to somehow be deeply connected to the soul. The only difference between him and the others was his soul injury. They couldn't be sure if this was really the cause, but it seemed very likely. Andrew just hoped that it wasn't permanent. It felt like his soul injury got better every day, especially since Melissa figured out a way to speed up the process.

She didn't have a lot of time for him, though, as she was helping the traumatized people Sarah had brought from the other camp.

With a sigh, Andrew went outside his cave to get some fresh air. He had begun to sleep alone in a cave since he had started screaming. He didn't want to worry the people even more.

Contrary to his expectations, the group didn't lose trust in him because of his weakness. They grew closer to him. He always felt some kind of distance between him and his people, but it was slowly disappearing.

"I guess I wore a mask for too long," Andrew mumbled while stepping into the open. It was pretty chilly at night now, and he actually felt cold.

The first thing he saw in the dim light of the slowly rising sun was a naked Alex, who was stumbling around with a confused look on his face.

"What the . . . ?" Andrew mumbled and quickly walked over to him.

"What's going on, Alex? Where are your clothes?" he asked the bulky man and tried not to look down.

He was pretty dirty and had some blood on him, but Andrew couldn't see any wounds, apart from a nearly healed bite mark on his shoulder.

"Oh boy," Andrew said, exasperated. Alex slowly noticed that someone was talking to him.

"Sarah attacked me!" he shouted as soon as he regained his bearings. "I told you, she is dangerous!"

"Listen, Alex." Andrew began, already feeling exhausted from the coming conversation. "It certainly is not okay that she attacked you."

"Not okay? She is insane, I tell you—"

"STOP!" Andrew shouted, with some anger welling up inside of him. Luckily, his skills had improved by now, and the anger had subsided somewhat.

Alex looked at him with a shocked expression, as if Andrew had hit physically him.

"You have been bothering her since we got here. For the Creator's sake, Alex, even I wanted to punch you for what you said to her. Just what is going on with you? Why are you becoming more and more hostile?"

Alex was speechless for a few moments, just looking at Andrew with wide, open eyes. Then his face was again scrunched up in anger, and he started shouting again. "I told you since the beginning that she is dangerous! She has attacked me twice now. And she isn't even human." He made a disgusted face and shuddered, as if he had eaten something gross.

Andrew couldn't help but look at Alex with a hint of disdain. "Alex. Look at yourself. Can you be considered fully human anymore?"

"This is different!" he immediately shouted and nearly poked one of Andrew's eyes out with the finger he held in front of his face. "The great system tells me that I am human. And she isn't. But I see what is going on."

Alex's face was distorted by a ridiculing smile. "You like them malformed, don't you?"

Andrew felt almost sick from this maliciousness. He felt emotions well up inside him again, but this time, he used them.

He didn't exactly know how he did it, but he pulled out the suppressed fear inside of him and somehow pushed it toward Alex.

One moment the man was smiling with narrowed eyes; the next, his legs began shaking wildly.

The moment only lasted for a few seconds, but it was enough.

"You went too far, Andrew," Alex said with a dangerously quiet voice.

"You too," Andrew replied, but wanted to appease him nonetheless. "We both made mistakes. Sarah also made mistakes. How about we talk about it and try to put it behind us? There is no point in driving a wedge in our cooperation."

Alex looked at him for a few moments and spat on the ground. "You wish. I will show people who you really are. You and your deranged little mistress. Just you wait."

With these words, Alex walked away. He was still naked, but probably too furious to notice or care.

Andrew sighed deeply and looked at the sky. "What have I gotten myself into?" he mumbled into the empty morning sky. But he was more concerned with what was going on with Alex. He had known him since the beginning, and he had always been nothing but supportive.

After Karen disappeared, he had begun to change. He was angry all the time, but only recently had he begun to act like a lunatic.

"Wait a moment . . ." Andrew mumbled, a shocked expression now on his face.

Alex started acting like this after the refugees arrived, and Sarah had warned him about someone. Denise. Sarah told him about her assumption that Denise had powers similar to his.

Andrew shook his head. He had talked to Denise. She had seamlessly melded into their group and was doing her job as part of the community. Everyone liked her.

Wait, did everyone like her? Why did he think that? He barely knew her.

Andrew felt a headache coming on and staggered for a moment as dizziness overcame him.

"Well, it doesn't matter," he mumbled. He started walking in the direction of Sarah's cave while trying to banish the distracting thoughts from his head. He had more important matters to deal with.

He rubbed his still aching head and mentally prepared himself for the second confrontation of the morning. "And all of this without breakfast. I must be cursed."

After a short walk, he arrived at the foot of the cliff below Sarah's cave, which was located pretty high above ground.

He shouted, but no one answered. With an annoyed sigh, he decided to throw rocks at the cave opening. The situation had to be addressed immediately before Sarah could make everything worse by letting herself be provoked again.

He lifted up a stone and wondered for a moment if he would even be able to throw it that high. He shrugged his shoulders, took aim, and let the rock fly.

He whistled when he saw the rock flying toward the cave in a straight line without slowing down. Level ten strength really changed something.

Right as the stone reached the cave, Sarah's head suddenly popped out, and the stone hit her forehead with an audible thud.

"Ahhh, you idiot!!" she screamed, and Andrew closed his eyes in horror. This would be even worse now.

Sarah rubbed her head and bared her sharp teeth at him. "I hope this is important, fish-face."

"It is. Please come down so we can talk. And sorry about the stone." Andrew held his hands up in apology, pointedly.

Sarah rolled her eyes and began climbing down. It was weirdly fascinating to watch her. Andrew had never really experienced her physical prowess until now.

She more or less ran down the steep cliff with feline grace. Numerous times, it looked like she would fall down at any moment, only for her to grab onto the wall at the last possible moment.

When she stepped in front of him, Andrew shook himself out of his daze. He didn't want her to tease him because he'd been staring at her.

Sarah stood in front of him with arms crossed and raised eyebrows. In the dim light of the new day, her eyes glowed a mysterious yellow. Her dark, wavy hair had grown and now reached her chin. This would have been a fascinating sight if there hadn't been a swollen bump on her forehead.

Andrew stifled a laugh and tried to be serious. Sarah looked at him with narrowed eyes, but luckily she didn't catch on.

As soon as Andrew remembered what it was he needed to discuss with her, his amused expression disappeared.

"Did you attack Alex?" He had to know if it was true first.

Sarah's imposing demeanor disappeared, and she smiled at him apologetically. "Maybe . . . ?"

"Oh, Sarah. We talked about this. You can't just attack and hurt people," Andrew said, groaning and rested his face in his right hand.

"I know, I'm sorry."

Andrew was so surprised by her apology that he looked at her with wide eyes.

"Don't look at me like that, you idiot. I know it's not okay to do something like that to our tribe. But let's face the facts. Alex is a major asshole." Sarah spoke in a surprisingly calm voice. "He threatened me. Provoked me. Insulted me. The. Whole. Time."

Andrew nodded in agreement. "I know. And he had it coming. Heck, even I got angry at his remarks. But still." He looked at her with serious eyes. "Not everyone knows this. A lot of people like him because he has protected us and hunted for food since the start. He wanted to convince people from the beginning that you were dangerous. And now he can claim you attacked him again."

Sarah made a sour face and threw her hands in the air in frustration. "I know, Andrew. But let's look at the positive—I didn't kill him, right? And I even brought him back!"

Andrew wanted to refute, but quickly realized that Sarah was right. He was honestly surprised when Alex told him about Sarah attacking him; he'd made it out alive and barely harmed. "Listen, I understand you. But we have to act smart now. I also lashed out at him when we talked about it. He threatened me afterward, and I have no idea what he will do now. I just hope he isn't stupid enough to cause unrest in the tribe."

Sarah didn't listen to him. She grinned with an excited expression and punched his shoulder. "You lashed out? Awesome!"

"Focus."

"Sorry."

Andrew sighed and started talking again. "I just need you to stay out of his way. Can you do that? I will try to speak with him and calm him down. I'm sure he'll listen to reason somehow."

"Yeah, sure," Sarah said with a snort and patted his aching shoulder. "And just so you know, he got to level ten. He is also on the Path of Conflict. Let me know if you need protection."

This news was quite concerning. Andrew understood why Sarah was on the Path of Conflict. But why Alex? He had assumed his path would lead more toward protection or hunting. This was worrisome.

"I will let you know."

He gave Sarah a grateful smile and let out an exhausted sigh. This had only been the start of his day. He wasn't ready for the chaos that would soon unfold.

"How about we go eat something?" Andrew asked. He was sure that with some food in his stomach, he would feel a lot better.

Sarah looked at him with a horrified expression. "Did you cook?"

"No?"

"Then sure!" Sarah shouted with an excited voice and started bouncing toward the cooking area.

Andrew was insulted, but he couldn't be all that mad at her. After the disastrous cooking experience with Melissa and Sarah, he tried cooking for other people. After he had caused someone to awaken a poison resistance skill, he stopped.

Sarah was quite far ahead when Andrew remembered that she always ate all the tasty mushrooms if left unchecked.

Andrew began sprinting after her as fast as he could.

CHAPTER THIRTY-TWO

The Source

After Sarah and Andrew had eaten, they decided to go to Tobias' cave together. Sarah had her vision of Dr. Becker to discuss, and Andrew wanted to talk to both of them about the situation with Alex.

"You could have let me have some more mushrooms, though," Sarah grumbled.

Andrew didn't bother to answer. He just kept walking silently beside her. When she didn't get a reaction from him, Sarah pushed Andrew into a puddle of muddy water and ran away laughing.

Of course Andrew had no chance of catching up with her now, so Sarah had to wait a few minutes in front of Tobias' cave for Andrew to arrive.

Dripping wet, he trotted over with an annoyed look on his face. He opened his mouth to say something, but then shook his head and went inside.

Feeling refreshed, Sarah followed. Tobias' cave must have been the best-lit cave in their entire camp. Dozens of torches were fastened to the walls deeper inside, illuminating the workspace of their self-proclaimed genius. Sarah knew he was probably right about that, but she would never admit it out loud.

The room they went into was extremely messy. All sorts of things were strewn about on the ground. Rocks, plants, animal parts, and lots of other things in all the variations one could imagine. Tobias was sitting beneath a torch with a large slab of tree bark in his hand, and he was scribbling something on it.

"Tobias?" Andrew asked the focused man, but he got no answer. "Tobias?" he tried again, this time a bit louder. But still, no reaction. Before Andrew could say anything more, Sarah had already opened her mouth.

"Wow, look at all this stuff! Would make awesome firewood!"

"What do you want?" came the immediate reaction of the scrawny man. He looked up at them with disdain in his eyes. "I am in the middle of transcribing the information about our people. I have no time to talk."

"You're what?" asked Andrew, perplexed.

Tobias looked at him with pity in his eyes. He began speaking very slowly and loudly. "I am writing down the status screens of our people. We will be able to make better use of our work allocation like this."

Andrew now looked even more annoyed than before. Sarah was slightly sorry now for pushing him into the water. Although . . . no, not really.

"Stop talking to me like that, or I'll lower the number of torches and resources you are allocated."

"What can I do for you?" Tobias asked in a friendly voice and sprang to his feet with a smile on his face.

Sarah and Andrew simultaneously closed their eyes in frustration. This man was insufferable.

Sarah was content for Andrew to lead the exhausting conversation with the man. "We're here to talk to you about important matters, so focus. First of all, do you have Alex's status transcribed yet? We could use some information about him."

Tobias thought for a moment and then answered. "Alex's status isn't transcribed yet, but I can do it now if you want. If you need information about other people, I'll have all one hundred eleven statuses transcribed by this evening."

Andrew nodded, and Tobias took a new tree bark into his hand and started scratching away. Sarah, on the other hand, was a little confused. "Aren't we one hundred and twelve people now?"

Tobias' hand stopped scratching on the tree bark. He looked up at her, clearly agitated. "Yes . . . yes, we are one hundred twelve people. But I thought I looked at every status screen. Why did I think that?"

He sank into deep contemplation but shrugged his shoulders. "Well, that's not important now. I'll transcribe Alex's status."

Sarah was even more puzzled now. She too felt that it wasn't important, but something in the back of her mind bugged her. The Tobias she knew would never be content with a realization like this.

"No, wait, it is important. Which status haven't you seen?" she asked the man, and he looked up at her with confusion in his eyes.

"I . . . uh . . ." he stuttered and held his head. "Is this really important? I think we can talk about it some other time."

Sarah had had enough, so she grabbed the scrawny man by his shoulders and shook him. Something wasn't right here. "Which status is missing?" she shouted at him, and he looked at her with a pained expression.

"It . . . I think . . . Denise's status is missing," he said with a face that looked like he was in pain. And then he lost consciousness.

Sarah was shocked when Tobias suddenly went limp in her hands, and she gently laid him down on the ground. "Andrew, what's going on here?" she asked and looked to her left, only to see that Andrew was already gone. He was walking toward the exit of the cave, as if everything were alright.

Sarah ran over and grabbed him. "What is going on with you?" she more or less screamed into his ear, and he looked at her with an angry glint in his eyes.

"I have important things to do. So I would appreciate it if you kept your lunacy to yourself," he spat, freeing his shoulder.

"Tobias just lost consciousness after telling us that Denise's status is missing! Something is really wrong around here! Don't you see that?" she shouted, but Andrew just looked at her with disdain in his eyes.

"Don't scream like that. I'm leaving now." He walked away.

Sarah stood in the now silent cave and felt fear bubble up inside of her. "What the fuck is going on here?" she asked herself.

The fear subsided as fast as it came and was replaced by calm. Something inside her told her that all of this was actually no problem. That she was making unnecessary trouble.

"Oh, hell no," she growled in anger. "I will not let this happen to me too."

Sarah pushed away the foreign emotions and thoughts inside of her and let the burning fury deep inside her very being wash through her. She intuitively infused this sensation with her magic power, and a burning sensation flooded her body.

<Warning! Body, mind, and soul are in danger of being damaged. It is recommended to immediately stop this action.>

The system prompt only motivated her to drive herself even further. Suddenly, she noticed something inside of herself. Deep, deep inside her soul and mind, hidden behind her own self. There was something that shouldn't be there. With all of her willpower, she ferociously burned it away, and she felt a sharp pain inside of her very being.

But it was successful. The foreign thing inside of her was no more.

<Unlocked the unique active skill "Soul Purge."

Soul Purge (Unique): Channel rampaging Magic Power and mental energy to purge any foreign influence in your soul. Warning: May cause damage to the soul.>

Sarah looked at the system prompt with a mixture of joy and murderous intent. This bitch had gone too far. She had somehow implanted something inside of Sarah's soul without her even noticing it. Thinking back, Denise had probably implanted it when they met. And it has been a long time since then.

Sarah felt a cold feeling wash over her body, and her neck hair stood on end. What if Denise had already affected the whole camp? Andrew and Tobias were obviously under her influence. Alex too, most likely.

Even though her very being was injured and she was terribly exhausted and dizzy from the purge, she had to act immediately.

"Shit!" Sarah cursed under her breath and began running. She knew of one person who may be able to heal something like this in other people. Melissa.

She was usually located in the nursery cave, so that's where Sarah went. She was in such a hurry that she noticed the attack a step too late.

Alex jumped down from a tree onto her back, and she gracelessly fell to the ground. At the same time, she heard multiple heavy footsteps coming closer. She wanted to stand up and fight back, but all of her limbs and even her head and tail were pressed down into the mud by heavy weights. She roared in anger and began thrashing with all of her might. But it was no use. Even though she had monstrous strength, she felt at least six hands holding down her limbs.

She heard the shouting of many different men and realized that Denise must have noticed somehow that she had purged her influence.

The only option left for Sarah was to use her mental skills. She pushed out as much magic power as she could through her horns, but there wasn't much left due to her purge.

She felt the grips on her body loosen and prepared another escape when she heard an angry voice. "Oh no, you won't!"

Sarah felt her mental power being pushed back inside her head. She tried to fight back, but it felt like something snapped inside her, and an immense headache overcame her.

Sarah was lifted up on her feet and saw the heavily sweating and panting Denise standing in front of her. Sarah could hardly stand on her own, so another guy helped her stand.

Denise started smiling with a malicious glint in her eyes. "You shouldn't have slapped me." She nodded to the other men.

Sarah felt like she was in a cocoon of bodies, so many people around her and holding her body still. She was so dizzy that she couldn't have fought back even if she wanted to.

They walked very slowly, so it took quite some time for them to move forward. Sarah tried her best to regain focus during the awkward march.

"I'd say a punishment is in order." Sarah heard Denise's quiet and gentle voice from in front of her. Sarah's head had begun to clear a little, and she noticed that they were walking down one of the tunnels they hadn't explored yet. It was the one with an insane amount of ambient magic power.

"I will rip you apart," Sarah growled, but she felt helpless. She didn't even dare use her acid breath because Bertrand was walking in front of her. This stupid giant.

Denise laughed with her pearly voice but didn't say anything else. The ambient magic power became denser the further down the tunnel they went. It had started to become visible to the naked eye.

Multicolored strands of energy were swirling through the air in complex patterns. Sarah would have been amazed by the beauty of it, but the situation made it impossible.

After some more walking, they finally reached their destination. Sarah's heart felt like it sank to the bottom of the floor.

They came into a wide cave where the magic power was wildly flowing through the air. And it was coming from a spatial rip in the air. Pretty similar to the one she had used to leave the spatial error, but this one seemed different somehow. It seemed more . . . orderly, like there was a pattern to the swirling energy.

And in front of it stood another man, carrying the unconscious Melissa over his shoulder.

Denise turned around and gave her a gentle smile. "I guess we came to the same conclusion. It is goodbye now, my dear. May you have a miserable end."

Sarah couldn't comprehend what had happened in the last few minutes and just stared at the hateful woman with fury in her eyes.

"Why?" she asked with a growl that sounded more like the voice of a ferocious animal than that of a human.

The men forcefully turned Sarah's head down while pressing her mouth shut, and Denise stepped in front of her.

"Because I can," she just answered and smiled brightly. Sarah also smiled, and forcefully opened her mouth.

With a swishing sound, a little bit of acid flowed out of the small slit and coated Denise's face. She stumbled back with a guttural scream. "My eyes! MY EYES!"

"Throw her in the rip!" she heard Alex scream behind her, and she was dragged to the spatial fluctuation. Sarah wildly thrashed around with her arms and legs, and the men had a hard time holding her still. Just as she managed to free one of her arms, she saw Melissa being thrown inside the rip. As soon as her body came into contact with it, she disappeared without a trace.

"You BASTARDS!" Sarah roared and threw more of them off of her. But she was already too close to the rip.

She felt a mighty punch in her back, and she flew forward, with an unfortunate man who was still holding one of her legs.

The last thing Sarah saw was the unconscious Denise being carried away by Alex and Bertrand.

CHAPTER THIRTY-THREE

The Dungeon

<Welcome to the dungeon instance XG78L. Analyzing participants.
Two pathless participants. Excluded from the selection process.
One participant on the Path of Conflict.
Selected dungeon type: Conflict.>

Sarah took a heavy breath when she finally felt herself surrounded by air again. The system announcement was still etched into her brain. She didn't really know what a dungeon was, but if it was designed after her chosen path, they were in trouble.

She looked around to orient herself. She was in a dark cave, but with very strange walls made out of a gray, dirty-looking material. The walls were completely straight, and the ceiling was at a right angle to the wall. It just seemed . . . unnatural, as if somebody had purposely shaped it that way. She looked around some more and saw that there were pillars of the same material in the cave.

Between the pillars were weird . . . things standing around in rows. They were all coated in a red and brown case and seemed to be hollow inside. Between them, there was a lot of stuff lying around in messy piles.

"What the heck?" Sarah mumbled under her breath. She felt a prick somewhere in the back of her head. It was telling her that she should know what the sight in front of her was, but she just couldn't say what.

She shook her head to get out of her daze and started to look for Melissa and the man, who had been unlucky enough to get transported to this place with her.

They were lying not far from her, Melissa still unconscious. The guy was awake, though, staring blankly at the ceiling. Sarah only now noticed that he was one of the kitchen crew. It was Neil.

Sarah quickly checked on Melissa to see whether she was breathing. With relief, she saw that Melissa's condition was stable, although she seemed to have some trouble breathing.

Only then did she turn around to Neil, who was still just lying on the ground. She went over and kicked him in the stomach first. He started wheezing and held his aching side while Sarah grabbed him by his collar and lifted him up.

He seemed to be a little out of it, his eyes darting around without focus. Perfect for her intention. With her other hand, she extended her claws and grabbed the guy by his head. He started howling in pain when her claws dug into his scalp.

"Deal with it," Sarah grumbled through gritted teeth while she sent her mind into his.

It didn't take as much power as usual with humans, probably due to his confusion. But it still wasn't easy. His brain activity was truly a mess. She still hadn't figured out much about the complex human brain, but she was pretty sure that it shouldn't look like this.

Sarah was looking inside him to figure out if the soul parasite from Denise also affected the physical mind. And there it was. There seemed to be . . . something burrowing in his mind. This something was probably the soul parasite, as it was sending out hardly noticeable signals into the brain.

She tried to somehow cut off the influence but only managed to disrupt the signal for a few moments. And then it started again, as if she had never done anything to it.

"Shit," Sarah grumbled and let Neil fall to the ground, where he curled up and held his head, whimpering. She knew she wouldn't be successful. But, she had to see for herself if she would damage something in the brain if she did something like this. Sarah kicked him in the head, and Neil fell unconscious.

After that, she walked over to Melissa and gently touched her head. This time, without the claws. It was a little harder to enter her mind without direct contact with her nerves, but it was alleviated by the fact that she was still unconscious.

Sarah looked deep inside Melissa's mind, which had very low activity. This was pretty fascinating, as she had never seen the mind of an unconscious person. She had no time for this right now. She had to see if Melissa was also infected.

And sadly, she was. But contrary to Neil, the soul parasite didn't seem to send out very strong signals. They were only miniscule and irregular. The soul parasite seemed somewhat suppressed. "That's my girl," Sarah purred and exited Melissa's mind. Now on to business.

She felt her instincts from her time in the swamp come back to her. They flooded her mind and body, and a strange excitement filled her. "I am so weird," she mumbled and began pulling the two unconscious people behind one of the strange, hollow objects.

She tied up Neil with some kind of rope she found lying around and tried to position Melissa as comfortably as possible. When she was somewhat content with this, Sarah started to scout.

She ran through the cave like a ghost, her senses sharpened to their utmost. The cave was rather big and filled to the brim with weird, red-brown objects, and she couldn't see or sense anything alive. The only thing that was noticeable was the insane amount of ambient magic power in the air. It was so much that it was almost suffocating.

She quickly reached the other end of the cave and started walking alongside the wall to the right. Some segments were collapsed here and there, and she made a big circle around them. No need for her to be buried underneath a few tons of stone.

Because of this, she nearly didn't notice the slight shimmer of light coming through a gap in one of the piles of debris. She came to a grinding halt and gingerly stepped closer. There were reddish spikes coming out of the rock with dangerously sharp tips.

"What the hell is wrong with these rocks?" she wondered out loud, touching one of the spikes. There was some kind of coating on it, and she smelled it. "It smells like . . . blood? What the . . ."

Sarah became more and more confused by the second, but she tried to focus on her goals. Finding a way out and looking for potential dangers.

While shuffling through the gap in the debris, she really had to watch out not to accidentally stab herself on one of the spikes. It probably wouldn't hurt her all that much, but she had learned in the swamp that one had to always be cautious around weird stuff.

The gap led up a slope, and the light got brighter and brighter. Just before the entrance, she had to shove away a large stone, which blocked her from exiting the cave.

With a grunt, she pushed it aside and stumbled outside when it crumbled away. She quickly regained her balance and scanned her surroundings. But her focus was immediately shattered.

"What the actual fuck?" she said, looking around. One tiny memory managed to slip out of her subconscious, and she realized what she saw in front of her.

These were enormous houses. And she was in a city. She more or less understood what that meant, but only parts of it. She couldn't imagine the number of people living in the building in front of her. The whole community of the caves would probably fit on only one or two floors.

The next thing she noticed was that this "city" was long past its prime. Most buildings were at least partly caved in, and everything was dilapidated. When Sarah's gaze wandered higher up, she just stood there for a few moments with a wide open mouth.

Parts of debris and sometimes even whole buildings were suspended in the air. Sharp winds were flowing around them, and smaller pieces of rubble were flying around like leaves in the wind. The sky was a myriad of different-colored strings that were flowing around like water. There was red, blue, green, purple, and every other color she could imagine. It seemed more like a fever dream than reality. After a few moments, she noticed that there was something substantial missing in this scene. There was no sound. It was perfectly quiet, as if she were standing in the middle of nothingness.

Sarah had no idea where she was, but she was pretty sure she was far, far away from the caves.

This scene was so alien that her brain could barely accept what she was seeing. She had seen a lot of weird stuff up until now, but this made everything else look insignificant.

When she had somewhat regained her bearings, the system gave her another shock.

<Welcome, Sarah Anna Fischer, to the modified dungeon instance XG78L-9 (Conflict). As it is your first time entering a dungeon, you will receive additional information.

This dungeon is an enclosed area. Nothing and no one can enter or leave during the time the dungeon is active. Your goal is to reach the objective of the dungeon. Upon completion, you will receive rewards and be able to leave. The objectives of dungeons are to help you grow and overcome new challenges.

Challenges:
- Defeat 100 normal enemies (0/100)
- Defeat 2 elite enemies (0/2)
- Defeat the dungeon boss (0/1)

Rewards (will be awarded at different progression states):
- +5 levels
- Achievement "Dungeon Conqueror"
- Special consumable "Genetic Material Sample"
- Upgrade for one random mutation
- Good luck surviving.>

Sarah couldn't even be mad at the system because the boiling rage inside of her was already directed toward a very tangible entity. Denise.

"I will rip you apart when I get out of here," Sarah swore with burning eyes as she made her way back into the building.

While she ran back to the location where she had hidden Melissa and Neil, she pondered what to do. The most important thing right now was to secure food and water. She guessed that she could survive a long time without it, as the ambient magic power was pretty high. And if she kept her usage of it on the low side, she wouldn't risk getting depleted any time soon.

The problem was the other two and the fact that she hadn't even seen an insect up until now. When she reached the hideout, only Neil was lying there on the ground. She panicked for a second, until Melissa walked toward her.

"Sarah . . . you . . . are here too . . ." Melissa said, breathing heavily. She seemed to have difficulty talking and even walking. She was stumbling around more than anything else.

"Sit down," Sarah said and gently pushed her to the ground.

"It is . . . so hard . . . to breathe." Melissa had a pained expression. "It even . . . hurts . . . my lungs. What's . . . going on?"

Sarah sat down next to her and told her about their predicament. Melissa looked a little bit spooked and glanced at her sidelong. "Will you . . . leave us?" Melissa asked in a quivering voice, the fear apparent in her cramped body.

"Don't worry," Sarah said and laid a hand on her shoulder. Melissa nodded gratefully, and her body loosened a little. She leaned her head on the wall behind her and closed her eyes. "So . . . tired . . ."

"Just stay here and rest for a moment. I'll be close by." Sarah stood up again.

With a determined expression, she prepared herself for another round of mutations.

CHAPTER THIRTY-FOUR

Incorruptible

Andrew was standing in front of the gathered crowd, his hands tied behind his back. Alex was standing behind him, and Denise was sitting on a simple chair made out of wood next to them. The upper part of her face was still bandaged, and only a few strands of her formerly luxurious hair could be seen.

"We are all here to decide Andrew's punishment." Andrew heard a booming voice coming from behind him.

Andrew let his head slump down in shame. He knew he deserved this. He knew all along. It was even a relief that this moment was finally here.

"Andrew brought a dangerous individual to us. Not only was she responsible for multiple assaults on members of our tribe, but she even critically wounded Denise! And if that isn't enough, she kidnapped two of our most cherished people. We are greatly weakened through the loss of Melissa and Neil," he roared in an angry voice, and the crowd started to confirm his accusations with shouts and gestures at Andrew.

"While it was a grave mistake by Andrew, he also did a lot of good for our community. Therefore, we will sentence him to step down from his position as leader. From now on, he will be responsible for caring for Derek and Till." Alex had obvious disdain in his voice. It was clear he thought the sentence too lax.

The crowd nodded, though they also didn't seem all that happy with this decision.

"I will take over the position of leader until we find someone more fitting. You can leave now." Alex closed the meeting and violently ripped off the rope that bound Andrew's hands. He clenched his teeth from the sudden pain but didn't dare say anything.

Something in the back of his head told him that this whole situation was off, but he quickly shoved the thought away. He had to accept his punishment. He was responsible for everything that had gone wrong.

"And now, apologize," Alex growled and shoved him toward the injured Denise.

Andrew stumbled with guilt deep inside his chest. He kneeled down and let his head sink in shame. "I am very sorry for your injury. It is all my fault."

"Yes, it is, but I am merciful. I allow you to keep living and wipe the asses of the idiots. Be grateful," Denise said in a mocking tone with poison in her voice, and Andrew nodded in affirmation.

"I am grateful."

"Good. Then fuck off and wipe some asses," she snapped at him, and Andrew scrambled to his feet and walked away hurriedly.

A strange relief flooded his mind when he thought about not having to worry about the well-being of their tribe anymore. He would only have to care for Derek and Till, who were in their condition because of him in the first place.

When he reached the cave where they were locked away, he scrunched up his nose because of the smell. Since Melissa had disappeared, nobody had cared enough to clean them.

Derek and Till were completely naked and sat on the ground with vacant looks in their eyes. Andrew noticed with surprise that they were very hairy now. The only places where skin could still be seen were their palms and around their eyes.

"Strange," Andrew muttered and thought about Sarah. They were probably also able to mutate. Andrew wasn't quite sure if it was good or bad that they hadn't lost their connection to the system.

He stepped in front of the two and kneeled down to the ground. "Derek? Till?" he called out to them with a gentle voice, and they looked at him with suspicion. They both scrambled on all fours and came to the wooden bars.

Hardly any intelligence could be seen in their eyes, and it broke Andrew's heart. Luckily, his skill kicked in and dimmed the pain.

"I am so sorry for not being there for you," he whispered to them, fully aware that they couldn't understand him. After he first visited them, he was so shocked that he walked away immediately. He had done his best not to think about them too much and overused his abilities to numb his feelings to it. But not anymore.

"Come with me. We'll wash you now," he told them in the same soothing and gentle voice as before, but they didn't seem to understand. So Andrew opened up the cage and held his hands out to them.

They still had suspicious looks in their eyes, but they took his hands. He gently pulled them along, and they started walking toward the river.

It took a long time to reach it because they were so excited to be outside for a change. They played around with the fallen leaves and ran after flies and other insects. It was quite exhausting keeping them together, but Andrew didn't mind.

It was a long time later when they finally arrived at the river. The former humans looked at the raging water with fear in their eyes and gripped Andrew's hands tighter.

"It's fine. There's no need to be afraid," he said and took out his personal brush. He first pulled Derek to the edge of the water and started washing his body.

Derek screamed with fright in the beginning because the water was so cold, but he seemed to enjoy getting clean after a while and sat down with a look of contentment on his face.

Andrew was strangely happy about Derek's reaction and felt something deep inside of him heal.

<Soul injury healed. Class elections are now possible. Listing available options:

Path of Leadership:
- Indomitable: Focus on Soul Power and Specialization Domination. Unlocking of specialization: Manifestation (Soul).
- Incorruptible: Focus on Soul Power and Specialization Equilibrium. Unlocking of specialization: Manifestation (Soul).

Path of Altruism:
- Pillar: Focus on Soul Power and Specialization Equilibrium.
- Path of Power: Focus on Soul Power and Specialization Domination. Unlocking of Specialization: Mental Warfare (Soul).
- Puppet Master: Focus on Soul Power and Specializations, Domination, and Adaptation.
- Soul Enslaver: Focus on Soul Power and Specialization Domination. Unlocking of Specialization: Parasitization (Soul).

Please choose carefully.>

Andrew felt like he had woken up from a long nightmare. It wasn't a physical change, but he felt lighter than ever. But the question was, what he should be choosing now.

He dismissed the option for the Path of Power immediately. He really didn't want to go down that path, as it seemed like he had to hurt a lot of people for that. The Path of Leadership also didn't matter to him anymore, as his job was now to care for Derek and Till.

So the obvious choice was the Path of Altruism. He wanted to confirm his choice for the system, but something held him back. He couldn't quite explain it, but something inside him told him that this wasn't the right choice.

He shook his head to banish the distracting thoughts and opened his mouth to confirm his choice of Pillar.

"I will choose the class Incorruptible," he heard himself say and held his hand in front of his mouth. What had he said just now?

"No, wait!" he shouted, but it was too late.

<You have chosen the Path of Leadership with the class Incorruptible. Your soul will now undergo a transformation. Please prepare yourself.>

Before Andrew could say anything more, the transformation began. Just like when he received his equilibrium specialization, his mind was sucked into a comfortable void, except this time, he could retain a stronger sense of self. He concentrated for a moment, and his body materialized. He looked at his ethereal hands and then around him.

He first thought that this space was empty, and physically speaking, it was. There was no sound, light, or anything else to perceive. But there was something else. This place was full of feelings. Full of personality. He soon realized that he was inside his very own soul.

He looked around in amazement, not really knowing what to do with all the information he had suddenly received about himself. It was a jumbled mess of so many facets of his personality that he soon wondered if he had gone crazy.

He delved deeper into his soul, which was obviously undergoing some sort of transformation. It was a complete mystery to him what exactly was going on. The only thing he knew was that this was probably the transformation of his soul that the system had told him about.

After some time, he noticed a giant accumulation of all sorts of jumbled emotions. They were blocked by some kind of barrier that felt very familiar to him. With a sinking feeling, he realized that all these emotions were suppressed by his skills. And they didn't just disappear. They accumulated over time until they broke out like they did when he injured his soul.

Looking over the giant mass of negativity, he realized that what had come out of him last time was only a small portion.

He had no idea what to do with this information, but he wouldn't just let it be. When he prepared to inspect it more closely, he noticed something else inside his soul. Something foreign. He concentrated on it and soon saw something . . . weird. It had grown tendrils that stretched throughout his entire soul. How could he have not noticed this sooner?

It felt strange, alien, and intrusive. And he instinctively knew it didn't belong inside him. His jumbled mess of suppressed emotions had to wait. This was way more urgent.

He analyzed it more closely and began to feel some kind of personality in it. He knew this personality. He thought hard for a moment, and then it struck him. Denise. This foreign thing belonged to Denise.

With anger billowing up inside him, he got ready to rip it out of himself, but then he noticed that a strand of it was connected to this foreign thing from the outside. Probably with its creator, Denise.

Andrew held himself back. He had to be smart about this. He had to do something without alerting Denise. It was just an assumption, but he couldn't think of anything else this thing could connect to.

Before he could even begin to think about doing something, a fundamental change occurred within his soul. Waves of powerful energy billowed through it, this time visibly. The tendrils of the foreign thing burned away like dry leaves in a fire and were pushed out of his soul.

When the billowing energy reached the strand connecting the foreign thing to Denise, though, it didn't burn the strand away. Instead, it encompassed the single tendril in some kind of cocoon. The strand tried to reach out again, but it couldn't get past the barrier.

After this spectacle, he felt clarity come back to him. He needed to get out of here. But it wasn't that easy. There was a large form of resistance holding him back, and it felt like he was getting sucked deeper and deeper.

He struggled and struggled, but was pulled deeper with every passing moment. Something inside of him just wanted to give in. To live inside this calming void, with no need to go back out into the cruel and difficult world ever again.

But he didn't want that.

"NO!" he roared with his whole soul, and the void shuddered from the power of his will. He pulled himself out of the soul space and into reality again.

When his senses came back to him, he was so overwhelmed by them that he keeled over and fell headfirst into the mud.

Derek and Till were shocked at first, but then they began to laugh. Andrew scrambled to his feet again and couldn't help but smile a little when he saw the two former humans laughing at him.

Not much time seemed to have passed, as the light around him was more or less the same.

"Come here, Derek. Let's finish cleaning you up," he said, and Derek came right to him, knowing what he intended to do. When Derek sat in front of Andrew again and let himself be washed with a content face, Andrew's face hardened.

Ice-cold rage bubbled up inside him. His skills were barely enough to suppress them far enough down so he wouldn't scream out loud. It all came back to him now.

Denise had taken Melissa from him. She had taken his people from him. She had humiliated and insulted him. So she would pay. And she would not go easily.

CHAPTER THIRTY-FIVE

Mutations and Status

Sarah moved some distance away from the sleeping Melissa and made herself comfortable on the ground. It was now time to decide which kind of mutation she would choose. She already had an expansive arsenal of deadly weapons, but her survivability was still somewhat lacking.

She remembered seeing the skill Fast Recovery on Andrew's status screen, so maybe she could find a fitting mutation. But she didn't get her hopes up. There hadn't been anything of the sort when she last checked.

She mentally summoned up the available mutation options, and a large screen filled her vision immediately.

<Mutation: Organs and Processes. Listing available options.
- Poison Concentration Organ (not recommended, 7 LF): A special organ located underneath the heart. Collects highly toxic waste and concentrates it. The product can be injected into the bloodstream for a short burst of lethality.

<Mutation: Skin. Listing available extensions to Dense Skin (0/3)
- Oily Film (1 LF)
- Contact Poison Film (1 LF)
- Acidic Film (1 LF)
- Magic Signature Suppression (2 LF)
- Multi-Layered Skin (2 LF)

Mutation: Bone Structure. Listing available extensions to High Density Bones (2/3)
- Vital Organ Shielding (2 LF)
- Bone Spikes (Elbow) (1 LF)
- Bone Spikes (Spine) (2 LF)

Mutation: Muscles. Listing available extensions to Strengthened Fibers (0/3)

- Short Fibers (explosive strength) (1 LF)
- Medium-Length Fibers (strength and endurance) (1 LF)
- Long Fibers (endurance) (1 LF)
- Magic Power Reinforcement (2 LF)

Mutation: Brain, Nerve System, and Sensory Organs. Listing available options.

- Protective Brain Webbing (2 LF): Protective webbing surrounding the brain. It cushions it and protects it from impacts.
- Sturdy Nerve System (3 LF): Impacts and wounds will impede the functionality of the nerve system less.
- Decentralized Nerve System (10 LF): Signals can be transmitted, as long as one nerve-string still connects the brain to the respective body parts.>

<For more options, increase your level and/or heighten your Life Force.>

She had hoped for some more mutation options because she had leveled up to twenty. While there were a few more options, they were not of much interest to her. Having studied all her options once before, she was pretty sure what she needed right now.

First, she would choose Vital Organ Shielding because this would exponentially increase her survivability. When she thought about it, the important organs were all pretty much unprotected inside her stomach. The lungs were somewhat surrounded by a rib cage, but still. She would feel much more comfortable like this.

Second, she decided she would choose the magic power reinforcement for her muscles. She guessed that with this, she would be able to give her muscles a momentary boost in strength. Thinking back, she really could have used it when she had been thrown in the dungeon.

And lastly, the decentralized nerve system. It was very costly, but for good reason. If she ever somehow injured her back, or if someone with a strong mind-altering power attacked her nerves, it would be over for her. But with this, she would be able to move even with a severed spine. At least she hoped so.

"Alright, do it, you stupid system! Gimme these mutations!" she shouted and mentally prepared herself for some serious pain. The system had told her the last time that it wasn't a good idea to mutate multiple parts of her body at once, but time was of the essence. She had no idea if enemies were looking for them right now. She had to be at fighting capacity as soon as possible.

When the timer hit zero, she lost all feeling and senses. It was like she was in the space of nothingness again, only she knew this wasn't the case. The mutation in her nervous system had probably shut it down.

This was probably her most comfortable mutation so far, if she ignored the subdued panic from feeling trapped inside her own body. She had never really thought about it that much, but she once saw an example of how badly mutations can go. The image of the grotesque bear cubs still swam before her eyes; they had barely been able to stay alive.

This thought only fueled the bubbling panic inside her. She was wrong. This wasn't the most comfortable mutation so far. This was one of the more horrible ones. She would prefer to feel immense pain if she could at least see what was going on with her body.

Holding her mind together with sheer resolve, she powered through this mutation. It took excruciatingly long to finish. Or maybe it just felt that way because it was so horrible. It was impossible to tell.

Her sensations came back all at once, which was way too much for her overtaxed mind. She dry heaved for a few seconds until she was able to make some sense of her surroundings again. She was lying on the ground, her face half buried in dirt. Great.

She still felt a little dizzy but had no time to waste. She stood up on her wobbly legs and tried to feel the changes inside her body. The first thing she noticed was that she was noticeably heavier. Which was most likely due to the Vital Organ Shielding. She curiously pressed her finger into her belly, just beneath her rib cage. Under her dense muscles, she could feel something hard. That mutation had gone well, at least.

Next, she tried to somehow feel the Decentralized Nerve System, but no matter how much she concentrated on her body, it was no use. She even tried to use her own abilities on herself, only to be disappointed once again. She had tried often to somehow influence her own nerve system with her abilities, but it just didn't work. She just hoped this mutation would work and wouldn't do something bizarre to her body.

The magic power Reinforcement of her muscles was something different, though. As soon as she thought about pushing some magic power into her right forearm, it began to vibrate with energy. After a few seconds, the arm even started swelling a little, with veins popping up. She tried to keep it active for a while, but it started to hurt pretty badly.

She let the magic power go and shook her arm out, which felt pretty sore and a little weak now. This was really only for momentary use. At least for now. Maybe she could unlock some mutations that made her muscles more sturdy.

Satisfied with her powered-up body, she took a look at her improved status screen, which was absurdly long by now.

Details:
Level: 20
Name: Sarah Anna Fischer

Class: Nightmare
Race: Mutant
Status: Normal
HP: 295/295 **SP**: 50/295 **MP**: 200/510

Achievements:
- How the hell are you still sane? Resistance to mind damage increased by 10%.
- Poison Gorger: Resistance to orally consumed poison increased by 30%.
- More Than Human: Higher success rate on special mutations.
- Junior Reaper (upgradable): You are able to slightly sense weak points in your enemies.

Affinities:
Mind (Mid) Body (Mid) Energy (Low)

Specializations:
- Mind (2/2)
  - Invasion
  - Nerve Control
- Body (2/2)
  - Adaptation
  - Mutation
- Energy (0/1)

Basic Stats:
Strength: 15
Dexterity: 22
Endurance: 20
Resistance: 19
Intelligence: 23
Force: 11

Special Stats:
Magic Power: 20
Life Force: 50
Mental Power: 31

Active Skills:
- Mind Infiltration (Invasion): While using Magic Power, you are able to invade the mind of another being. Invasion is facilitated if the being has been poisoned by you.

Passive Skills:

- Poison Body (Adaptation): You are able to increase your resistance to hazardous substances and reinforce your body with their properties in combination with your Specialization "Mutation."
- Poison and Acid Resistance: You are highly resistant to various poisons and acids. (Overcoming new or stronger poisons or acids strengthens this ability.)
- Walking Hazard: Your body liquids are highly toxic and acidic. You are now naturally producing a strong nerve toxin and acid inside your body. (Consuming new or stronger poisons and acids strengthens this ability.)
- Mutated Glands: Toxin and acid glands are incorporated in certain mutations.
- Metamorphosis (Mutation, 48/50): You are able to mutate your body. The amount of mutations is dependent on your Life Force. Due to your Specialization "Adaption," there will be less Life Force needed, and you will have fewer limitations. Your Class, "Nightmare," will influence your mutations.
  - Skin:
    - Dense Skin (1 LF): Dense and leathery skin. More force is needed to penetrate the skin, and shallow wounds close up faster.
  - Bone structure:
    - High Density Bones (2 LF): Incredibly robust and dense bones. Higher stamina consumption due to increased weight.
    - Predator Teeth (1 LF)
    - Retractable Claws (2 LF)
    - Vital Organ Shielding (2 LF)
  - Muscles:
    - Strengthened Fibers (1 LF): Increased muscle strength. Muscles are slightly tougher and stronger.
    - Magic Power Reinforcement (2 LF)
  - Brain, Nerve System, and Sensory Organs:
    - Predator Eyes (1 LF): Higher sensitivity to movement. Higher chance of spotting camouflaged beings.
    - Optimized Brain Structure (Battle) (6 LF): Optimized structure, focused on movement and decision making.
    - Decentralized Nerve System (10 LF): Signals can be transmitted, as long as one nerve-string still connects the brain to the respective body parts.
  - Organs and Processes:
    - Magic Power Nourishment System (5 LF): Your body is adapted to run only on Magic Power. You are able to sense Magic Power

in other living organisms and are able to feed on it. Most matter that enters your digestive system and lungs will be converted into Magic Power. Warning: High potential of cell breakdown if your Magic Power is empty for too long.

- Acid Gland (not recommended), (4 LF): A gland located in the throat, which produces highly corrosive acid. Can be spit out with moderate pressure.
- Extension: Gaseous acid (1 LF)

○ Special Mutations:

- Nightmare's Tail (class specific), (5 LF): A long and flexible tail with an exoskeleton made out of spine-like bone segments. Can be stretched over its original length, but will leave the vulnerable muscle and sinew under the exoskeleton exposed. Poison gland incorporated in the tip.
- Nightmare's Horns (class specific), 5 LF): Two large and curved horns located on top of the forehead. Directly connected to your brain through nerve strings. Amplify mind related skills and enable them to work without direct contact. Warning: Strong pain and disorientation if broken.

- Suppression (Nerve Control): Your emotions will influence your nerves less. Warning: Instinctual behavior is also suppressed.
- Struggle (Conditional Passive): Your Resistance is increased in dire situations.
- Slightly Crazy: Most things won't bother you that much. If certain conditions are met however, there is a slight chance that you will go berserk.
- Mean Eye: There is a chance that other beings will shortly freeze in fear when they look at you. Higher chance with sentient beings.

Her stats had improved quite a bit, especially her resistance, which had risen by a whole nine points through her reaching level twenty and the mutation of her bone structure. She wasn't sure if the nerve system mutation also changed something; it was hard to tell.

She also began to see a pattern in her increasing stats. On every level, she would gain one magic power, four life force, and three mental power points. She had no idea why she got more of the former two special stats than magic power, but this was something to ponder at a later date. Every point in these special stats heightened her HP, SP, and MP, though she could only guess for now which increased which.

And for every ten points in each special stat, she gained heightened basic stats. This was all she could think of right now, as she hadn't really looked at her status in a systematic way until now. She had just been overwhelmed by everything. If she got back alive, she would start to document her stat increases with Tobias, as this would for sure enable them to figure out how the system worked. At least if she didn't kill him first due to him being an exhausting prick. And of course, if the whole ripping Denise to shreds went well.

Sarah grinned while thinking about her improving body. It was a truly exhilarating feeling to get stronger and stronger with each passing day.

By now, she had thoroughly exhausted herself. Not only had she not gotten any rest after the incident back at the camp, but she had more or less immediately gone out to explore. She really needed some shut-eye right now.

Already swaying a little from side to side, she made her way over to where Melissa lay huddled on the ground. She laid herself next to her but positioned herself so she would be able to keep tabs on Neil too.

It didn't take long for Sarah to fall into a somewhat peaceful slumber.

CHAPTER THIRTY-SIX

Clarity

After an unknowable amount of restless sleep, Sarah woke up again. Every time she had woken up before, she had made sure that Melissa was still next to her and that Neil was still tied up.

And luckily, not much had changed. The only difference was that Melissa was awake now. Melissa was sitting next to Sarah, looking at her. When she noticed Sarah was awake, she blushed a little and cleared her throat. "I thought I'd keep watch and let you sleep a little."

Sarah looked at her with a raised brow and wondered what kind of 'keeping watch' she'd been doing.

"But you didn't—"

"I did keep watch."

"But—"

"I. Did. Keep. Watch."

Melissa looked at her with such an intense gaze that Sarah dropped the subject. No use quarreling with this stubborn woman. Sarah sat up and noticed that Melissa looked a lot better. "Didn't you have trouble breathing?"

Melissa nodded and gave her a crooked smile. "I did. And I know now why it hurt to breathe. I got the skills Magic Overload Resistance and Acid Resistance. The very air here is harmful for humans, but I guess the system didn't want me to die just yet."

Sarah nodded in understanding. Given her constitution, it made a lot of sense for Sarah to be unaffected by this environment. Since her body ran purely on magic power, the air here was like a feast for her.

Sarah's mind had fully awoken, and she remembered the uncomfortable discussion she'd need to have with Melissa. "Melissa, I need to talk to you about something very important."

Melissa looked at her curiously but nodded in affirmation.

"So, you . . . You have some kind of parasite in your soul, and most likely the whole camp does too. Denise implanted it, and it influences you in her favor." Sarah tensed up her body, just in case Melissa attacked her.

"Oh, good. I was so afraid that you would still be under her influence," Melissa said, slumping and letting her head fall against the hard wall. "On the other hand, I guess I'd be pretty much dead by now if you had been."

Sarah looked at Melissa in surprise. "You knew? How are you not affected by it?"

Melissa nodded gravely. "I do. And I still am a little. But, I suppressed it so far that it feels more like someone is whispering weird stuff in my ear. It's easy to ignore. But sadly, I only started to notice a few days ago." Melissa's face contorted, and she looked down to the ground in shame. "You see, I . . . Or, no, let me say it differently. A lot of people have a great liking for me."

Sarah only lifted one of her eyebrows and snorted.

"Not like this!" Melissa retorted in anger but calmed herself again. "Yes alright, also like this. But many others who don't see me like this do like me a lot. But recently . . . they started treating me more coldly, like they'd stopped caring about me. And I started to think that I deserved to be treated like this. That was the moment I started doubting my own thoughts. I first suspected Andrew of this, even though I couldn't explain why. But . . . well, now it's clear who did this."

Sarah looked at her with a frown. Something didn't sit quite right with her about what Melissa had told her. "And you just did nothing?"

Melissa glared at her, and her lips became small lines. "Don't be too fast to judge. How do you think you were able to notice it? Why do you think it took Denise so long to take over? You have no idea how hard I tried to prevent this whole shitshow. And let me tell you, it's not easy to do while simultaneously hiding it from this freakin' parasite in my head and not going crazy over the thought of something foreign being in my very soul."

"I'm sorry," Sarah said seriously and looked into Melissa's angry eyes. "I judged you too quickly."

Melissa's anger melted away, and she nodded in approval.

"So . . . did you get it out?" Sarah asked tentatively.

Melissa snorted. "Of course I did. Do you think I'd let this thing stay inside me any longer than necessary?"

Sarah nodded in understanding and let herself slump against the wall. She hadn't even noticed how tense her body had become.

They sat there for quite some time before Melissa spoke again. "You know, if I look at this rationally, I should be freaking out right now. I have been kidnapped and thrown into some dangerous, foreign place where even breathing harms me. But I feel strangely . . . freed. I didn't know I had felt burdened to this extent."

"Guess that happens when you have someone around who permanently dampens your emotions," Sarah mumbled, causing Melissa to chuckle.

"Yes, you might be right. But, it's not just that. I . . . When, do you think, was the last time someone asked me if I was okay?"

Sarah looked at Melissa with a confused face because of the sudden shift in their discussion. "I don't know. Yesterday?"

Melissa smiled wryly and shook her head. "It's been a long time. And I don't even like to remember because it was a pretty horrible moment. I had just killed someone."

Sarah didn't quite know what to say. She saw how troubled Melissa was but had no idea how to soothe her or help her. But, before Sarah could say something stupid to lighten the mood, Melissa continued.

"You see, I like helping others. I like what my skills can do and how I can support our community. But . . . people don't really see me as a person. Either they see me as some sort of stress relief station, or they look at my breasts and only think about . . . you know what. Nobody even thinks about asking how I am doing, or that I could be too exhausted to help them."

Sarah frowned upon hearing this. And, she couldn't keep her mouth shut. "Why do you even care what other people think about you? Why don't you just send them away when they bother you?"

Melissa snorted and looked at her with doubting eyes. "You are the last person who can say that to me."

Now it was Sarah's time to get a little angry. "What are you trying to say, huh? Like I care what others . . ."

"Stop," Melissa said resolutely and held up her hand. Sarah's mouth closed, but her anger hadn't subsided.

"A lot of people in the community obviously don't like you. And you are . . . let's say, a rather special person. But you still try so hard to fit in, even if it is clear that it will never be possible in our group. But there are people who like and accept you, and you still try to fit into the bigger picture. Why?"

Sarah felt like Melissa's words had hit her deep in her soul. She didn't want to admit it, but she knew Melissa was right. Why had she tried so hard to fit in? Why had she tried so hard to be part of a community that didn't fully accept her?

Sarah took a deep breath and let her head hang down. "I guess you're right. Sorry for getting angry," she mumbled. Melissa took Sarah's right hand into hers. They were warm and soft, but they still gave her the strength to confront reality.

"Thinking back, I always thought that I had to fit in. That I have to try really hard to be part of a community, even if I'm odd. And yes, I know that I am different than most people. I can't really explain why I have this need inside of me. It just feels like it has been a part of me for a long time. Maybe even from before all of this happened."

Melissa scooched closer and took her in her arms. "I guess we both have our problems. And even if no one else likes you . . . I do. So don't worry about being alone."

Sarah smiled, and emotions welled up inside of her. Just like the first time she had met Melissa, she had managed to lift a heavy weight from her heart just by being there for her.

"Thank you, Melissa. You are the only person who isn't shit in this crazy world. And I care about how you feel."

Melissa laughed out loud, and Sarah couldn't help but also smile a little, even if she had no idea what amused Melissa so much.

"I guess I can count that as a compliment?" Melissa asked and smiled teasingly.

Sarah didn't know why, but Melissa seemed to shine brightly at this moment, even with all the dirt on her face and her blond hair a tangled mess. She looked down in a hurry to hide the furious blush on her face.

She heard a slight giggling from her side, which only heightened her embarrassment. Anxious to escape the uncomfortable situation, Sarah cleared her throat and changed the subject.

"Do you think you can heal Neil over there?" Sarah asked while still staring down. Melissa's hands, which were still holding hers, cramped a little at her question.

"I think so, yes. Until now, I had to be extra careful not to alert Denise to my tampering. But I guess that's not important anymore," she said with a sigh. "The sooner the better?"

Sarah nodded, and they stood up together. She immediately regretted changing the subject as Melissa's soft hands released hers.

While cursing herself inwardly, Sarah walked over to the still unconscious Neil, with Melissa close behind her.

"Should I do something?" Sarah asked. Melissa was standing there without moving an inch.

"No, it's just . . . the last time I ripped something like this out of someone else . . . it didn't go well," Melissa replied with a quivering voice.

"It's fine," Sarah soothed and turned to face her. "You managed to do it for yourself. You will be able to do it for someone else. And if something goes wrong with him . . . let's say, he won't be able to harm you."

Melissa looked at her with complicated feelings in her eyes but nodded. Without saying anything more, she crouched down next to Neil. Sarah also crouched down and gripped Neil's neck with both her hands. If he even showed a hint of aggressiveness, she'd snap his neck like a dry twig.

Melissa put her shaking hands on Neil's chest and closed her eyes. They sat there for a long time, but nothing changed. Sarah concentrated on her magic sense, and only now did she see something happening.

Magic power seemed to concentrate in Melissa's hands, only to vanish like a lie. That was where the conversion of the energy into . . . whatever Melissa was producing with her skills took place.

"He's free," Melissa said in a shaky voice and pulled her hands back.

"Just like that?" Sarah asked, feeling almost disappointed by the anticlimactic conclusion.

Melissa snorted and looked at her with furrowed brows. "That's what you think. You don't want to know how this disgusting thing defended itself. It almost felt like it had some kind of will of its own." She shuddered at her own words and frantically cleaned her hands on Neil's clothes.

Sarah quickly overcame her strange disappointment, and a small glimmer of hope blossomed in her heart. Maybe when they got out of this mess, they could save the others. It didn't matter if they liked her or not; nobody deserved to be in the claws of that insane bitch. She wondered how the system would define Denise's state of mind, considering Sarah had judged herself to be slightly crazy.

"Let's hope he wakes up," Melissa mumbled, ripping Sarah from her thoughts.

A loud grumbling sound could be heard from Melissa's stomach. She looked down worriedly and then up at Sarah again. She didn't even have to say anything before Sarah was on her feet again.

"Don't worry. I won't let you starve to death. Can I leave you alone with him?"

Melissa nodded and smiled. "He's tied up and has a slight soul injury. I doubt he will wake up for another day or so. And while you're away, I'll start looking for a water source in this cave. Maybe there's something trickling inside."

Sarah looked at her with concern. "Just don't go outside. I have no idea what's going on out there, but . . . this place is not normal."

Melissa looked at her curiously, but Sarah held up her hands. "I'll explain later. I have to scout some more and get you something to eat. I need you alive and well to be able to tell you stories."

Melissa gave her a grateful smile, which caused Sarah to blush again. Now seriously, why did this always happen to her?!

Feeling flustered and insecure, Sarah turned around and ran away. She was already too far gone to hear Melissa's fearful, whispered words.

"Don't die."

CHAPTER THIRTY-SEVEN

Dungeon Exploration

Sarah had been walking through the ruined city for quite a while. Even though the sun wasn't visible through the oddly colorful sky, the natural light had begun to dim. The strangest part was that even though there was barely any light anymore, everything was still perfectly visible. This place got stranger and stranger by the minute.

During her scouting, she hadn't encountered even one living creature, not even a plant. She had sharpened her physical and magical senses to the extreme, but nothing popped up. The eerie silence of her surroundings started to get to her, and she began to imagine sounds in the distance. It was unnerving.

Every now and again, she would come upon exceptionally bizarre parts of the city. Some of the houses looked like they had been melted down and cooled again in only a few seconds. They twisted and bent into impossible shapes in the sky. Some parts of them were even suspended in midair, as if they had forgotten to fall down. It all looked like it had come straight out of a dystopian novel.

A loud humming sound suddenly assaulted her ears, and Sarah tried hard to ignore it. The sound got worse by the minute. As it got louder and more erratic, she looked around in alarm to find the source, but there was nothing around her. She looked up into the sky and was once again flabbergasted.

There were gently flowing strings of color, which began to bulge and twist above her. An especially thick red string started to slowly flow down.

The humming sound grew louder and became more erratic, so Sarah held her hands over her ears. The thick red string flowed lower and lower until it gently touched one of the buildings.

The color didn't fully block her sight, so she could see what was happening to the structure beneath it. The building began twisting and turning like it was alive. Now she understood what the heck had happened to the structures around her. The red string was getting lower by the second.

"This is not good," Sarah mumbled in shock. She started to run away, but it was no use. The red string was huge and began blocking out more and more of the sky.

Sarah slid to a halt and looked around her. "There!" she shouted to no one in particular, and she made her way to a hole in the ground. There were better things in life than to delve into unstable constructions, but it was definitely better than being bent out of shape by a weird energy string.

Sarah looked up again, only to see that the string was even closer now. Way too close. There was no more time to lose. Sarah jumped inside the hole and extended her claws.

She scratched over the surface, which tugged painfully at the roots of her claws. After a few seconds, she came to a grinding halt and clenched her teeth against the pain. But it wasn't over yet. The humming was still getting closer.

The red energy started to push its way inside the hole from above her. With no other choice, Sarah started jumping from one side of the wall to the next. It was very painful, and she, more than once, bumped into outcroppings.

After another leap, there was no more wall. Crying out in fright, she fell down and crashed to the ground. Sarah groaned in pain but forced herself to look up again. She could still see the red string through the hole in the ceiling, but it didn't come down any further.

With a sigh of relief, she let the tension flow out of her body, and with it came the pain. She looked down at her body and saw several bruises and open wounds. It wasn't too bad, but it was definitely painful.

The problem was her left hand. The claw on her thumb had been more or less ripped out and was only slightly attached to her finger now. She tried to retract it like her other claws, but was met with stinging pain.

"Fuck, this is horrible!" she groaned and gently grasped the useless claw with her other hand. She gritted her teeth, and ripped it out.

Searing pain erupted in her thumb, and she let out a small whimper. "Why do the fingers need to be so sensitive?" she mumbled through gritted teeth and took a deep breath to calm herself again. After some time, the pain reduced, and her finger wasn't bleeding anymore.

Sarah breathed out in exhaustion and started to take in her surroundings. There was life. Everywhere.

Her senses bombarded her with information about the different little creatures surrounding her. There was also a literal carpet of plants with dense magic inside of it. Her immediate surroundings were void of any life, though, probably due to their close proximity to the hole in the ceiling.

Thinking about the horrifying red string of twisting death, it made a lot of sense that nothing could live on the surface.

Still holding her injured finger, she inspected the life forms around her more closely. Every surface was covered in turquoise moss-like vegetation, with glowing yellow flowers sprouting in various places. On top of the moss, giant snails were crawling around and happily munching away at the moss. There were also lots of little flies hopping from one flower to the next. Apart from these three life forms, there was nothing else.

Creeping closer, Sarah inspected the giant snails more thoroughly. Their shells came just below her midsection, and their giant eyes were as big as her fists. They were softly glowing a brownish color, and she could even see parts of their organs through their semi-translucent flesh. A thick mucus covered their skin, and they left trails of the substance behind them.

Sarah's face contorted. "Ugh, this looks so gross." But, it was still necessary to test whether the system counted the snails as enemies. If so, this quest would be very easy.

Because she didn't want to touch the slimy things, she reached out with her mind. There was very little nerve activity in the snails, but trying couldn't hurt. Sarah reached out to their brains and nerve systems, but the snails only shuddered in response. They didn't even stop eating.

With a frustrated groan, Sarah got a little closer. More testing was needed. She opened her mouth wide and covered the snail in her acid breath. And then . . . nothing. The moss, the snails, and even the flies were completely unaffected. Sarah was getting worried. Two of her attacks were rendered useless.

The next step was to test her poison. Her tail shot forward with lightning speed and punctured the snail in front of her, which finally gained results. The snail quickly pulled itself inside its shell and closed the opening.

Sarah inspected the tip of her tail, only to see that it was slightly sizzling. Those snails seemed to be acidic. Great.

Sarah waited a few minutes until blackened goo started to flow out from the shell. It only took a few more minutes for the shell to fall on its side, and Sarah could see the shriveled remains of the snail inside. The once brownish, glowing flesh was now blackened, and the glow had faded. Looked pretty much dead to her. At least her poison was somewhat useful.

Contrary to her hopes, the system didn't count the snail as an enemy. "It would have been too good to be true," she mumbled dejectedly and scooped up a bit of the blackened flesh. She gagged a little when she felt the slimy consistency of it, but she forced herself to take a bite.

She gagged some more when she tasted it. Not only was it sizzling wildly in her mouth, proving her assumption of it being acidic, but it even tasted unimaginably horrible. Not even Andrew's cooking came close.

But as horrible as it tasted, it topped her MP off. These snails were practically walking—no, slithering packs of magic power. The problem was that Melissa probably couldn't eat this stuff. Sarah had even hurt herself a little while eating it. She had to find another source of food. And more importantly, water.

Seeing as there was abundant life surrounding her, there had to be some source of water somewhere.

To get used to the horrible taste, Sarah started to eat more and more of the snail. She had hoped that the taste would become more bearable after a while. It didn't.

<Compatible genetic material consumed. Incomplete. More genetic material is needed for special mutations.>

Sarah looked at the system message with annoyance. She would definitely not want to become slimy. It didn't matter how strong it would make her; snail mutations were off the table.

Sarah shook off the disgust she felt and decided to just go somewhere at random. There were a total of five tunnel entrances in this place, and she had no way of knowing what she would encounter. So she just walked to where she was looking at the moment and started sneaking forward.

All her senses were on high alert, and the sheer amount of information her brain was battered with was almost too much to process. This was the first time her magic sense had been activated for so long, as it was exhausting for her brain. To her pleasant surprise, it felt more and more normal the longer she used it.

She walked through the winding tunnel for a long time, snacking on a snail here and there, until she got into some kind of cave. She wasn't quite sure if this place was natural or not because everything was covered in moss. The only new organisms in this cavern were big mushrooms here and there. They were big enough for her to sit on.

"They look so soft and squishy," Sarah mumbled with a longing look in her eyes. They really looked softer than anything else she had experienced until now. Except maybe Melissa's hug.

While she basked in the precious memory, something large jumped at her from the ceiling. It was incredibly fast and stretched out its claws to dig into Sarah's unprotected backside. To its surprise, its prey moved even faster and stabbed something into its stomach.

With an evil grin, Sarah punched the creature in the face and pulled her tail from its stomach. The creature tried to lash out at her, but she swatted away its appendage like a fly.

The creature sprang back a short distance and snarled at her. Now Sarah had a chance to take a closer look at it. The creature appeared vaguely humanoid. It had black, slimy skin and looked at her with disgustingly big yellow eyes. Its arms were way longer than its legs, and it stood hunched over on all fours. Its open mouth showed rows of sharp, long teeth.

"Disgusting," Sarah said, her face contorted. "Why does everything here have to be so gross? Can't there be something tasty-looking?"

The creature seemed confused for a moment but pulled itself together and tried to run away. It seemed to have trouble walking and stumbled every now and again.

Sarah grinned and leisurely started following it. It didn't take long for it to reach a hidden tunnel behind a carpet of moss. But before it could enter, Sarah pounced on it.

"Is that where your friends are? Thanks for showing me," Sarah said and started breaking its limbs one by one. The creature tried to scream, but only a bubbling sound came from its maw. It seemed like Sarah had hit right into its organs with her poison tail.

She turned it around and began studying it some more. It still tried to crawl away from her, but every time it tried, she just dragged it back.

It was breathing haggardly now, and yellow foam started to come out of its mouth. After some more time, it wasn't able to crawl anymore and just looked at her with hate-filled eyes.

Sarah had concentrated on it the entire time, all of her senses on high alert, but she hadn't felt anything. No indication of mind or soul invasion. Not even the smallest flare of magic power inside the hideous body.

Satisfied with her observation, she stomped on the creature's throat and shattered its neck. Its body jerked one last time and then it lay completely still.

<Normal enemy slain. Progress: 1/100>

Fire burned in Sarah's eyes while she grinned her sharp-toothed smile. As hard as it was for her, she had to suppress her fighting fever for now. First, she had to make sure that Melissa wouldn't starve to death. So she scratched a few marks into the tunnel and looked at the remains of her foe with a frown on her face.

"I guess I need to try eating you too."

CHAPTER THIRTY-EIGHT

Spiraling Down

Andrew was chopping firewood on the main plaza while waiting for his test to unfold. During the past few days, he had observed Denise's and the others' behaviors.

What at first seemed like an almighty control over everyone appeared to have certain conditions and strict limitations. He had seen Denise test people's limits. If she pushed them too close to something they didn't feel comfortable with, they began showing signs of resisting her influence.

Sadly, Denise could partially overcome this factor. She found out more and more about the circumstances under which people would do something they normally wouldn't. Just yesterday, he had observed her ordering someone to steal food.

The same person was later beaten up by otherwise harmless people. This happened because Denise had apparently noticed that some sort of betrayal was the trigger. Like this, she managed to shape the camp more and more to her will.

A strange incident had happened just a short while ago. For some unknown reason, Denise had begun laughing wildly for a few moments and shouted, "Serves you right!" while grinning manically. After people started staring at her, she hastily pulled up her façade again.

A plus point for Andrew was that she wasn't able to sway people with her beauty anymore. She didn't have much hair left, and horrifying scars were visible underneath her bandages. It was puzzling to Andrew how her skin had already healed from the damage. The only logical solution was that she either had a particular skill or was at a much higher level than everyone else. Seeing how she had been able to influence even Sarah, the latter was much more likely.

Andrew's heart beat faster for a few seconds when he saw Denise walking to the center of the plaza. How she was able to navigate herself so flawlessly without her eyes was also a wonder to him. He still remembered vividly how they carried the injured Denise out of the caves. Her face looked like it had melted.

Her chin held high, she walked up to one of her servants, as Andrew called them. His name was Hans, and he was one of the better-looking men in the group.

"Where's my food?" she demanded in a sharp tone while snapping her fingers.

Hans turned around with furrowed brows and rubbed his chiseled chin. "How would I know? Go to the kitchen crew; they'll have it ready for sure."

Denise was visibly shocked. She had been carrying out this simple command to Hans for days now, so it definitely shouldn't fall into the category of going over the limits. However, Andrew had tampered with her influence in Hans' soul without Denise or the man noticing. Andrew had weakened its effect without touching the soul parasite itself.

"Bring me my food! Now!" Denise screamed at the scared-looking Hans, who held his hands up to calm her. Denise's voice began shaking, and her hands were trembling. Even through the parasite, which was still embedded in his soul, Andrew could feel her trepidation. This reaction was well beyond what he had expected. His goal had only been to see how she would react if her skills didn't work as planned. He hadn't wanted to agitate her this much. For now at least.

"Listen, Denise," Hans said in a calm voice, "I know you have . . . Well, your eyes . . . I know it's difficult for you, but I am needed here. And you can orient yourself just fine. I hope you can understand that."

"TURN AROUND AND LOOK AWAY!" Denise screamed, her voice cracking. Andrew felt a strong surge of magic power wash over the clearing. Everyone in the vicinity dropped what they had been doing and looked away. Andrew scrambled to do the same, and turned just enough that he was still able to see Denise out of the corner of one eye.

Denise was panting heavily, and sweat was running down her forehead.

"What is—" Hans tried to say something, looking around with fear in his eyes, but he was interrupted by Denise's fist in his face.

Andrew stood there, shellshocked, as the small, delicate woman threw the big man to the ground like he weighed nothing. She sprang on top of him and continued hitting him in the face. Hans tried to defend himself, but she swatted his arms away like they were feeble twigs.

When Andrew heard the first crunching sound and saw blood splatter, he turned his head. The sickening sound of flesh pounding on flesh and the occasional crunching of bones continued for a few moments until Hans stopped howling in pain.

A deadly silence fell over the clearing, only disturbed by Denise's heavy breathing. Andrew's heart felt like it would jump out of his chest at any moment. If it hadn't been for his skills, he would have shat his pants from fear by now.

The look on her face had shaken him to his core. The uncontrolled rage and fear that had not only been visible in her expression but also through the parasite had paralyzed him.

For a long time, nothing else happened. After Denise's breathing had calmed down somewhat, she spoke again. This time, her voice was calm again. It was even gentle.

"Go now. Don't look back, and don't talk about the sounds you have heard. Hans tripped and hurt himself," she told the people, and another powerful wave of magic power washed over Andrew.

Like the others, he started walking away but risked a sneak peek behind him. Denise lay on the ground, probably unconscious. This was his chance. He looked around suspiciously, but nobody paid him any attention. He gulped, but his mouth was dry from nervousness. It was so strong that he had a hard time suppressing it. With cautious steps, he went closer to the motionless Denise. It would all be over if he could kill her.

When he was just a few steps away, he stepped on something soft and squishy.

He jumped back in shock, only to notice that he had stepped on the barely breathing Hans. His foot was drenched in blood, and he froze in horror. But this was no time to hesitate. With a few deliberate steps, he stepped even closer. But, before he could do anything, he felt a heavy hand fall on his shoulder.

"What are you doing so close to her?" he heard Alex's gruff voice behind him. Andrew wanted to turn around to somehow get Alex off of him, but a punch had already landed in his stomach. The force of the punch lifted him up slightly, and he fell to the ground while wheezing in pain. He looked up at Alex with blurred eyes while forcefully trying to breathe.

When he began vomiting, Alex crouched down next to him. "I know what you had in mind, filth. Don't think I didn't notice the looks you gave Denise. Trying to sneak up on her when she is unconscious and vulnerable. You are despicable, Andrew."

He spit on Andrew's head before standing up and walking to Denise's side. He had probably lifted her up, as Andrew heard Alex's heavy footsteps walk into the distance. Andrew had no idea what exactly was going on, though. He was still doing his best to get at least a little air inside his lungs.

While lying in the dirt and his own vomit, he began to ask himself where everything had gone wrong. Had it been when Denise came? That was definitely part of it. Or had it been even earlier, when he had sent Sarah to deal with the violent group? Maybe. Or maybe had it been even earlier, when he had awakened his abilities?

Tears ran down his face when he realized that everything had gone wrong from the moment he had opened his eyes in this cursed world. Death, suffering, betrayal, more death, and more suffering. And there was no end to it.

The powers they had received were a curse disguised as a blessing. He started to wonder which twisted mind had devised this torture for them. Who had thrown them into this mess? Who had given them these fucked-up abilities, which made a joke out of free will?

The system. The Creator. The administrators.

A burning rage awakened inside him, and he screamed out his long-suppressed anger and pain. But only a weak gurgling sound came out of him, and his stomach cramped painfully.

He sobbed on the ground for a while until he was somewhat able to breathe again. While holding his aching stomach, he stood up and stumbled to Hans.

Hans wasn't breathing anymore. He was dead. His empty eyes stared into the sky, still with a look of shock and betrayal in them.

Andrew averted his gaze and gritted his teeth. He stood up again and started wobbling away.

He was sick of all of this. He'd had enough of being pushed around by circumstances. Only now did he realize that he was weak. He was pathetic. The only thing he had been able to do was order people around.

This had to change. He had to become stronger. He had to become so strong that no one and nothing would be able to take things away from him. Not even the administrators.

With gritted teeth, he started focusing on his new ability, Soul Manifestation. He had used it to infiltrate Hans' soul and lessen the influence Denise had over everyone. He had never even thought of using it as a means to attack someone, but it was his only chance.

With a growl, he forced a part of his soul out of his own body and into a pointed shape. A reddish shimmer shot out of his chest, and a wave of exhaustion overcame him. But he wouldn't stop. He had no idea if this would even work. But he had to at least try.

He tried again and again and again while walking through the forest, and his proficiency increased at an insane rate. Despite his rage and fear, his focus was unparalleled.

When he finally arrived in front of his new cave, he broke down and fell to the ground. This wouldn't do. He had to stand up again. He had to get stronger.

But he had to train. He had to know if his skills even affected other people.

While trying to get to his feet, he heard a rustling sound in front of him. He looked up in fright, only to see the empty eyes of Derek and Till in front of him.

A grim determination rose up in him, and he forcefully suppressed every feeling of guilt inside of him.

<New active skill unlocked:
Emotion Eradication (Equilibrium): You are able to forcefully eradicate feelings inside of you. Warning: Overuse of this ability will permanently damage your ability to feel respective emotions.>

He only gave the prompt a quick glance while immediately activating the power. A wave of calm overcame him, and all his uprising guilt vanished.

He went over to one of the two former humans and laid a hand on his shoulders.

"Come, Derek. I need to show you something."

CHAPTER THIRTY-NINE

Going Berserk

"Are you sure you want to do this?" Sarah asked in an uncertain voice. She was looking down at the crouching Neil, who held a chunk of moss in one hand and a still-glowing yellow flower in the other.

"You told me that this made you stronger, right?" he asked in a firm voice, his eyes fixated on the plants in his hands.

Sarah nodded with a frown on her face, and her tail twitched nervously. When Neil started his profession as a food tester, Sarah had volunteered to try the unknown substances, like moss, first. And, to her shock, it even managed to knock her out for a moment.

The poison in this plant and its flower was so potent that it overwhelmed her resistance. She was actually looking forward to seeing if this new plant gave her abilities an upgrade if she ate enough of it. But first, she had to deal with this blockhead.

"You know that I nearly died, right? Why risk your life when I saved it just a little while ago?" Sarah asked in a harsh tone and crossed her arms. Melissa stepped beside her but didn't say anything.

"That is the problem," Neil told her with a gentle smile. "I had to be saved. I am too weak. I don't want to imagine what Denise might have done to me if I had been in her control much longer."

Before Sarah could interject, he held up his hand and spoke again. "Your concerns are valid, for sure. But we sit in a conflict dungeon and have to kill enemies. I don't want to be pushed around by forces I can't control anymore. I want to have power of my own. And this here," he said, lifting up the plants for Sarah and Melissa to see, "this is the fastest way to do it. Or rather, the only way that is known to us." With these last words, he gave them a crooked smile and gingerly bit into the moss.

Sarah wanted to spring forward and slap it out of his hand, but Melissa held her back. "It is his decision, Sarah. And I understand him well. Honestly? I'd do it myself if I had free body specialization slots."

Sarah didn't let Neil out of her sight, but she nodded. She felt a little guilty about even telling him, which might eventually resulted in him torturing and maybe even killing himself. But as Melissa had said before, it was Neil's decision.

Even though he had only eaten a small part of the plant, it didn't take long for him to spasm. While already twitching heavily, he bit into the flower and swallowed it too.

The screams didn't take long to come. He screamed and coughed until blood came out. His body bent in impossible shapes until loud cracking and snapping sounds could be heard.

Melissa turned around and ran away while gagging. Sarah could hear her throwing up in the distance, but Sarah stayed next to Neil.

"Push through, Neil," she said in a quiet but firm voice. "Melissa didn't heal you for nothing. Survive and pay her back."

She had no way of knowing if he had even heard her. But after some more time, the spasms and screams subsided, and he lay on the ground, motionless.

Melissa returned to her side, and Sarah felt a shaking hand slip into her own.

"Is he dead?" Melissa asked her with a quiet and trembling voice.

"Nope," Sarah answered and looked down at Neil with a smile on her face. "He's only getting started."

Magic power spread inside his body in violent waves and seemed to change something within him. Sarah had never seen the awakening of a specialization before, but she was sure that this was how it looked.

His distorted body began twitching and cracking again. But this time, his limbs seemed to snap back into place.

"Looks like he got something good," Sarah said with a glint in her eyes. Melissa turned her gaze away again.

It took a long time, but the transformation stopped eventually, and Neil lay still again.

"He made it through," Sarah told Melissa and pressed her hand gently, "but his brain activity is pretty low. He'll probably be down for a while. I'll get more of that mushroom for you and maybe even progress the quest. We need to get out of here as fast as possible."

Melissa looked at Sarah again and also pressed her hand. "You're right, but there is no getting out of here if you are dead. Don't overdo it."

Sarah smiled a little and flicked Melissa's forehead. "Don't worry too much. I know how to take care of myself."

Melissa looked at her with narrowed eyes and rubbed her aching forehead. She even started to get a blue bump.

Without losing any time, Sarah turned around and sprinted away, ignoring the angry shouting from Melissa to stay still.

Sarah smiled and sighed contently as she thought back to Melissa's grumpy face. "This is the best."

When she made her way out of their hideout, though, another feeling started to expand in her body. Excitement. A raging, boiling excitement.

With a light spring in her steps, she ran over to the hole in the ground, where she had descended the last time. This time, she took the descent a little more carefully, so she didn't repeat the graceless fall from last time.

She let herself fall for the last part, and she landed with a heavy thump. This caused the surrounding snails to look over her for a moment before they resumed eating.

First, she sat down next to a snail, patted the shell, and started munching on the moss and flowers. The snail was seemingly irritated by the strange creature beside her but soon resumed eating again.

"You know you're dessert, right?" Sarah asked the snail, which stopped for a moment to look at her. Their eyes met for a few seconds, and they both stood still.

And then they resumed eating.

After Sarah's first experience with the poisonous and acidic moss, she passed out for a moment, but her poison resistance had begun to adapt to it. Even though she was more resistant, it took a heavy toll on her.

"This stuff is swerrioulys . . ." When she tried to say something, it quickly became a jumbled mess. Her sight swam, and her body started to feel numb.

"Iss twhis the mowement two swop? Nwo iw iwn't!" she shouted, still not able to speak properly, and stuffed her face with some more moss.

It didn't take much more for her to pass out.

Not long after, she woke up because she felt something nibbling at her arm. She groggily turned her head, only to see that her dessert had decided to try and take a chunk out of her.

The snail froze when she looked it in the eyes and stayed still for a few moments. And then it began munching on her again.

A smack and a poison injection later, Sarah walked down one of the tunnels while chewing on the blackened flesh of her dessert. The snail had somehow managed to have a betrayed look in its fist-sized eyeballs.

But even the foul taste of this meal couldn't dampen her mood. After a few hours, her poison body skill received an upgrade.

<Poisonous Magic Power: Your magic power is slightly changed in its composition. If another being comes into deep contact with your magic power, or other energies converted from it, they will receive magic power poisoning.>

"This is awesome!" she shouted, now fully capable of speaking again. The moss had seemingly not contained ordinary poison but something that affected the magic power in her body itself. So far, she had no idea how magic power could be poisonous or what exactly it did to other beings. But, thinking back to her experiences, it probably affected her mind somehow.

"There is only one way to find out," Sarah mumbled with a fire in her eyes, tossing the empty shell away.

Cracking her hands and neck, she started sprinting forward in an excited manner before reminding herself to stay careful. There was no need to get herself killed.

When she reached the cave where she had fought the mutant, she felt five presences with her senses. They were all clustered together around the entrance, where she had left the corpse.

A wide grin formed on her face, and the mad fire in her eyes intensified. The rage, shame, and helplessness she had felt due to Denise flared up inside of her and snuffed out her last concerns. All these emotions had been suppressed, but they had smoldered and only became bigger over time. And now they had nearly erased all rational thinking.

Still grinning widely, Sarah openly marched into the cave, her eyes locked on the five mutants without blinking. Somewhere in the back of her mind, she registered that while they looked similar, they all seemed to have different specializations.

When the mutants noticed her, they started bellowing with cracked voices and baring their teeth.

Sarah roared back her defiance, accompanied by a disruptive mental wave. It made the mutants shudder in pain and fear. Her roar switched seamlessly to laughter, and she jumped forward. She grabbed the first mutant by the neck and simply twisted with all her might. The tough flesh and bones bent beneath her force, and the head nearly ripped off completely.

Next, she jumped in the middle of the still-swaying mutants to inject each of them with a full dose of the beloved poison from her tail.

Snapped out of their daze by the sharp pain, they began lashing out at her. But, being poisoned not only by physical but also magical poison, their movements were sluggish and unprecise.

Sarah's battle-attuned brain lit up like a firework, and she surrendered to her instincts. Ripping out flesh here and breaking a leg there, she started butchering the mutants, who screamed in fear and pain instead of anger.

Sarah still received injuries, though she barely noticed them. They were shallow and only further increased her fury and madness.

One of the smaller creatures suddenly latched onto her back and bit into her right shoulder. With an angry roar, Sarah pulled the head away and bathed it in her acid breath. The mutant screamed in unimaginable pain as its eyes started to melt away.

Letting the dying one fall to the floor, Sarah looked at the last remaining mutant. It wanted to run away, but Sarah sprang after it. She ripped it apart with gusto, its body an unidentifiable mess after only a short while.

When no enemies were left, Sarah's consciousness started to slowly come back. With a frown, she looked around at the mess she had created. Blood, gore, and limbs were splattered across the floor and walls.

Sarah looked down at her bloodied hands, chunks of flesh still stuck under her claws. Her hands were perfectly still. The scene and her actions made her somewhat nauseated, but at the same time, she felt free like never before. It had felt so incredibly good to just give in to the wild abandon that had overtaken her. She even felt a little refreshed.

She had always feared the part of the description about her slightly crazy skill. The thought of going nuts had always been a constant worry.

"But this is actually not that bad," she said while clenching her fists. The gore produced a slight squelching sound, and Sarah frantically started shaking her hands out.

"Ew, ew, ew!" she shouted, removing all the slimy flesh that stuck to her body.

Having finally removed everything, she shuddered. "I guess everything has its downside," she mumbled, walking over to one of the mushrooms. First, she had to get Melissa and Neil some food to eat.

And afterward, she could go wild.

CHAPTER FORTY

Cockroach

"You want what?" Sarah asked with a frown on her face.

"I want to accompany you. I want to help," said Neil with an annoyingly bashful smile on his face.

"But . . . you're so . . . frail. You'll be ripped apart in seconds." Sarah poked a finger into one of his rather unimpressive-looking forearms.

Neil looked at her dejectedly and crossed his arms in front of his chest. "I may be right now, but I will get stronger. I am on the Path of Conflict now, just like you. And my . . . skills necessitate me getting . . . well, hurt."

"Show me," Sarah told him with resolution in her voice. Neil looked like he'd reject her, but then he glanced to the side with a sigh and showed her his specializations and skills. But not everything. "You're a smart one, huh?" Sarah mumbled with a smile.

"Not like someone else here," Melissa quietly mumbled from behind her. Sarah turned around to glare at Melissa, but she innocently smiled back at her.

Now it was Sarah's moment to sigh, and she distracted herself with Neil's information in front of her.

<**Specializations:**
Body (Mid):
Adaptation
Evolution (New)

Active Skills:
- Fear Suppression (Adaptation): Suppress the effect fear has on your body for a short while. Warning: You still feel the fear.
- Rapid Regeneration (Evolution): You can rapidly regenerate your body for a high Magic Power cost. Potentially fatal damage to your body and/or mind

will trigger a stronger version of this skill, using all your available Magic Power. If there isn't enough Magic Power to heal all the damage, non-crucial parts of your body will be converted into Magic Power to enable this process. Warning: Using this skill on healthy body parts may lead to tumors.

Passive skills:
- Heightened Regeneration (Evolution/Adaptation): Your body heals and recuperates faster on its own, as long as you have above 50% Magic Power remaining. Negative effects on your body are lessened.
- Cockroach (Evolution/Adaptation): Every time you come close to death and survive, your body will undergo an evolution, which will strengthen you.
- Poison and Acid Resistance: Your body is adapted to handling extreme amounts of poison and acid.
- Magic Energy Resistance: Your body can contain a high amount of foreign and/or distorted Magic Power without getting damaged. Warning: The soul might still suffer from the effects.

Neil was still looking off to the side, obviously feeling ashamed. Sarah smiled gently, stepped forward, and laid a hand on his shoulder. "There is no shame in the name of your skill. Carry the insults of the system with defiance, as they will only make you stronger."

Neil looked at her with tears in his eyes and also laid his hand on her shoulder.

They stood like this for a while, wiping away the stray tears that streaked down their faces. Sarah finally had someone to share her pain with.

Melissa, on the other hand, could only look on in confusion at the incomprehensible scene in front of her.

"Alright, Cockroach," Sarah said, and laid her arm around his shoulders.

"I'd prefer you not call me that," Neil mumbled dejectedly.

"Cockroach?" Melissa asked with confusion on her face, and Neil buried his face in his hands.

"Let's go hunting!" Sarah shouted, trying to gloss over the embarrassing situation she had created for Neil, and she began dragging him away.

It took quite some time to get underground with him; he wasn't as fast as she was. When they finally got down there, Neil looked around in awe.

"This place is so strange and beautiful. I mean, the sky outside is fascinating too, but scary after what you told me."

Sarah wanted to answer when her senses warned her of imminent danger. She turned around to face the incoming threat and prepared to shoot out her tail to poison whatever was attacking her, but she was too slow.

A being of enormous mass barreled into her from one of the tunnels and knocked her to the ground. Too many limbs attacked her from above, and her brain and nerves were on fire from trying to react to everything.

And as fast as the being came, it also disappeared from above her again. She looked around in confusion, only to see Neil lying in a tumbled mess on top of one of the mutants next to her. Only this mutant had too many limbs.

Neil was thrown off of the being and flew through the air a few meters, only to fall to the ground with his arms bent at unnatural angles. Even though she was worried about the fool, she had to react now.

She pounced on the being and started swinging her claws at it. To her surprise, it blocked her. Sarah and the mutant went back and forth, wildly swinging at each other and trying to somehow overwhelm their opponent.

The mutant was massive, though still somewhat weaker than Sarah, but his five arms made the difference. She tried her best not to look too closely at the disfigured face with its two gaping maws, which split the slimy black skin from top to bottom of its head.

Sarah tried to use her tail but immediately regretted it. It used up too much of her attention to use her tail in a fight, which caused her to pause for a fraction of a second. The being noticed this gap and tried to disembowel her with one of its claws.

She felt the sharp claw rip through her skin and muscles like they weren't even there, but the claw got stuck in her protective bone plating.

Even though the pain was excruciating, she had to use this time wisely. When the creature tried to pull its claw out of her stomach, she used the pulling force and jumped forward. She pumped her whole body full of magic power and felt her muscles swell painfully.

With a mighty roar, she dug her claws deep into the creature and began ripping it apart. With a nasty tearing sound, three arms and a portion of its upper body were ripped off, and the creature screeched in pain and rage.

But it still wasn't dead.

Weirdly shaped bones and guts seeped from its open side, but it was still attacking her with its remaining arms. Sarah's enhancement of her muscles receded, and she was momentarily weakened, having trouble defending herself against the creature.

A moment of dizziness overcame her, and the remaining claws loomed dangerously over her head. But a snail flew at the mutant's head and threw it off balance.

Neil stood a short distance away, breathing heavily and holding his bloodied side. "Finish it already!" he roared at her, snapping her out of her daze.

Sarah jumped forward, threw the being to the ground, and began pummeling its head. Bones and teeth cracked under her fists, while Neil threw himself onto its remaining arms, so it couldn't defend itself anymore. She had to cave in its head until the abomination finally stopped moving.

<Quest progress:
Defeat 100 normal enemies (6/100)
Defeat 2 elite enemies (1/2)
Defeat the dungeon boss (0/1)
Eat 100 snails (7/100)
You have gained multiple levels.>

Sarah looked at the system prompt, and her face became hard. Neil, on the other hand, shouted in joy and triumph, only to whimper in pain after straining his still-injured body too much.

"We did it, Sarah! This was so fucking scary! I think I am in shock or something," Neil shouted with a slight tremor in his voice.

"We did it. But it was a shitshow," Sarah answered and looked him in the eyes. "The only reason I am still alive is because of your interventions. And it was also dumb luck that you even succeeded and are still alive. We need to get better at fighting."

She had noticed with resignation that she wasn't adept at using her various powers. She had a lot in her arsenal but usually just stuck to one thing during a fight. Thinking back to the fight when she had tried to use her tail, it had taken up too much concentration. They had nearly died fighting against an elite enemy. There was still another one somewhere out there, not to mention the dungeon boss.

"Uhh, Sarah," Neil mumbled and looked down at her in horror. "You . . . you still have an arm in your stomach."

Sarah looked down and noticed that the claw, including the ripped-off arm, was still sticking out of her. And with this realization came the pain.

She gritted her teeth and ripped out the arm. Another wave of pain overcame her, and her blood splattered on the ground and began sizzling.

Not thinking too much about it, she grabbed a little of the glowing moss and pressed it onto her wound. Contrary to her expectations, the pain subsided somewhat.

"Huh," she said, not quite understanding the weird effect of the plant.

"Are you okay?" Neil asked and touched her shoulder gently.

"I'm fine, Cockroach, thanks," she answered with a smile and patted his hand. "This moss seems to help with the pain. But I'm probably only surviving this because of my poison body." She wondered for a moment if she had gotten even crazier. She soon concluded that this would only be helpful to her in this crazy world.

"Do we go back and rest?" Neil asked and helped her stand up again.

"Go back? Rest? Are you insane? We came to fight, and that's what we'll do. And while we're at it, we'll train on how to get better at it." Neil's gentle smile disappeared.

"But . . . we're injured. Is this a good idea?"

"Can you move?"

"Yes?"

She punched his shoulder and he stumbled. "Then get your shit together. We are fighting against time. Who says these creatures can't find our hideout? This elite enemy probably found our place of entry because I killed a few of its kind around here. Who says they can't follow us back to Melissa? And besides . . . I have some open business with Denise."

Neil's fear-filled eyes hardened upon hearing the bitch's name, and he started smiling again. Only this time, it wasn't his usual gentle smile, but one filled with malice and anger. He nodded and punched her shoulder.

She smiled and nodded in appreciation. As if of one mind, they began moving deeper into the cave system while talking about their skills and how best to use them.

The hunt had begun in earnest.

CHAPTER FORTY-ONE

Mutation Upgrade

A single long, hook-like claw came from her left, and Sarah ducked, trapping the arm from below. It had missed her by a hair. Not missing her opponent's slight loss in balance, she kicked into one of its legs, causing it to fall.

Before it even touched the ground, Sarah's elbow thundered into its breast, shattering every bone in its chest cavity. When it finally smashed into the ground, it couldn't scream anymore. It just weakly gurgled and tried desperately to breathe.

Sarah stretched her aching body and stomped on the neck of the creature underneath her. She let out a content sigh and turned around to see how Neil was doing.

He was still fighting the two mutants he had taken on, but they were pretty much done for. Multiple broken claws stuck out of his body and he was covered in blood. But it didn't even bother him. Throughout their multiple hunts over the last few days, he had gained the ability to completely ignore pain. His cockroach ability made wounds and pain inconsequential.

They had learned how to use their abilities to their highest potential and to generate some sort of fighting style best suited to each of them. Neil's approach was to let his opponents' weapons get stuck in his own body and then hit and stab them to death with a hard, heavy stick he had found lying around. It looked pretty gruesome and took a while, due to his lacking strength, but it got the job done.

Sarah had to be more careful. She didn't have such a potent healing ability. In the beginning, she disrupted her opponents' nerve systems and injected them with her magic poison. Afterward, her fighting style revolved around either crushing her opponent instantaneously or, if that didn't work, slowly whittling them down with her poison, acid, mental magic, and small cuts from her claws.

During these fights, she had noticed that her magic poison affected every individual differently. Generally, the most prominent aspect of their opponents' supernatural abilities had been somewhat inhibited. This hypothesis had been confirmed after she had tested it out on Neil. It had taken several hours for him to be able to heal properly again, which caused him to develop a certain amount of resistance to this kind of poisoning. So, he hadn't even been that mad at her. Well, at least afterward.

She looked at the carnage surrounding them and scrunched up her nose. These mutants smelled horrible. They had killed so many by now that she thought she'd have some sort of resistance to the acrid smell by now. But it never got better.

"Maybe that's some sort of skill? Or mutation?" she mumbled, but she couldn't bother thinking more about this question, which was impossible to answer for now. While listening to Neil beating the guts out of his opponents, she decided to study her status screen again.

Details:
Level: 29 (+9)
Name: Sarah Anna Fischer
Class: Nightmare
Race: Mutant
Status: Normal
HP: 450/475 (+180) **SP**: 266/475 (+180) **MP**: 698/870 (+360)

Achievements:
- How the hell are you still sane?: Resistance to mind damage increased by 10%.
- Poison Gorger: Resistance to orally consumed poison increased by 30%.
- More Than Human: Higher success rate on special mutations.
- Junior Reaper (upgradable): You are able to slightly sense weak points in your enemies.

Affinities:
Mind (Mid) Body (Mid) Energy (Low)

Specializations:
- Mind (2/2)
  - Invasion
  - Nerve Control
- Body (2/2)
  - Adaptation
  - Mutation
- Energy (0/1)

Basic Stats:
Strength: 18 (+3)
Dexterity: 23 (+2)
Endurance: 23 (+3)
Resistance: 19
Intelligence: 24 (+2)
Force: 11

Special Stats:
Magic Power: 29 (+9)
Life Force: 86 (+36)
Mental Power: 58 (+27)

Active Skills:
- Mind Infiltration (Invasion): While using Magic Power, you can invade the mind of another being. Invasion is facilitated if the being has been poisoned by you.

Passive Skills:
- Poison Body (Adaptation): You can increase your resistance to hazardous substances and reinforce your body with their properties in combination with your Specialization "Mutation."
- Poison and Acid Resistance: You are highly resistant to various poisons and acids. (Overcoming new or stronger poisons or acids strengthens this ability.)
- Walking Hazard: Your body liquids are highly toxic and acidic. You are now naturally producing a strong nerve toxin and acid inside your body. (Consuming new or stronger poisons and acids strengthens this ability.)
- Mutated Glands: Toxin and acid glands are incorporated in certain mutations.
- Poisonous Magic Power: Your Magic Power is slightly changed in its composition. If another being comes into deep contact with your Magic Power, or other energies converted from it, they will receive Magic Power poisoning.
- Metamorphosis (Mutation, 48/86 Life Force used): You can mutate your body. The amount of mutations is dependent on your Life Force. Due to your Specialization "Adaption," there will be less Life Force needed, and you will have fewer limitations. Your Class, "Nightmare," will influence your mutations.
    - Skin:
        - Dense Skin (1 LF): Dense and leathery skin. More force is needed to penetrate the skin and shallow wounds close up faster.
    - Bone Structure:

- High Density Bones (2 LF): Incredibly robust and dense bones. Higher stamina consumption due to increased weight.
- Predator Teeth (1 LF)
- Retractable Claws (2 LF)
- Vital Organ Shielding (2 LF)
- Muscles:
  - Strengthened fibers (1 LF): Increased muscle strength. Muscles are slightly tougher and stronger.
  - Magic Power Reinforcement (2 LF)
- Brain, Nerve System, and Sensory Organs:
  - Predator Eyes (1 LF): Higher sensitivity to movement. Higher chance of spotting camouflaged beings.
  - Optimized Brain Structure (Battle) (6 LF): Optimized structure, focused on movement and decision making.
  - Decentralized Nerve System (10 LF): Signals can be transmitted, as long as one nerve-string still connects the brain to the respective body parts.
- Organs and Processes:
  - Magic Power Nourishment System (5 LF): Your body is adapted to run only on Magic Power. You are able to sense Magic Power in other living organisms and are able to feed on it. Most matter that enters your digestive system and lungs will be converted into Magic Power. Warning: High potential of cell breakdown if your Magic Power is empty for too long.
  - Acid Gland (not recommended, 4 LF): A gland located in the throat, which produces highly corrosive acid. Can be spit out with moderate pressure.
  - Extension: Gaseous acid (1 LF)
- Special Mutations:
  - Nightmare's Tail (class specific, 5 LF): A long and flexible tail with an exoskeleton made out of spine-like bone segments. Can be stretched over its original length, but will leave the vulnerable muscle and sinew under the exoskeleton exposed. Poison gland incorporated in the tip.
  - Nightmare's Horns (class specific, 5 LF): Two large and curved horns located on top of the forehead. Directly connected to your brain through nerve strings. Amplify mind-related skills and enable them to work without direct contact. Warning: Strong pain and disorientation if broken.
- Suppression (Nerve Control): Your emotions will influence your nerves less. Warning: Instinctual behavior is also suppressed.

- Struggle (Conditional Passive): Your Resistance is increased in dire situations.
- Slightly Crazy: Most things won't bother you that much. If certain conditions are met, however, there is a slight chance that you will go berserk.
- Mean Eye: There is a chance that other beings will shortly freeze in fear when they look at you. Higher chance with sentient beings.

Her growth made her extremely happy. The increases in her basic stats were small in number, but they made a big difference when it came to fighting. Every point gained felt like there was a little bit more power in her punches, a little bit more oomph to her mental assault, and a tiny bit more speed to outmaneuver her opponents. It was intoxicating.

To her annoyance, she was once again bottlenecked. Level 29 just didn't seem to want to increase, and she didn't know why, but she instinctively felt what she had to do—fight a strong opponent. They had found the lair of the second elite enemy, though it had made no effort to search for them; nor had they dared to stick their heads into its lair. They only knew where it was because Sarah had felt its insane mental activity from a long distance away. This was not an enemy she had been keen to encounter.

<Congratulations! The first objective of "Kill normal enemy" has reached its maximum of 100/100. Hidden objective reached: Kill the normal enemies with the help of one of the pathless participants of the dungeon.

You have gained an "Upgrade to one random mutation." Due to reaching the hidden achievement, it will be upgraded to "Upgrade to one random special mutation."

"Nightmare's Horns" will be upgraded to "Nightmare's Stalwart Horns." The mutation will begin shortly.>

"Shit!" Sarah cursed and her head snapped to Neil. "Protect me!" she shouted, and even though he was confused for a moment, he didn't hesitate to run to her. She didn't wait for him, as she ran toward the nest the mutants had just stormed from, and she sat on the ground in the darkest, most hidden corner.

"Are we getting attacked?" Neil asked in a calm tone, his eyes darting around the slightly glowing room.

"No. I'll mutate. If I scream too much, gag me somehow. And if you see—" She wanted to say more, but the mutation process had begun.

Luckily, she didn't have to worry about screaming anymore. Sadly, the process was horrible. She lost control over her body and only dimly felt aware of her surroundings. But this was soon pushed into the back of her mind, as the pain coming from her forehead was nearly unbearable. It felt like her horns were pushing out of her head from the inside, while something new tried to take their place. The process was not gentle.

She nearly passed out at one point but forced herself to stay conscious. They were still in enemy territory.

When the pain finally subsided, she turned to the side and gagged for a moment. Her head spun; just opening her eyes made her feel dizzy. So she lay on the ground for some time, until her tumultuous head had calmed down enough for her to stand up again.

Neil glanced at her from where he was standing and soon looked back to the entrance of the cave.

"Is everything alright?" he asked with worry in his voice, and Sarah patted his back weakly.

"It's fine," she said and straightened her cramped back. "I just have to get used to this, but I am not in fighting condition anymore. Let's get the fuck out of here, before something stronger than these things tries to take a bite out of us."

Neil nodded and they started hurrying away. They had used different entrances every time they had entered, and this strategy had proven useful so far. They had never been ambushed upon entering the cave system.

It didn't take long, though, for Sarah to stumble and fall to the ground. "Damn, I'm still too disoriented. Carry me!"

Neil didn't hesitate. He had only lifted her a little before he groaned and fell on top of her.

"What the fuck are you doing? Is this your way of hitting on a woman? I can tell you, this doesn't work," Sarah sputtered, trying to shove Neil away.

"You're just too freaking heavy!" Neil shouted while scrambling to his feet. His face was bright red and he looked like steam would soon start to come out of his ears. "You're at least twice as heavy as a normal person!"

Sarah smiled contently, thinking about all the dense muscle and bones that made her body so heavy. "Alright, stop being a wuss now and carry me."

With a despondent sigh, Neil crouched down in front of her and turned his back to her. She climbed on top of him with some difficulties and he groaned beneath her weight. He started walking away, but couldn't run anymore. "Why the hell do you still eat so much? I mean . . . wait, Sarah. Is this the tip of your tail I can feel pressed against my back?"

Sarah's claws slid out and she gently held his neck. "Do you have a problem with how much I eat?"

"No?"

"Good boy. Now walk a little faster."

Neil groaned again but picked up the pace.

Not feeling any need to look for the right way anymore, Sarah could finally take a look at her new mutation.

<Nightmare's Stalwart Horns (class-specific, 10 LF): Two large, sturdy, and curved horns located on top of the forehead, directly connected to your brain

through nerve strings. Amplify mind-related skills and resistances and enable them to work without direct contact. If another being tries to influence you with mind-related skills, they get strong Magic Power poisoning. You can detect if another being wants to influence your mind and/or soul and can locate it.>

Sarah grinned involuntarily. This was exactly what she needed right now. She was wondering if this mutation had been influenced by her experience with Denise or by her wish to be more resistant to mind and soul influences. Considering these horns had a similar effect from the beginning, it might have been a coincidence.

In any case, it was terrific. It even heightened her basic stat resistance from 19 to 21 points. This could only be good.

She got stronger and more deadly every day. She had even become more resistant to outside influences. And the defeat of the next elite enemy and the dungeon boss would only make her even stronger.

The day of her revenge grew closer.

CHAPTER FORTY-TWO

Assault

Andrew thrust down the shovel in his hands, ignoring the pain it brought to his shoulders and hands. Bit by bit, he closed the second of the two graves he had dug out.

Blood ran down the shaft of the shovel from his blistered hands, but he didn't stop. With his next thrust, the shovel broke apart with a loud crack. He took the sharpened stone that served as the shovel's blade, went on his knees, and continued digging.

When the ordeal was over, he rammed two thick branches into the earth at the top of the graves and started carving names in them.

When he finished, he stood there silently for a few moments. "Your sacrifices will not be forgotten. You have died for a good cause."

He stood there for a while longer until the silence was once again broken. But this time, by heavy footsteps.

"You can't even care for two idiots properly," Alex said with a disgusted voice and looked at the graves. "Well, I guess one can say that you got the job done properly this time, right? Death might be the better alternative, rather than staying alive after what you did to them."

Andrew slowly turned to Alex and looked at him for some time without saying a word or moving.

Feeling increasingly uncomfortable, Alex stepped closer to Andrew in a threatening manner. "Why don't you answer, you—"

Alex didn't finish his sentence or come closer. An incorporeal, greyish spike had shot out of Andrew's hand, directly into Alex's chest.

Alex started screaming in fear and agony and tried to get away from Andrew, but Andrew calmly followed him, making sure to stay out of reach of Alex's massive arms.

Andrew pushed even more energy into the spike, which was still embedded in Alex's chest. Alex tried to pull it out but couldn't even touch the incorporeal energy.

The spike started shaking and rippling and became stronger with the more energy Andrew pumped inside. And with an audible popping sound, the energy ripped apart and imploded.

Alex stopped screaming and moving. He just stood there, a short distance away from Andrew, with a vacant look on his face.

Andrew stepped closer and looked Alex in the eyes. A thin thread of saliva began flowing from his open mouth.

"I'm sorry, old friend," Andrew said and grabbed Alex by his head. Through the connection to Denise, he sent the impression of a fierce and dangerous beast, which overwhelmed both him and Alex. And then, he stabbed his stone knife into Alex's throat.

Alex's body shuddered slightly and his hands weakly pulled the knife out of his neck. His vacant eyes stared at the bloodied blade until he fell to the ground.

Andrew stepped over Alex's dead body and started walking toward the center of the camp in a wide circle. He heard multiple people running through the forest. With satisfaction, he noticed they were running in the wrong direction. Just as planned.

Suddenly, pain shot throughout his very being. With an enormous amount of willpower, he pushed down the feelings that wanted to rise inside of him.

"Not now. Not yet," he groaned, holding his chest. After a while, the wave receded and he was left panting in exhaustion.

When he calmed down again, he started running. There was no time to lose.

He ran through bushes and shrubbery, which caused cuts and injuries on his legs, but he didn't stop.

With a loud cracking sound, he broke through the last bush and into the main clearing in front of the caves.

A lot of people were running around in a hurry, trying to build up some defenses out of various objects. Andrew didn't care about them. He ran straight to the center. His goal stood before him.

He built claws out of his soul energy and pumped them as full as possible. Denise turned her head in confusion when he was just a short distance away and opened her mouth to shout something, but it was already too late.

Andrew crashed into her with as much force as he could muster and ripped with his energy claws into her body and her soul.

He immediately overcharged them, and they imploded with loud ripping sounds inside her soul.

Denise roared in pain and anger, and they fell to the ground together.

With surprising force, she pushed him down and rolled on top of him. He could see that her soul was in a very bad state. Tattered and ripped apart, but for some reason it was still functional enough for her to defend herself.

"You will not kill me!" she roared and started punching him with full force. Andrew tried to block, but his arms were swiped to the side like his strength meant nothing. Denise was way stronger than expected.

"No one will kill me!" Denise continued roaring and started to rip at his soul with every punch she delivered. He desperately defended himself, sure he wouldn't survive such an injury.

But she was too strong. "I will get my wish! I WILL REVIVE HER!" she cried out, and with the last word she punched into his stomach, and with the fist came a tremendous wave of energy, which rippled through Andrew's entire being, cracking and tearing.

With horror, he felt the big lump of darkness inside him rip apart. It had swollen to a much bigger size by now, and it was completely open.

<Warnin&! Unidentifi@d, unst]@#œ energy source has been set free inside of "//. You and your immediate UA/()roundings are in mortal danger! Looking for s@l()%ions.>

It began with a wailful cry from behind him, and then it felt like he had plummeted straight to hell.

Inhuman screams echoed around him, and he could barely keep his consciousness inside the storm of madness.

All the guilt he had never had the chance to feel washed over him, and he nearly gave up then and there. But seeing one of his people fall lifelessly on one side of him brought him back from the brink.

With an agonized roar, he stretched out his soul as far as it could go and stabilized every living soul he could feel around him. He didn't have time to pinpoint Denise's soul; he had to worry about her later.

The force of the madness multiplied and he could barely hold on.

<War/UAQN! I/"HD@i28/gad9UJnu OUHAa / »GAD aoe9dè !>

The souls around him lost their stability more and more, so he ripped even more of himself out to stabilize them. The pain was unimaginable.

Then, the first soul started to break down. He had to do something. He had to protect it. So he did the only thing he could still think of in his crazed state.

He pulled the soul deep inside of him and protected it from the storm of madness.

The next soul was set free suddenly, as the body of the person died because of the stress. This time, without his intention, the soul traveled along his soul tendril and nestled inside of him, right next to the first he'd retrieved.

One after another, the people around him started to die or break down, and the amount of souls inside of him increased more and more. He tried to hold off the souls, but it just didn't work. He knew instinctively that he had made a horrible mistake.

His soul began to crack and rip. There was just too much inside of him now. He felt like he would burst at any moment.

And then, something fundamental inside of him cracked and ripped, something he had never before noticed.

His whole world turned upside down. And the last thing he saw before darkness engulfed him was a surprisingly clear system message.

<Connection lost.>

CHAPTER FORTY-THREE

Into the Dark

"Finally!" Sarah shouted and immediately regretted it. The many snails in her stomach sloshed around sickeningly.

Neil smiled at her and then went pale. Sarah ran over and pressed her hand to his mouth. "Don't throw up! Do you want to lose the progress?" They had had to learn the hard way, that throwing up snails would reset the progress one had made eating them.

Neil's eyes widened in fright and he took on a look of strong concentration.

Intending to get the reward before Neil could throw up again, Sarah mentally prompted the system to get on with it. The answer was disappointing.

<Eat snails (100/100) complete.

Error. Reward not specified.

Solution. The reward of the dungeon will be enhanced.>

Sarah didn't know if she should be happy or not. They had hoped that finishing this partial quest would bring them some kind of benefit before they attacked the final enemies. But alas, it would not be.

"Well, at least we get some better rewards in the end. Could be worse," she mumbled to quell her disappointment and to drown out the sounds of vomiting from behind her. Sadly, it was futile.

Resigned, she looked at the quest again, but the part about the snails was still marked as complete. Considering the system's sadistic humor, this was truly a nice surprise.

After Sarah had waited some time for Neil to calm down again and eat a little bit of mushroom, she stepped closer to him.

"Are you ready?"

Neil clenched his fists and teeth and cold sweat was running down the side of his head. But he still nodded.

"Good boy," Sarah said with a smile and patted his head. "Now remember, I'll distract the elite enemy first. It's most likely able to do some mind magic stuff, so you'll be done in for, if it attacks you first. I'll occupy it, and you ambush it. Easy peasy. This will be no problem for us."

Neil looked a bit more confident now, but he apparently couldn't help but feel self-conscious about the fact that he was responsible for dealing the decisive blow to the creature.

Sarah's face became more serious and she grabbed him by his shoulders. "You can do this. We can do this. Now let's go."

Without waiting for a response, Sarah walked down the dark tunnel. For some reason, nothing was growing in the proximity of the second elite enemy. Coupled with the massive mental signal she received, even over a great distance, this enemy was cause for concern. She had also felt it stretch out its mind toward them curiously, so there was no way of making a surprise attack.

Luckily, it hadn't made a move on them yet. Their success depended on how far they could go without it reacting to them.

They walked and walked, but the elite enemy did nothing more than keep track of them.

This was somehow very disconcerting for Sarah. Whatever the reason to ignore their approach, it couldn't be good.

Sarah was so focused on the enemy that a thought came a little too late.

"Wait, Neil. Can you see well?" she asked her companion.

"No? It's freaking dark down here. I swear if something just jumps out from the next corner, I'll piss my pants." He was half-joking and looked around in fear.

"Shit," Sarah cursed and hastened her steps.

"What is it?" Neil asked, stressed about her reaction.

"This place is too normal. You can always see in this weird place, even if there is no light. That the darkness here seems to work normally, in combination with the elite enemy and the completely absent vegetation and slugs, is a very bad sign. It probably . . . does something to its surroundings. Ever meet something that could have such an intense effect on its surroundings?"

Neil gasped in realization and grabbed the hem of Sarah's shirt so he wouldn't lose her in their dark surroundings. "Just once," he replied. "The administrator. Do you think . . . do you think we are closing in on the dungeon boss? And that it's on the same level as one of them?"

"I don't know," Sarah said, feeling quite shocked herself. But the time to think about this was over.

"Wait here," Sarah instructed Neil, and she began walking ahead.

"Sarah, wait! We have to go back again!" Neil said with panic in his voice.

"And then? Come back another time and then get slaughtered? This thing has already noticed us. There is no telling if it will follow us and attack us with Melissa around. Do you want that? We are neck-deep in shit, Neil. There is only one way to go now. And it is forward."

With these words, she turned around and started running with all her might. By now, she had started to sense an oddity in the ambient magic power. It seemed to flow in the direction of the enemy, which was probably the boss and not just some elite enemy.

The pounding of her feet and the drumming of her heart were the only sounds she could hear in the darkness. She saw a dim light in front of her. When she was close enough to see what it was, a primal part of her mind screamed at her to turn around and run away.

An enormous blob of pulsating flesh towered in front of her. From one of its sides, a shriveled-up body with thin limbs stuck to it, looking like it had already been dead a long time. The thin skin on the flesh blob was black and slimy, and it continuously oozed some kind of liquid on the ground, which was why it was surrounded by a pool of it.

The sight was so wrong and horrifying that Sarah's mind blanked out for a split second.

And then, the thing attacked. Her mind and body were overwhelmed with pain and other sensations, which should only be possible in nightmares.

Sarah screamed in fright and tried to defend herself. But it was useless. It was like trying to stop a landslide with her bare hands.

Her body fell to the ground and started convulsing. Just when she started to panic, an odd thought came to her mind. *It's . . . not that bad*? While it surely was one of the most horrible feelings she had felt in her life, certain mutations were even worse than this.

This realization caused her to laugh out loud, even though her body was still convulsing from the pain. She could feel the irritation through the mental attack, which caused her to laugh even more. And then, it suddenly stopped.

Sarah stood up again, thinking that Neil had hit it with a fatal strike. But he was still some distance away.

She looked at the thing in confusion, only to see that several impossibly large blood vessels had burst open and even ripped open its skin, leaking thick, yellow blood on the floor.

The thing still trembled slightly but looked like it would die pretty soon.

"Did you kill it?" Neil asked in wonder and looked down at the mess with disgust.

"I don't think so," Sarah answered and poked the fleshy blob with one of her fingers. But it didn't react.

She hesitantly stretched out her mind and soon connected with the thing. And then she knew why it had died so suddenly. Its entire mind seemed damaged and infected by something almost corrosive.

And there was only one answer to it—the magic power poisoning, which everyone experienced once they tried to infiltrate Sarah's mind. The effects were catastrophic.

"It was my magic power poisoning," Sarah answered in surprise. Nothing had ever reacted with more than discomfort and disorientation to this ability.

Neil looked at her in awe and then at the beast again. The tremors in its body grew weaker and weaker until they stopped completely.

"I know I shouldn't be disappointed but . . . that was somehow anticlimactic," Sarah muttered, only to receive an annoyed look from Neil.

"Just be happy that—" he started to say but was interrupted by the system.

<Defeat elite enemy (2/2) Complete.

Reward: Genetic material (Regeneration) will manifest.>

Sarah's gaze was fixed on the message. "Regeneration," she whispered, feeling immensely happy to finally receive a chance to get an ability like this.

"Sarah," Neil said and tugged at her arm, but she ignored him.

A red marble had begun to manifest out of nowhere in front of her face. Not even her magic power sense noticed something out of the ordinary. It just . . . appeared.

After a few seconds, the marble started growing and just floated in the air. It was reddish, with brown streaks running through it.

Sarah grabbed it and immediately contorted her face in disgust. It was squishy and wet.

"Sarah!" Neil said with more insistence, but she still ignored him. Not wanting to wait any longer, she ate the gross ball and swallowed immediately. Her whole body shuddered, but it was soon forgotten.

<Genetic material (Regeneration) acquired.

Scanning the body for compatible genetic fragments.

Compatible genetic fragments found. Enhancing the Mutation option.

New Special Mutation option available:

Restoration (30 LP): The speed of regeneration is heightened. Magic Power will be consumed if not enough nutrients are available. Heavily mutilated or lost body parts can be regenerated, apart from the brain. A minimum of 60% of the body mass is required, to enable this ability. If the body mass falls below 60%, you will fall into a comatose state until you are sufficiently regenerated. Only possible with at least 40% remaining body mass.>

"SARAH!" Neil shouted, and Sarah turned around, annoyed.

"What? The boss is defeated. There is nothing else here. What's the problem?" she shouted back in anger, feeling annoyed by getting pulled out of her revelry.

"We didn't defeat the boss, Sarah! Look at the damn notification!"

Sarah opened up the notification again, and her pale skin became even paler. "Shit. We only killed the elite enemy. But where is the dungeon boss?"

Neil said something, but a new system message popped up in front of her, which blocked out everything else.

< Multiple levels gained. Recording of Dr. Alain Becker available.

Error. Forced interruption of the recording function due to immediate danger.>

"Immediate danger," Sarah whispered with wide eyes and looked around the room. But there was nothing here.

"Neil, we're in danger. Stay sharp," she commanded, and Neil immediately stopped his nagging, and they stood back to back.

They stood there for a long time, and Sarah could feel the cold sweat running down Neil's back. Just when she thought that the system had given her a false alarm, something happened to the corpse of the flesh blob.

The flesh started to lose its glow, and then it shriveled and shrank together and began getting smaller and smaller. The room grew darker than before, now pitch black.

Sarah noticed in alarm that the ambient magic power had started to flow again. Faster and faster it flowed until it was more like a raging river, shooting toward the corpse.

"No, not the corpse," Sarah said in shock. She grabbed Neil and sprang away from it.

A few seconds later, an explosion of magic power and kinetic force extended from the flesh blob, and its remains were splattered onto everything around it.

Even though they were already some distance away, Sarah and Neil had been flung through the room like leaves in the wind.

Luckily, they flew into the tunnel and lost a lot of their velocity before slamming into the soft ground. Even so, it hurt like hell.

Sarah immediately jumped up and saw that Neil was still lying on the ground. A quick check on his mental activity showed her that he was only unconscious.

A relieved sigh slipped through her lips, and she focused forward.

A small, humanoid figure floated in the cavern. Even though it had pitch-black skin, it shined with a bright, grayish light.

"A . . . kid?" Sarah said in shock upon watching the thing for a few moments. The being in front of her looked exactly like a human child.

The child slowly turned around in the air until it was facing her. It opened its eyes and Sarah could only see pitch-black holes. Upon gazing at her, its face contorted in a mixture of rage and fear.

This wasn't what she had imagined, but it was the dungeon boss. The display of supernatural power in front of her was just too insane. She had never seen anything or anyone display this kind of power.

When Sarah shifted her feet into a fighting stance, the dungeon boss seemed to interpret this as a signal to start the fight. The glow became even brighter, and violent streaks of energy blasted from it, disintegrating the stone walls it touched.

And with another child-like scream, it started flying at her.

CHAPTER FORTY-FOUR

Perspective

Sarah slowly opened her heavy eyelids. Her vision was blurred and her thoughts heavy. It took a moment for her to fully realize that she was awake and lying on hard ground.

She then noticed two voices saying something—her name.

With her eyes now focused, she sat up and sucked in a sharp breath, which caused her to cough heavily.

"Sarah! I am so glad you're alive!" Melissa said, and then Sarah felt her warm and soft embrace envelop her. Sarah leaned into the embrace and weakly held one of Melissa's arms.

Sarah looked around for a moment and spotted Neil sitting next to them, hastily wiping away a tear. He smiled at her and let out a shaky breath. Sarah was deeply touched by the two people sitting next to her and worrying about her. It was something so small, but the mere thought that they cared so much about her made her feel warm and accepted as never before.

"Are you . . . are you crying?" Neil asked with a surprised look on his face.

"Shut up and come here," Sarah said with narrowed eyes, and Neil hesitantly scooched closer and hugged both of them.

"I am alive," Sarah said, her voice breaking with emotion, and she started crying. Melissa and Neil held her shuddering body. The memories of the unimaginable agony, and the fact that she had been way too close to her soul being annihilated, shook her to her core.

From where Melissa was touching her, a warm sensation spread inside her body and soul and eased her pain a little. Like this, they just sat there for a while, until Sarah had let everything out.

Neil and Melissa gently parted from her, and Melissa laid a hand on her cheek. "Do you feel better?"

"Yeah. I'll be fine," Sarah replied with a hoarse voice and struggled to ask the next question. "How does . . . how does my soul look?"

"Surprisingly fine," Melissa answered with a confused look on her face. "Your soul seems like it has been half ripped apart and then patched up again to be tougher than ever before. I honestly have no idea what all this means. But it seems like you'll be fine after you have had a bit of time to process all of this."

A heavy weight lifted off Sarah's chest. She had feared that her soul was somehow crippled or that she was incomplete. It was a huge relief that her very being was intact.

The next part to worry about was her body. She gritted her teeth and looked down at herself. Melissa had dressed her in new clothes; her old ones had probably been ripped to shreds. And underneath the clothes was flawless skin. Even her foot had regrown. The only worrying part was that she looked rather skinny. The process had tapped on her body mass.

Another weight fell from her, and a short laugh escaped her lips. "I even have my foot back!"

Sarah felt Melissa's hand stiffen, which was still resting on her. "What do you mean you have your foot back?" Melissa asked with a horrified look in her eyes.

Sarah's tail whipped around uncomfortably under Melissa's frightened gaze. Sarah swallowed hard and started talking about the boss fight after the moment Neil had lost consciousness.

Recalling the events made Sarah realize her madness in the heat of the fight, but she had come to accept this part of her. Melissa and Neil didn't judge her for it either, so she had no reason to hide any detail from them.

It had been brutal, dirty, and horrifying.

"But I survived, and that is everything that counts," Sarah said resolutely and gently laid her right hand on Melissa's shoulder.

Melissa's lips quivered and her eyes became wet again. "Thank you, Sarah. Thank you for going through this to get us out of here."

Neil vigorously nodded his head in agreement and patted her shoulders.

Sarah scratched her neck in embarrassment and just nodded. She felt uncomfortable, so she quickly changed the subject. "So how do we get out of here now?"

Neil just pointed to a far corner of the cave, and Sarah turned her head.

A white, slowly rotating sphere of energy hung in the air and gave off a soft glow. "Why does it look so different?" she asked in wonder.

"Don't know," Neil answered and rubbed his chin. "Maybe because it's stable? I mean, the other looked . . . well, unstable. With all the energy rippling through the air and everything. This one here looks so clean and perfect. Maybe because the system created it?"

Melissa and Sarah could only shrug their shoulders. It didn't matter in the end, so the subject was quickly forgotten.

"We'll get ready to leave. Just rest here, and we'll go get everything," Melissa said with a pat on her shoulders and stood up.

"Get what?" Sarah asked.

"Mostly cloth, these weird ropes, and other interesting stuff I have found lying around," Melissa replied. "It will soon be winter back at the caves. We'll need every bit of clothing we can get."

Melissa smiled at Sarah and kissed her forehead. "We'll be back soon." She turned around, and Neil started following her, after waving goodbye.

Suddenly alone, Sarah didn't know what to do with herself, until she remembered that she must have received the rewards from the quest.

With bubbling excitement inside of her, she prompted the system to show her all the missed messages. It was a true flood of information that popped up.

<Restoration successful. A stable condition was reached. Returning to normal operation.

You have unlocked the specialization Disintegration. You have gained the active skill Disintegration Infusion. You have gained the passive skill Tempered Soul.

You have leveled up multiple times.

You have reached level 40. Requirements met for a class upgrade. Upgrade available upon activation. Warning: Due to the weakened state, there is a chance for cell and/or soul breakdown.

General system change: Dr. Alain Becker's recordings can now be watched upon activation. Available recordings: 2.

You have completed the quest! You have gained the following rewards (rewards are enhanced due to the eat snail subquest):

6 levels gained. Levels could not have been added due to pending class upgrade. Changed rewards to System Question: Clearance Level 1. Available upon activation.

Achievement Dungeon Conqueror gained.

Dungeon Conqueror: +1 to each Special Stat per Level Up.

Achievement Junior Reaper has been upgraded to Budding Reaper.

Budding Reaper: You can slightly feel physical and mental weak spots in your enemies.>

Sarah had never seen so many notifications at once, and she had never gained so many boosts to her power. It was immensely regrettable that the class upgrade would have to wait until she had rested some more. But luckily, there was something else that sounded delicious.

"Activate system question," Sarah mumbled and another screen popped up.

<System Question: Clearance Level 1 has been activated. Please state your question.>

"Why do you exist?" Sarah blurted out but was quickly disappointed.

<Error. Clearance Level is too low. Please state another question. Warning: Attempts remaining: 2 out of 3.>

"Damn system," Sarah mumbled and thought over what she would like to ask. The system didn't like being asked questions too sensitive in nature, or else it wouldn't have given her limited attempts to ask questions.

She would wait for Melissa and Neil to come back and discuss it with them.

<Warning. System Question: Clearance Level 1 cannot be deactivated. The decision to wait longer to ask the question will automatically cancel the System Question.>

Sarah wanted to swear at the system but decided against it. It seemed rather touchy about this question thing, as if it didn't even want her to have it. She didn't have another option and had to be careful what to ask, so she decided to ask the system something she had been curious about for a long time.

"What are the different paths for?" she asked, and this time the system didn't reject her.

<Paths are ways to power. Upon selecting a certain path, your being will merge with it, which means that they are the only means to advance your Magic Power Level. The decision to renounce the path will result in the decay of your being and in some cases death.>

Sarah's mouth gaped wide open. "So . . . we're damned to always follow our path if we don't want to die or decay? Seriously?" She wasn't quite sure if this was something she had wanted to know, but at least she could warn the people close to her now.

At least for now, she didn't want to leave the Path of Conflict anyway. But what of the future? What if she someday didn't want to fight anymore? Was this really what her life would be? Conflict or death?

Sarah shook her head and smiled. At least the system didn't count her relationship with Melissa as a renouncement from her path. For now, that was all she needed.

To cheer herself up again, she decided to open up her status screen and take a good, long look at all of her gains. And they were truly impressive.

Details:
Level: 40 (+11)
Name: Sarah Anna Fischer
Class: Nightmare (Upgrade Available)
Race: Mutant

Status: Weakened (All stats decreased by 50%)
HP: 520/640 (+165) **SP:** 200/645 (+170) **MP:** 780/1205 (+335)

Achievements:
- How the hell are you still sane? Resistance to mind damage increased by 10%.
- Poison Gorger: Resistance to orally consumed poison increased by 30%.
- More Than Human: Higher success rate on special mutations.
- Budding Reaper (Upgradable): You can slightly feel physical and mental weak spots in your enemies.
- Dungeon Conqueror: +1 to each Special Stat per Level Up.

Affinities:
Mind (Mid) Body (Mid) Energy (Low)

Specializations:
- Mind (2/2)
  - Invasion
  - Nerve Control
- Body (2/2)
  - Adaptation
  - Mutation
- Energy (1/1)
  - Disintegration

Basic Stats:
Strength: 25 (+7)
Dexterity: 27 (+4)
Endurance: 30 (+7)
Resistance: 25 (+3)
Intelligence: 28 (+4)
Force: 22 (+11)

Special Stats:
Magic Power: 40 (+11)
Life Force: 109 (+33)
Mental Power: 80 (+22)
Pure Energy: 1 (+1)

Active Skills:
- Mind Infiltration (Invasion): While using Magic Power, you are able to invade the mind of another being. Invasion is facilitated if the being has been poisoned by you.

- Disintegration Infusion (Disintegration): You are able to infuse any part of your body with the energy of "Disintegration."

Passive Skills:
- Poison Body (Adaptation): You are able to increase your resistance to hazardous substances and reinforce your body with their properties in combination with your Specialization "Mutation."
- Poison and Acid Resistance: You are highly resistant to various poisons and acids. (Overcoming new or stronger poisons or acids strengthens this ability.)
- Walking Hazard: Your body liquids are highly toxic and acidic. You are now naturally producing a strong nerve toxin and acid inside your body. (Consuming new or stronger poisons and acids strengthens this ability.)
- Mutated Glands: Toxins and acid glands are incorporated in certain mutations.
- Poisonous Magic Power: Your Magic Power is slightly changed in its composition. If another being comes into deep contact with your Magic Power, or other energies converted from it, they will receive Magic Power poisoning.
- Metamorphosis (Mutation, 53/86 Life Force used): You are able to mutate your body. The amount of mutations is dependent on your Life Force. Due to your Specialization "Adaption," there will be less Life Force needed and you will have fewer limitations. Your Class "Nightmare," will influence your mutations.
  - Skin:
    - Dense Skin (1 LF): Dense and leathery skin. More force is needed to penetrate the skin and shallow wounds close up faster.
  - Bone Structure:
    - High Density Bones (2 LF): Incredibly robust and dense bones. Higher stamina consumption due to increased weight.
    - Predator Teeth (1 LF)
    - Retractable Claws (2 LF)
    - Vital Organ Shielding (2 LF)
  - Muscles:
    - Strengthened Fibers (1 LF): Increased muscle strength. Muscles are slightly tougher and stronger.
    - Magic Power Reinforcement (2 LF)
  - Brain, Nerve System, and Sensory Organs:
    - Predator Eyes (1 LF): Higher sensitivity to movement. Higher chance of spotting camouflaged beings.
    - Optimized Brain Structure (Battle) (6 LF): Optimized structure, focused on movement and decision making.

- ■ Decentralized Nerve System (10 LF): Signals can be transmitted, as long as one nerve-string still connects the brain to the respective body parts.
  - o Organs and Processes:
    - ■ Magic Power Nourishment System (5 LF): Your body is adapted to run only on Magic Power. You are able to sense Magic Power in other living organisms and are able to feed on it. Most matter that enters your digestive system and lungs will be converted into Magic Power. Warning: High potential of cell breakdown if your Magic Power is empty for too long.
    - ■ Acid Gland (not recommended, 4 LF): A gland located in the throat, which produces highly corrosive acid. Can be spit out with moderate pressure.
    - ■ Extension: Gaseous acid (1 LF)
  - o Special Mutations:
    - ■ Nightmare's Tail (class specific, 5 LF): A long and flexible tail with an exoskeleton made out of spine-like bone segments. Can be stretched over its original length, but will leave the vulnerable muscle and sinew under the exoskeleton exposed. Poison gland incorporated in the tip.
    - ■ Nightmare's Stalwart Horns (class specific, 10 LF): Two large, sturdy and curved horns located on top of the forehead. Directly connected to your brain through nerve strings. Amplify mind related skills and resistances and enable them to work without direct contact. If another being tries to influence you with mind related skills, they get a strong magic power poisoning. You can detect if another being wants to influence your mind and/or soul and can locate it.
- • Restoration (30 LP): The speed of regeneration is heightened. Magic Power will be consumed if not enough nutrients are available. Heavily mutilated or lost body parts can be regenerated, apart from the brain. A minimum of 60% of the body mass is required to enable this ability. If the body mass falls below 60%, you will fall into a comatose state, until you are sufficiently regenerated. Only possible with at least 40% remaining body mass.
- • Tempered Soul (Unique): Your soul is highly resistance to damage and invasion.
- • Suppression (Nerve Control): Your emotions will influence your nerves less. Warning: Instinctual behavior is also suppressed.
- • Struggle (Conditional Passive): Your Resistance is increased in dire situations.

- Slightly Crazy: Most things won't bother you that much. If certain conditions are met however, there is a slight chance that you will go berserk.
- Mean Eye: There is a chance that other beings will shortly freeze in fear when they look at you. Higher chance with sentient beings.>

Her new disintegration skill certainly sounded powerful. She was changing more and more into a true nightmare. If she understood her stats correctly, she could even infuse this power not only in different parts of her body but also in her poison or acid.

And what was up with her stats? She had never experienced such a huge jump. She wasn't sure where it had come from. Probably a mixture of her new skills, specialization, level-ups, and maybe even for reaching over one hundred points in life force. Once again she thought to herself that they needed to study the system more, to understand how it worked. But that was also something for the future. Now, she'd revel in her improvements.

Sarah grinned from ear to ear. She couldn't wait to try her new skills out. And she knew exactly on whom she could test them. Her grin grew more sinister as she thought about Denise again. "I'm coming for you," she growled and clenched her fists.

It wasn't long before Melissa and Neil came back. They waved from afar and smiled at her. They both had enormous bags strapped to their backs, and Melissa seemed to struggle under the weight. But, she stubbornly took one step after another.

"That's my girl," Sarah mumbled and smiled a toothy grin. She stood up and stretched her stiff body. She already felt the weakened state slowly fading away and her strength coming back.

"Ready to go?" Melissa asked with a smile. Neil gave her another big bag, which had been strapped to his back, and Sarah took it with a nod.

She turned back to Melissa and gave her a bright smile. "Let's go."

Melissa took Sarah's hand, and they started walking toward the white, rotating sphere.

A lot waited for her on the other side. A new home she would build with Melissa and Neil. Even more power with her class upgrade. And finally, her revenge.

She couldn't wait any longer for this.

About the Author

Gonoa is the author of *The Wish*, a post-apocalyptic LitRPG originally released on Royal Road. Although he has tried numerous times to read and write non-fantasy stories, he hasn't succeeded thus far; his addiction to the genre sits too deep. Resigned to this, he has made a diabolical plan to spread his fantasy mania to as many people as possible. Gonoa lives in Europe, and in his free time, he enjoys cuddling with his cats.

Podium